THE SOUL GARDEN

BY RHYS HUGHES

W HEN THE WAR CAME, PAUL WAS EVACUATED ONE MORNING. HE WAS PUT FIRMLY ON THE TRAIN AND WAVED OFF INTO THE WEST. London, they told him, was a death trap, even though his side was going to win anyway. These words filled him with anxiety and hope at the same time, but both emotions faded in force as the hours passed. He fell asleep and dreamed of a garden.

He often had the same dream. The garden was large but without any sense of space or freedom. There was no story, just the old orchard trees and the paths between them, a crumbling brick wall, low bushes bright with ripe berries in the muted twilight, a structure that seemed to be a decayed shed, a large butterfly in a spiderweb. He trembled for no reason.

He awoke and found that the train had arrived at his destination. It was the village in Devon to which he had been assigned, suitably remote and safe, or so it was claimed. His guardians waited for him on the platform, distant cousins on his mother's side of the family. He had never met them before. They put him at his ease. They were awkward but friendly.

His new home was a short walk from the train station. The house was large and oddly shaped but there was nothing menacing about it. The front door led to a passage cluttered with bicycles, hat stands and gardening tools. Paul knew that his hosts were rather disorganized people. He had been warned. The rooms were dim, filled with the detritus of generations.

"Never throw anything away, that's our trouble," said Albert. He patted his guest on the head and turned to his wife.

"Could throw it all away," she said, doubtfully.

"Never know when we might need some of it. A bent spanner, a broken old gramophone, a mouldy blunderbuss."

"The gun is an eyesore."

"Best to keep it, all the same."

"In case we are invaded," his wife agreed.

"Now *that's* unlikely."

Albert laughed and guided Paul into the living room. They perched him on a chair too high even for an adult. He was given weak tea and sandwiches and a promise of a tour of the house later.

"And the garden," said Christabel, the wife.

"Overgrown, it is," said Albert.

Paul took off his school cap and devoted himself to the meal. But soon his eyes were roving around the room, examining the assorted objects on shelves, a curious selection of books, parts of machines, jars of powders and liquids, dusty figurines, brass lamps, empty picture frames, paint brushes, vases, candlesticks, wax apples, briar pipes, green bottles.

"Soon get used to everything," said Albert, cheerfully.

"He already is," said Christabel.

"Anything is possible, but not everything is desirable. That's my motto. It has stood me in good stead, anyway."

"But *has* it?" wondered his wife, and he paled.

"We are doing alright," he said.

Paul had been prepared for eccentricity. In fact, he was mildly disappointed by the banality of the oddness of his hosts. They should have been dangerously insane, sword swallowers or fire eaters. That would have been more entertaining than this cryptic dankness. He asked:

"May I see my room?"

"Certainly, but the garden first. The garden is unusual. Bet you never saw a garden like this one in London."

"Do they even have gardens there?" his wife said.

"Don't be foolish, dear."

Albert showed Paul where the back door was. It opened with a loud squeal of rusty hinges. Tall grass lay beyond. Gnarled trees and ivy-covered boundaries of stone blocks. No, it wasn't the garden in his dream. It was utterly different, a wedge of neglect, a former vegetable plot run riot, creepers and tendrils snaking across the width of the area. Vast mushrooms sprouted from rotten branches that had sheared off from gloomy trunks.

"But this is only half of it," said Albert, and he squinted into the distance, a sigh that was a failed laugh emerging from his mouth. He nodded at infinity, or somewhere in its environs. Both hands thrust deep into the pockets of his tweed jacket, he turned on his heel and re-entered the house. Paul lingered and tried to see what lay beyond the limits of human perspective. The stone walls converged to a point, but the point was illusory.

"Can any garden be so big?" he asked when he returned to the living room. Albert was on his knees building a fire in the grate with sticks and anthracite. It was a delicate operation. He said:

"It was an orchard originally but somehow it ended up as a garden. This is one of the last houses in the village."

And as if that explained everything, he rolled up a page of newspaper and thrust it deep into the pile of sticks.

Paul licked his lips. The ball of paper began to uncurl.

"The garden turns a sharp corner right at the end? That's why we can only see half of it from here, I suppose."

Albert stood and shrugged. He groped for a box of matches on the glossy mantlepiece. "I've never ventured down there to check. Brambles and thorns. It doesn't seem worthwhile to me."

"Now I'll show you your room," he added.

PAUL WAS GIVEN the room of their only son, Bobby, who was away at sea. They said he was out East somewhere but were reluctant to be too specific. They had already got into the habit of being secretive. It was less cluttered than the other rooms in the house, but contained a fair share of oddities, curios, ornaments, and souvenirs, not to mention heirloom furniture. There was an iron bedstead, a cabinet full of books, a rack for hats.

Most imposing of all, yet strangely inconspicuous in some manner, was a wardrobe of truly impressive dimensions. As soon as he entered the room, Paul was mystified as to how it had been carried up the stairs and conveyed between the door jambs. It was wider than the doorframe. It was all of one piece with no joints visible, not the sort of thing that can be dismantled and put back together. Its presence here seemed impossible.

The enigma of its existence ought to be explained, but Albert didn't ask if Paul wanted anything. The opportunity to inquire was lost. Paul was left alone, wondering how much Bobby had really made his mark on the room. Nothing here evoked an individual. It was all an amalgam of generations. The woodcuts on the walls, the sabre hanging in a scabbard above the door, even the drapes on the window spoke of a mixture of eras.

And the wardrobe was a monolith among weeds. When Paul stretched on the bed and stared at the ceiling, it loomed over him, implacable, immense. In his mind he turned it over, used it as a boat to sail down a river. It could easily accommodate him and his possessions. A playful idea. The daydream faded. It was quiet here, unlike in the city, no passing vehicles hissing like the waves on a beach. The darkness had weight, it was solid. Yet there was a blueness within it and he found he could see everything.

He was fast asleep and on the threshold of the dream about the garden. His eyes snapped open. The blueness shimmered as if he had slid under the sea. The wardrobe seemed more obvious than before, a block of night, a tomb. He stilled his breathing. Now he could hear footsteps, very distant, quite methodical. They echoed weakly. Was someone moving about downstairs or out on the street? He concentrated, lifted his head higher.

The pillow he had been resting on was damp with sweat. He felt feverish, a spasm racked his body. He exhaled slowly, fighting the urge to sob. There could be no doubt. The footsteps were coming from inside the wardrobe. Slowly they grew in volume. Distant, too remote, as if coming along a path of broken stones, the echoes were trapped within its wooden sides. Paul chewed hard on his lower lip but tasted no blood. He shivered.

Fear had gripped him, but something strong deep within his mind was now gripping the fear. If any grip was relaxed, anything might happen. Paul felt more like a disinterested bystander than an active participant. He remarked to himself with curious aplomb, "Just someone inside the wardrobe," and then he threw off the bedclothes and sat up, waiting. For some reason, it was easier to listen when he wasn't encumbered by the sheets.

The footsteps were accelerating. Whoever was making them was speeding up from a walk to a run. The handles on the wardrobe door, loops of iron, were eyes watching Paul's reaction. Paul knew he had to appear unconcerned. Did the wardrobe sway slightly? In the tangled blue shadows it was difficult to be sure. The footsteps stopped. The feet, shod or bare, that had made them were standing on the other side of the locked door.

"But they sound more like hooves," he said quietly, then horrifying himself with his boldness he called out, "Are you the Devil?"

But his voice failed at the end of the question, became a croak.

His body was absolutely rigid, the wardrobe seemed to regard him with an amused expression or a malign one, he wasn't sure which. The circular handles gazed at him intently. They wanted to remember him, he thought. He realized he had resumed breathing, but his breaths were shallow. He felt lightheaded. Then the wardrobe door rattled, just once.

There was silence for a moment. The footsteps resumed, growing fainter as Paul struggled to control his convulsive lungs. They were retreating into depths that simply shouldn't have existed. At long last they faded away to nothingness, but Paul remained where he was, ears straining, until the grey light of dawn and the singing of birds heralded daytime.

Paul lay down but was unable to sleep. He wondered why the Devil would be inside a wardrobe. Logic told him it was a ludicrous idea. The footsteps must have some other source. Perhaps he was going mad. His father had told him the tale of a man with a tumour in his brain who saw ghostly figures in his kitchen. No, that couldn't be right. The wardrobe was a creature in its own right and had been playing malevolent tricks on him.

ALBERT SAID, "You look worn out."

Paul sat at the table in the living room and ate the toast that Christabel had placed in front of him. He grimaced.

"First night in a new bed, I expect," Albert added.

"It was fine," said Paul.

"Guess you'll want to explore the village today?"

"Of course he will," confirmed Christabel, "and make new friends. It must be a bit disconcerting for him."

"Stranger in a strange land? Out in the sticks with the yokels. Here with the daft ha'pennies of Devonshire."

"No, it's alright really," answered Paul.

Albert smirked his approval.

"Tough lad, no namby-pamby nonsense with him. Get some fresh air down by the river. There's an old bridge."

"I'd quite like to see the garden again."

"What for? All weeds."

"It's very interesting," said Paul.

"Bit of a jungle, mind," Albert remarked, "But there's a good view from a skylight in the attic. Only window in the house that faces that direction. Hardly ever use the attic these days."

"Full of clutter," said Christabel.

"The clutter that got in the way of the clutter down here," was Albert's idea of a witticism. He laughed as he filled his pipe with some obscure tobacco, lit it with a match and allowed it to go out almost at once. "So we removed it. Deuce of a job to get it up there."

"Show me the way," pleaded Paul.

"Ain't nothing to it, my lad. The passage leading to your room? Keep on to the end of it. There's a door in the wall, but it doesn't look like a door at first. It is flush with the wall, see. Need strong fingernails to prise it open. The cavity it exposes has a spiral staircase."

"Every step creaks with a different note of the scale," said Christabel, "and makes a hell of a din if you fall."

"Play a Music Hall song on it, if you're clever."

"Thank you," said Paul simply.

He finished his toast. He pushed his plate away, as if it was his past and a hindrance. He rose to depart.

Albert ignored him, Christabel had returned to the kitchen. Paul climbed the stairs to the landing, took the corridor that led past his room, soon found the hidden door and managed to open it. The spiral staircase wasn't as dramatic as he hoped it would be. It was made of unvarnished wood and colorless. He ascended in a tight helix. His head rose above the level of the attic floor into a dusty world under the sloping roof.

Cobwebs sagged from the rafters, furry with dust motes, desiccated flies, a bone-dry moth of immense size. Paul was struck by the idea that he was inside a vast wardrobe, not an attic at all. He shook his head, balanced himself on rickety floorboards, blinked in the dim light.

The knick-knacks here were of a wider variety than those downstairs. In a corner stood a pipe organ, the relic of some unconsecrated chapel, with yellow keys like stained teeth. Paul wandered erratically towards the window, touching objects, spinning an old globe on its pivot, swinging the pendulum of a warped grandfather clock in a smashed case, brushing the spines of ancient volumes in green leather with tingling fingertips.

He found a flashlight and to his surprised delight it worked, though it was weak. He switched it off again to conserve the dying battery. There was a brass telescope. He picked it up and carried it to the window, setting it down, leaning on it as if it was a crutch. He sneezed.

The pane of the skylight was grimy. He wiped it with the sleeve of his shirt and made a porthole. He could see the garden spread below, the boundary walls undulating into the distance, two wavy lines meeting at a point far away. With a serious expression, he tried looking with the telescope. At first he had difficulty adjusting the focus. He persevered.

The lens was faulty, perhaps. He saw a brown door at the farthest end of the garden, ordinary enough, but the image shifted, chromatic aberration made it seem he was peering through a rainbow and abruptly he lost focus. He lowered the telescope, sighed, turned to search for other interesting objects. He found a magnifying glass and a walking stick.

He knew there was something odd about the stick when he picked it up. It was heavy and the word *Calcutta* was inscribed on the bulbous pommel. With a quiver of delight, he realized it was a swordstick, a secret rapier, the weapon of a cultured assassin. He drew it out gingerly. The blade needed oiling but it was in relatively good condition. He smirked.

As he was crossing the attic to the spiral stairway, he noticed a knothole in a floorboard. He threw himself flat in the dust and pressed his eye to it. He saw shadows beyond as thick and flowing as treacle. He aimed the flashlight beam through the hole. Although the bulb was weak it provided enough illumination for him to perceive that he was directly above his bedroom. The wardrobe was there, the top just a few feet below him.

On that flat surface he saw strange carvings, tendrils or tentacles, entities that were both plants and sea creatures.

This minor adventure gave him an idea. He stood and descended and went into the garden with the swordstick. Albert and Christabel were elsewhere. Free to do whatever he pleased, he risked incurring their displeasure. He planned to slash his way to the end of the garden, to the brown door. Just because the door of the wardrobe was locked didn't mean the garden door was too. He must find out the truth for himself. He plunged into the growth and soon was lost among the ferns and brambles and rose bushes.

THEY FOUND HIM an hour after the onset of night. He had managed to cut a path one quarter the length of the garden. He was exhausted by the effort, sitting on the ground among the dripping sap, the sword next to him, his flashlight bulb pulsing slowly. Albert picked him up.

"Bit of an explorer, eh? Just like our Bobby."

"Needs a slap," said Christabel.

"I was the same when I was a lad. No real harm done." Albert regarded the fuss his wife was making as amusing but unnecessary. She pretended to be in a worse mood than she was, but she did resent the time spent worrying when they hadn't been able to find him anywhere in the house. They assumed he had gone to the river and fallen off the bridge.

"Tired out, yes? Manual labor," said Albert, suddenly in a political frame of mind. He added, "Imagine doing that kind of work day in and day out for ten or twenty years. Or worse, being down the mines. Not much fun, is it? Poor pay, injurious to health. This is why we need a different kind of government after the war. Thank your lucky stars, lad."

But he didn't mention what Paul ought to be grateful for. He carried him back to the house and set him down in the most comfortable chair in the living room. Christabel brought him a cup of tea. Albert crouched

and continued his political speculation. Paul yawned.

"Oh, leave the boy alone." Now it was Christabel's turn to be sympathetic and she stroked Paul's hair tenderly.

"Not everything in the world should be delved into," Albert said, his voice growing melancholic. "Often things have other reasons for existing. I have no idea what's at the bottom of the garden. But I bet it ain't fairies. Or pots of gold. Probably just blackberries when the season's right. It's a lesson for us all. The effort is almost never worthwhile."

"There's a door," said Paul.

"There's *always* a door," countered Albert, "but it doesn't mean a blooming thing. You left the sword behind."

"Didn't you bring it?"

"Nasty old thing. My grandfather was in India. Brought it back with him as a memento. I never liked the look."

"It'll rust in the garden," pointed out Paul.

"Best thing for it," said Christabel, but she held out the flashlight. "Didn't forget this, though, did we?"

Paul nodded. He could collect the sword tomorrow. He hoped it wouldn't rain during the night. They allowed him to rest in the chair until he felt strong enough to climb the stairs to bed.

He should have fallen asleep immediately, but something in the room had a disconcerting effect on him. He lay on his back and felt he was moving, pushing his way through the tangled garden. The muscles in his arm twitched as if he was still swinging the blade. And then the footsteps began, distant, remote, the irregular rhythm. He stared at the wardrobe. The handles were eyes. He gulped and waited. The hooves clattered.

This time he wouldn't call out. He would say nothing. It wasn't the Devil in there, it *couldn't* be the Devil. It was somebody else. The hooves were just shoes, wooden clogs, or it was an acoustical trick? He waited. These footsteps were coming from a great distance.

Louder and closer, but now they seemed to slow down. The first time he had heard them, they had accelerated into a run. This time they were cautious, perhaps aware of Paul on the other side, approaching him with greater stealth. What if he had the key to the door this time? It would swing open and then the world beyond would be exposed to Paul's gaze. Or would the inhabitant within block the view? The steps diminished.

Almost imperceptibly, the wardrobe vibrated. Paul held his breath, waiting for the sound of the turning of the key in the lock. He felt clammy all over. His eyes ached. Then the door moved. Whoever was inside was trying to open it but had no key. Paul was safe again, just for one more night. The steps retreated but only a few paces. There was silence.

Paul waited under the sheets, icy, shivering, until the fear became like the turning of a gigantic wheel over his body, and he shook himself out of the cold sheets and moved towards the wardrobe. The idea that the knothole in the attic had given him returned. He nodded.

The keyhole could be peered through. It was better to get the ordeal over and done with as rapidly as possible.

There was no need to kneel or squat. The keyhole was at eye level. Just a matter of leaning forwards and pressing his orbit to the gap. He saw nothing at all, just blackness, but felt a slight breeze on his eye. There was wind inside the wardrobe. And now he smelled a sweet scent. Flowers of some kind. Also mild decay, a rich aroma of humus, ancient soil. He groped for his magnifying glass and tried again. Still only blackness.

Now he took the flashlight, switched it on, held the feeble beam to the hole and tried to look inside. But the flashlight was bulky and wouldn't allow him to shine and see at the same time. Yet there came a sigh from the other side as the beam played over the form of whatever lurked behind the wooden door. A sigh of sadness deeper and more intense than terror, a whisper of infinite resignation. Whatever existed in the wardrobe was timeless, eternal, trapped and despairing, a victim as well as a menace, a void.

Paul fell back, shaking his head, his chest constricted.

The flashlight fell and broke.
Slowly, he kneeled.

BOBBY TURNED UP one day, on leave. Unlike his parents, he wasn't reticent about what he had been doing. He had sailed to India in a troop ship. He was going to be based there from now on. The Japanese were surely planning to invade. He was tall and jovial and took to Paul immediately, showing him the photographs he had taken of his barracks, the forests, the trees. His family had a connection with India, he said. "Vast place, it is."

He added, "Swamps and tigers too. Whole country is overgrown, just like the garden of this house." And if this joke wasn't enough, he dipped into one of his pockets and pulled out a box of matches. "Seen anything like these before? They might *look* familiar but they aren't."

"Bengal Lights," he explained, after a suitable pause.

Paul watched as Bobby struck one.

The head flared up, white streaked with blue and spitting, and it burned for a long time without eating the wooden stick that Bobby was holding. "Used by the Signals Corps. Toxic, though, so you must take care, realgar and orpiment, a dangerous mixture. But safe in capable hands. Come on." He nudged Paul and took the flaming brand to the back door. "Let's take it into the garden. It's too smoky here. Fumes filling the house."

Paul opened the door.

"Look at that," said Bobby, as he cast the brand into the distance. "Who's been cutting at the plants?

"Like a rhinoceros charged through," he added.

Paul was tongue-tied.

The Bengal Light finally spluttered out. It had burned a circle around itself that still glowed with tiny sparks.

Bobby held up the box of Bengal Lights, shook it, opened it, rummaged inside. Some of the sticks were tipped with more of the flammable chemicals than others. He was seeking a fat example.

"Here's one for you," Bobby said, and Paul accepted the precious gift. His mind reeled as he realized that here was a key to the secret of the wardrobe. Not *the* key, but a key nonetheless.

"Great," said Paul, and Bobby replied:

"I won't be wanting my room back. No need for you to move out. See that shed over there?" He pointed to the decayed shack next to a lichen-covered pear tree. "There's a camp bed inside. Often slept on it in the past. Prefer it to a soft bed, in fact. You can stay in my room."

Paul nodded. He clutched the precious stick.

Bobby emitted a laugh.

"Life's a strange old thing, mind."

It was a commonplace observation that suddenly struck Paul with a terrific force. He felt a great weight on his soul. The footsteps in the wardrobe carried a weight too. The density of oblivion.

Paul went into his room after supper and lay down and waited. He felt he would never sleep again, but this feeling was deceptive. He must have dozed off despite his reluctance. He was awakened by the sound of the hooves inside the wardrobe. Now they paced from side to side. Whoever they belonged to had decided to remain near the door.

They ceased. Paul scarcely dared to breathe or blink. Five minutes passed before he slipped silently out of bed. He moved in a crouch to the wardrobe and stood until his eye was level with the keyhole. Darkness and a feeble sigh. With trembling hands, Paul took the Bengal Light and struck it on the rough surface of the iron lock. It flared up, threw a garish glow over his face. Whimpering, he inserted it into the keyhole, propelled it with a flick. It dropped inside. He fixed his right eye to the hole once again.

The Bengal Light was spluttering a yard away from the door, illuminating an area larger than the bedroom. Paul felt the saliva in his mouth turn oily. He was unable to swallow. There was a garden in the wardrobe. Not a garden like the one that belonged to the house. The walls that formed its boundaries on each side were much higher and stronger.

There were trees, old and gnarled but some laden with fruit, and the scent of night blooms wafted to him on the currents of hot air generated by the Bengal Light. Low flat stones made a path into the distance. On a slightly rounder stone sat a figure with its back to Paul, but he knew it was clutching its knees. Then it gradually turned and gazed with an anguished but infinitely weary expression at the keyhole. Paul was horrified, captivated. The figure was a man but there was something wrong with his lower legs.

Then he blinked and Paul's stomach twisted inside him. The eyelids closed upwards. The man's eyes were inverted. Now the man smiled and Paul realized his mouth was upside-down too. The smile was a grimace of despair. His flaring nostrils sucked in the smoke of the Bengal Light. His nose was also inverted. In fact, his entire face was wrong. Somehow it had flipped on his head. Paul shook but was unable to retreat. He retched.

The man walked forwards and lifted an arm. His fist was clenched and then he opened it to reveal an empty palm.

What did this gesture mean? Paul felt a desire to rescue him but also a deep aversion to him, a blend of horror and intolerable sadness. He needed the key. It was the only answer. A key to the wardrobe door! The man began to stamp on the Bengal Light, putting out the flame.

Paul fell back, gasping. A few wisps of smoke came out of the keyhole. He said to himself again and again, "I will let him out. I wouldn't keep an animal in a cage. I won't let him remain there."

The burning Bengal Light floated before him as an afterimage. It scorched the walls as he turned, turned the bed into a lake of fire, incinerated his hands as he held them up to repeat the enigmatic gesture, opening and closing them. He sat on the edge of the bed and wept.

BOBBY LEFT AFTER TEN DAYS. He was summoned by telegram unexpectedly and had no time to say farewell to Paul. Then enemy bombers were reported in the area. It seemed the village was no longer a sanctuary. A new military establishment a short way along the coast, a radar station, made the region a target. Albert said the children had to be evacuated again.

Paul realized he would never learn the secret of the wardrobe and it would torment his soul for the rest of his life.

On his last day in this house, he made a supreme effort to reach the far end of the garden. He did so when Albert and Christabel were out shopping. When he opened the back door, he was confronted by a wedge of charred earth. Even the shed that Bobby had occupied was a ruin. Its walls had vanished and only the blackened wooden roof remained.

Paul approached it and saw the same patterns carved into the timbers as he had seen on the top of the wardrobe. Had the enemy already bombed the garden without his knowledge? No, that was a ludicrous idea. Then he understood that the sparks from the discarded Bengal Light had started a fire in the roots of the grass, one that had spread very slowly.

It had devoured the shed and most of the vegetation as far as he could see. This made his task easier, though grimier. He walked forwards, crunching soft granules of carbon underfoot. He soon passed the farthest point he had reached with the swordstick. He found the blade melted and cooled into a new shape, a deformed scimitar, a bizarre, cruel, and useless weapon. He stepped over it and kept going. Ash billowed around him.

The fire was dead and it had eaten everything right to his destination. But as he proceeded, he learned a curious truth. The convergence of the walls wasn't a trick of perspective. The garden was shaped like a long isosceles triangle and came to a sharp point. Wherever the other half of the garden might be, it wasn't here. There simply wasn't sufficient space. He was channeled by these walls to the elusive brown door, which was covered in soot but still standing firm. Paul pulled at the handle. Nothing happened.

The door was shut, but there was a key in the lock. He tried to turn it, but it was stuck. He extracted it and saw that it was the wrong key, too small for such a door. He pocketed it and rested his forehead against the wood. Whatever was beyond, whether adventure or paradise, suffering or nothingness, was forbidden to him. That was the only explanation.

He stumbled away at last, turned and loped back to the house. Albert was standing in the kitchen. He seemed unsurprised that Paul had made a desperate attempt to find an ultimate meaning in a pointless activity. He remembered his own youth and smiled indulgently.

He said, "We're packing you off right now. A bus is on its way. I reckon you'll have a fine time in your new home. Anything you forget, we can send it on as a parcel. Brave face, lad.

"But clean it first, you grubby rascal," he added.

THE WAR ENDED, but Paul went to sea. He wanted to emulate Bobby despite the victory. Years passed. Something happened, an accident. It was kept a secret by the military. Albert and Christabel heard only rumors. But one morning Albert was reading the newspaper and an item caught his attention. He read it aloud to his wife, who was at the sink, peeling potatoes.

"Something I heard in the pub stuck in my mind. Harold was talking about his brother who was missing in action. Then he gets a contract to provide some of his prefabricated houses and lots of the words were blacked out. But he held it up to a light and found he could read it from the other side. The prefabs were intended for the *really* badly wounded."

"What's odd about that?" wondered Christabel.

She used the point of her knife to dig out an eye from the potato she was holding in her strong chilled fingers.

"Thing is," said Albert, "they were too mangled to be alive. Yet they were alive anyway. Get it? How can you send chaps like that back home or even tell the loved ones? Better to say 'missing in action' or something. Makes sense, if you see it from their point of view. Well, Harold began thinking that maybe his own brother was one of them. He said he always had a feeling his brother was trying to send him messages in his mind. I don't know how that works, but the trauma, whatever it was, altered his brain."

"Just banter and ravings," was Christabel's opinion. She paused to see how Albert would react to her skepticism.

He slapped the table with the newspaper. "Reckon this confirms it. If you read between the lines, anyway. The government has established a new hospital for hopeless cases,

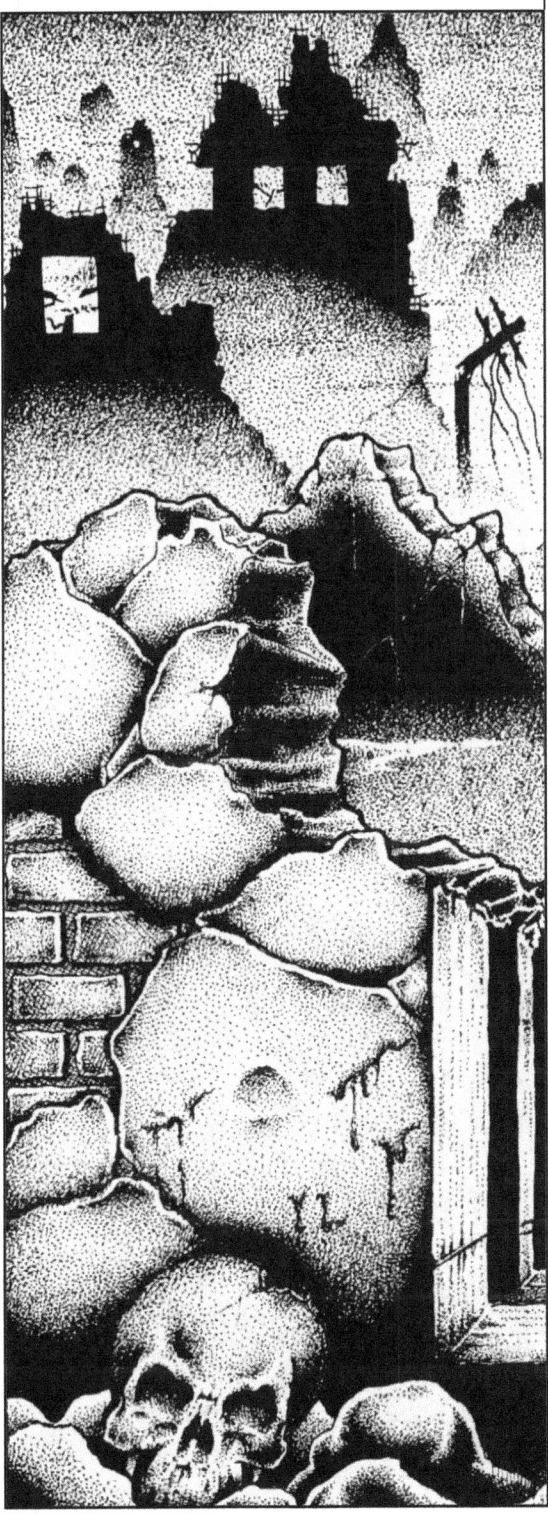

you know, the ones that can't go home. They are denying it but a minister had a slip of the tongue."

"Where is the hospital located?" asked Christabel.

"That's the point. They won't say. Somewhere very isolated, maybe on an island that's off-limits to visitors. Maybe it's not even on the map. Could be on military land or in a foreign country."

Christabel washed the peeled potato in the bowl.

"Paul went missing too."

"Not in action," said Albert, "but maybe that doesn't matter. What was his role? If he was working in the engine room and there was a snag." He shrugged and sipped his cup of tea. "Ah well."

"He was a fun little blighter, though, wasn't he?"

"They soon grow up."

"What are these hospitals like then?"

"How the blooming hell should I know that? Harold didn't describe them. And I didn't want to question him about the voices in his head. That wouldn't be polite. Might drive him barmy."

"If your tale is true, they have taken Paul to some place where he can be looked after for the rest of his life."

"But what *kind* of life, eh? That's the question."

"Must do *something* with them."

"That's just what worried Harold. What kind of something? I'll pop down the pub later and show him the paper. Here," he said in a more practical tone, "I am thinking it's time to get rid of some of this clutter. We can start with Bobby's room, rent it out to a lodger. Could do with the extra cash but nobody is going to want to stay here with all the junk."

Christabel nodded abstractedly and continued peeling and washing. At last she said, "Study the shape of these, Albert."

"Homegrown, delicious."

"But they don't look right to me."

"Who cares what they *look* like, dear? It's what they *are* that matters. That is a general rule for life. The war seemed terrible, didn't it? It looked awful. The craters, the wreckage. But it was the best time of our lives.

I should have been a philosopher, but I never had a chance."

He turned to the crossword, licked a pencil.

"Anything is possible," he said, and then after a pause, "but not everything is desirable." He clicked his tongue.

IN THE FACILITY, in the enclosed garden, waiting. It is a beautiful prison but lonely. He walks towards the door, lies down on the grass under a tree to sleep. Night falls. He tries to dream of a different garden. His mind refuses to find the right images in his subconscious. Once they came so easily and then they were driven so deep into his soul they were lost forever. They remain inside, he is sure. His soul is cluttered with fragments of broken memories, splinters, shards so jagged that some cut him in unknown places.

He abandons sleep, sits on a stone, clasps his knees. A spanner, broken old gramophone, mouldy blunderbuss. These are the decayed images he is trying to evoke. He concentrates on them, but he feels too anxious to continue. The door behind him rattles gently as if it is being deliberately pushed. A breath of wind from another world follows it. The garden brightens. He hears a hissing like one of the rare snakes he has been warned about. A Bengal Light

has come through the keyhole and landed on the grass.

Paul stands up. He turns and steps forward, opening his clenched fist. On his palms rests an object. He smiles. Twenty years have passed in agony and his future has passed with them. But the pain has finally subsided to a dull burning. He shuffles forwards, resisting the impulse to run and hurl himself at the door. His hooves kick the sparks high as he walks. All his features are upside-down. He holds the key he has been keeping for so long, moves to the door and inserts it. He turns the key. The door opens.

Rhys Hughes has lived in many different countries and currently lives in India. "The Soul Garden" was conceived in Goa but written down in Sri Lanka. Rhys began writing at an early age and his first book, Worming the Harpy, *was published in 1995 by Tartarus Press. Since that time, he has published more than fifty other books and his work has been translated into ten languages. He recently completed an ambitious project that involved writing exactly 1000 linked narratives.*

FINDING THE HOLLOW MAN

BY DAVID SURFACE

TO: *Maryanne Bishop*
FROM: *Kathryn James*
DATE: *2–15–2016, 9:11 PM*

RE: *Request for interview*

So you've found me.

In my day, it took some digging to find a missing person. Especially one who did not want to be found. These days, all you have to do is push a few buttons.

I don't understand what you want from me. This story you want to interview me for—is it a crime story, or a love story? Or a ghost story? A good story can't be too many things, or else it starts to fall apart. You should know that—you're a writer, aren't you?

You want to know if I'm the same Kathryn James in those news stories from fifty years ago. Am I the same fourteen year-old kid in those black and white photos, that skinny girl strapped to the stretcher, pale-faced and smeared with mud, being carried out of that black hole by all those men with flat-top haircuts and serious faces? When you ask if that was me—in all the ways you understand those words—I have to say yes, that was me.

You say you don't believe the newspapers tell the whole story. Nine children go into a cave, only one comes out... You say there has to be more to it than that.

Let me ask you this—if I didn't tell the whole story to the police, the social workers and psychologists, if I didn't tell my teachers or my friends, or my own mother, what makes you think I'll tell you?

You say you can wait till I'm ready. Really? How long, exactly, are you prepared to wait?

You think you're a patient woman? You don't know what patience is. You don't know what it means to wait, without hope or reason. To wait in the cold and dark without even a goddamn glimmer of light.

○ ○ ○

If I agree to tell you my story, there are going to be certain conditions. And I will expect you to honor them.

My conditions are this—that you tell my story exactly like I tell it to you here. Don't change a word. I will not have lies put in my mouth. If you promise not to change what I say, I promise to give you the truth. It's as simple as that.

I'll wait.

○ ○ ○

The truth is that this is not really my story. It's Billy's. His and mine, maybe. But there is no story without Billy.

The first thing you need to know is that it wasn't Billy's fault, like some people said it was. Billy never held a gun to any of those kids' heads. They followed him into that cave for the same reason I did. Because they wanted to. That's the gift that Billy had. Making people do things they'd never do otherwise, making you see things you knew

could not be true. That's how it all started with the Hollow Man.

I heard Billy tell the story of the Hollow Man in the playground at school, in the backyards of our families and friends after dark, later in old cemeteries, in well-worn spots in the woods or by the river where we went to smoke and drink on those long high school Friday nights.

The story of the Hollow Man grew over the years, like stories do. At first I thought Billy was just making it up as he went along. Later I realized that he was revealing more and more of the real thing, piece by piece, giving us what he thought we could handle.

The story starts with the Civil War, which was all around us back then, in the books they gave us to read in school, in the monuments to the Confederate dead, and the rusted cannonball the size of a baseball that sat on my father's desk, the one he'd dug up from a cornfield just a few miles away.

A hundred years before, when that cannonball was shiny and new, the story of the war was written on people's bodies, the ones that were still walking on whatever limbs they had left, and the ones that would never walk again. Back then, the dead were everywhere, Billy told us, like fruit that rots where it falls because there's too many to pick up.

In nature, nothing goes to waste, including the dead. The wild dogs and crows took their share, but there were also people who helped themselves, doctors and surgeons who needed bodies to cut open and study. When the war was on and the dead were everywhere, the doctors could take their pick. But when peace came, the dead were hard to find, so they went back to scrounging in all the places where the dead get thrown away and forgotten. Prisons, asylums, and poor houses all make good picking-grounds, if you get there quickly enough. The quicker the better. Executions are the best. They run on schedule, no guesswork, no waiting.

That's what brought the doctors to our town—in a place as small as this one, a hanging is always big news. The way Billy told it, the doctors went straight to the jail and talked to the man who was to be hung, asked permission to take his body after the hangman was done with it. The man got angry and refused, so the doctors waited till after the hanging, then bribed the undertaker and took the body anyway.

It was hot, the hottest part of summer, not a good time to travel with a dead body, so the doctors decided to do the dissection right there. They needed a place that was cool, dark, and secret, so they went deep into the cave at the edge of town and did what they wanted to do. After they'd removed and studied the man's heart, his lungs, liver, and everything inside of him, they stuffed his empty body full of rocks and sank him deep in the blue hole near the mouth of the cave—the same place where people go nowadays to picnic and take pictures of their kids next to the wildflowers and the pretty blue water.

You can guess the rest of the story—the strange noises, shadows moving across the cave walls where no shadow should be, the horrible shape glimpsed from the corner of your eye. You probably had a story like that in the town where you grew up. Every town does. The kid decapitated in a school bus crash. The old man burned to death in his bed. All the mutilated dead coming back to make us look at the worst things life can do.

But the Hollow Man was different. All those other stories are public property; they belong to everyone. The Hollow Man belonged to Billy. You should have seen him tell it, the way his voice grew quiet and big at the same time, the way his glasses caught the firelight and threw it back at us. When Billy said that in the deepest, darkest parts of the cave, the Hollow Man still walks, looking for what was taken from him, you didn't just believe it was true, you *knew* it, like you knew the feel of your own skin wrapped around you.

The other thing you need to know about Billy is how invisible he was, most of the time. You know the kind—smaller, weaker, quieter than the other boys, until he opened his mouth and turned his power loose on you. Nature gives gifts to the small and

weak, and the bigger and stronger animals hate them for it.

Jordan was like that. While the rest of us were getting caught up in the tale Billy was telling, you could feel Jordan getting angrier and angrier, until one night he finally snapped and called Billy a liar, right there in front of everybody.

Billy didn't back down. He just sat there, peering at Jordan through his glasses. *It's true,* Billy said. *Look it up.*

I spent the rest of that weekend in the library, looking for proof. Afraid that I wouldn't find it. I didn't want Jordan to be right. I finally found what I was looking for in a binder of old newspapers, buried among all the other stories about politicians and crop prices, an article called *Dead Man's Cave.* I looked closer and there it was. The two doctors, the hanged man, the secret dissection. It was all there.

I learned things that I never knew before, things Billy never told us. For one thing, the Hollow Man had a name. Caleb Wilkins. He was thirty-one years old when he died, was what the paper called a *laborer,* and had killed a man in a drunken brawl at the local tavern, probably over money.

I'd always liked the part of the story where the condemned man got angry at the doctors and refused to let them have his body. I pictured him raging in his cell, tearing up the papers they'd brought him to sign and throwing the pieces in their faces, like Jesus throwing the moneychangers out of the temple.

What's hard to understand now is why Caleb Wilkins refused to give up his body in the first place. If you believe in heaven and hell, like most people did back then, or even if you don't and you think death is the end, like turning off a light-switch, either way it doesn't matter what happens to your body after you die, because you won't be in it.

So why was Caleb Wilkins so afraid to let them cut up his body after he was dead? Was it because those answers—that your soul goes to heaven or hell, or that there is no soul—are both wrong? What if something else happens? What if part of us knows, deep down inside, that there's no escape and that we're all trapped in our bodies forever?

Those were the kind of questions I thought Billy could help me understand.

I brought it all to him. The xerox of the newspaper article, the names, the dates, the facts. Billy let me come in and spread the papers across his bed where we looked at them together for an hour or more. Before long, I started to get the feeling that Billy wasn't really looking at the papers anymore. That's when I glanced up and caught him looking at my chest. He looked away, but I saw the color in his face change.

Then Billy started talking. He started out by saying that he and I had known each other for a long time, wasn't that true? I said yes, yes it was. Then he started saying things I didn't understand. He talked about how growing up isn't something that just happens to you—it's something you *do*, a process of trial and error where every mistake brings you closer to where you need to be. I didn't understand what he was going on about, but whatever it was, I could see it was making him suffer. His voice shook, and he couldn't look me in the eye. The more he talked, the worse it got. It was a hard thing to watch. I found myself praying that he'd stop, but he just kept going.

Billy said that growing up isn't something you can do by yourself. You need other people—maybe that was something we could do for each other. He said all this, trying not to look at me, while I waited for him to get to the point. When he finally did, it was so tortured and twisted that I almost didn't recognize it. He said that we should *do things. Try things.*

I have, in my sixty-five years, heard more than enough talk about what men and women do with each other with their bodies, but I swear to God, I have never heard anything more horrible than those few awkward, child-like words.

I confess, I'd had thoughts about being with Billy, but those were more like dreams or music, nothing hard and real like what he was talking about now. I'd always felt that what Billy and I had was something special and fine, almost holy. But after what he'd just said, I didn't feel like he wanted *me*—it was more like I was a *thing* he wanted to use for his own selfish purpose,

like it was some kind of science experiment.

I told him I wasn't sure and asked him if I could think about it. He told me that was fine, and for a moment it almost looked like he felt relieved.

That Friday night, I took the papers I'd copied at the library and brought them with me to that spot in the woods where we all liked to gather. Jordan was not impressed. He said that just because some stupid old drunk got hung and cut up, that didn't prove the Hollow Man was real.

That's when I heard Billy say something. I didn't understand it until he said it again, loud enough for all of us to hear.

"I saw him. I saw the Hollow Man."

Everyone got real quiet then. What I felt was a whole other kind of horror—that Billy had said such a foolish and unnecessary thing, all because he'd let anger and pride get the better of him. But once you've stepped over that edge, there's nothing left to do but keep going, and that's what Billy did, conjuring the Hollow Man, word by word, right in front of our eyes. He told us how one day he'd gone deep into the cave, deeper than ever before, when he felt someone watching him, looked up and saw a figure standing on a ledge high above. *The Hollow Man was naked,* Billy told us, with pale fish-like skin, split wide open (that's how he said it—*split wide open*) from throat to crotch, all yawning raw and empty inside like one of those carcasses you see hanging in the butcher shop. He told us about the wet, rattling sound the figure made, like when you suck the last of a drink through a straw— and how even after the Hollow Man slid back out of sight, he could still hear that rattling sound echoing in the darkness.

It was too much for Jordan. He really went off, called Billy a liar and told him how we were all sick of his stories, how we'd been sick of them for years, but no one had the guts to say it till now. He went on and on about how Billy was just hungry for attention, and what a needy, pathetic little freak he was.

Billy just sat there and took it, staring at Jordan with the firelight flickering in the lenses of his glasses. Then he said it. He told Jordan that if he didn't believe him, he should follow him down to the cave right now and see for himself.

While the other kids were putting out the campfire and getting ready to go, I managed to get Billy by himself for a moment. I was angry—if Billy was telling the truth about what he saw, why didn't he tell me first? And if he was lying and asking me to believe him, that meant he thought I was a fool, no better than the rest of them. I was just about to say all of this to him, when he looked me in the eye and told me he didn't want me to come with them.

If he'd told me to go to hell and slapped me in the face, I couldn't have felt more hurt. I knew he was trying to protect me, but I didn't care. Whatever was going to happen to Billy, I wanted it to happen to me.

"Do what you want," he said. "I don't care." Then he walked away. I let him get far enough ahead of me, then I fell in line with the others and started after him.

o o o

TO: Maryanne Bishop
FROM: Kathryn James
DATE: 2–17–2016, 9:09 AM

RE: Request for interview

I apologize for leaving you hanging. It's not because it was getting late and I needed to sleep—I haven't slept. To be honest, it's because I need to write the rest of this story in the daylight. When I'm finished, I think you'll understand why.

Let me ask you this—have you ever been inside a cave? Not one of those tourist attractions with hand-railings and staircases and spotlights, all lit up like Hollywood—I'm talking about a *real* cave, the kind that makes you work and sweat for every yard you go, the kind that holds its secrets. That's the kind of cave we had, and it was open to anyone with enough courage and a flashlight, until the town decided it was dangerous and tried to seal it off. But kids love forbidden places. Put a sign over the gates of Hell that says KEEP OUT and kids will run right into the fire, every time.

We followed Billy through the woods and felt the trail dropping down lower and lower. I could feel the air getting colder the farther down we went. Then there it was, a jagged black wound, torn in the side of a limestone cliff, half-hidden by moss and tangled vines. I could feel the cave breathing its damp, cold breath over my skin, my hair lifting in the breeze pouring up from underground.

We went slowly into the mouth of the cave and walked along the ledge that ran beside a little river that disappeared underground. The ledge got narrower and narrower until we all had to walk single-file. I could see Billy out in front, shining his flashlight ahead into the dark.

As we got deeper into the cave, the roof got lower and lower until we had to crawl. Being flat on my belly with all those tons of rock just an inch over my back and not being able to stand up made me feel like screaming. Instead, I just tried to make my mind go blank and kept moving.

When we finally got to a place where we could stand up again, I heard a rushing sound like a waterfall, so loud it was hard to talk, so we all kept walking in silence. The rock floor under our feet got rougher and rougher and suddenly I realized we were climbing over jagged stones right in the middle of the river. The roar of the waterfall was deafening now, though I still couldn't see it. I tried not to imagine what would happen if one of us slipped on a rock and got sucked away in that freezing cold water. I couldn't think of anything worse than getting pulled over the edge like that and falling blind into whatever was down there.

By the time I got to the other side, I looked around and saw flashlights bobbing and waving in different places, some nearby, some far away. I realized the group had split up, following different paths over the rocks. I could hear people yelling back and forth to each other. The water was too loud to understand what they were saying, but you could tell from the sound of their voices that they were scared.

I watched all those flashlights waving around in the dark disappear one by one, till there was only one—then it was gone too. I started to panic, then I heard a deep, raspy voice right behind me say, *"I'm the*

Hollow Man… I want your internal organs…"
I turned around and saw Jordan, shining a flashlight under his chin and laughing. I yelled at him, but I was glad—not glad to see him, just glad not to be alone in the dark.

The two of us kept climbing along the side of the river toward the spot where I'd seen that last flashlight disappear. The rocks got bigger and higher until we couldn't go any further. Jordan pointed his flashlight up the wall to an opening that looked big enough to crawl through. I watched him climb up the rocks and disappear through the opening. A moment later his head popped back out and he reached down and pulled me up into a dark place away from the sound of the river and the waterfall.

I looked at Jordan. His hair was wet, there was dirt smeared on his face, and his eyes looked wilder than I'd ever seen them. I remember he asked me which way I thought we should go—it was the first time he'd ever asked me for help. Then I remembered a trick Billy had showed me—shut off your flashlight and look around for some sign of light to walk toward.

I told Jordan to turn the flashlight off. He hit the switch, and the darkness dropped on us like a weight. I tried to swallow my panic and looked for some faint glow, some slight change in the darkness. But there was nothing but blackness. It felt like being buried alive.

I don't think I started crying until Jordan put his arms around me. He didn't say anything, he just held onto me like he was trying to keep me from running away, and if he hadn't been holding onto me so hard, maybe I would have. When I felt him kiss the top of my head, it seemed like the most natural thing in the world. And when he put his mouth on mine and then put his hand under my shirt, I let him do it because it made me forget about the dark and about the panic. I couldn't see anything; it was like being blind and that made it easier to do the things we were doing.

Suddenly there was a light shining in our eyes. I couldn't see who it was behind the light, but I knew it was Billy. I said his name and the light swung away from us and I heard footsteps running away, echoing in

the dark. Jordan clicked on his light just in time to see Billy's back disappear around a corner—I was glad I couldn't see his face.

When Jordan put his hand on my shoulder I shoved it away and started walking. I heard Jordan calling out behind me but I didn't turn around or stop. I didn't want to see him, ever again.

Without the flashlight, I had to keep my hands on the walls of the cave to feel my way. The tunnels kept twisting and turning until I wasn't sure which way I was going. When I saw a glow up ahead, I moved toward it and saw someone sitting against a rock with a flashlight lying on the ground, throwing a pool of light. It was Billy. I heard him saying something, one word again and again, and I moved closer to hear what it was.

"Stupid," he was saying over and over. "Stupid, stupid, stupid…"

I told him to stop. That's when he started yelling at me. He said a lot of ugly things, some I've forgotten, some I can't forget. *"Do you know what it feels like to have your insides ripped out?"* As soon as he said that, he started laughing. He laughed and laughed like he was never going to stop, and that scared me worse than anything. I reached out to touch him, but he pushed my hand away and ran straight out of the light.

I followed the sounds of Billy's footsteps until I couldn't hear them anymore. It was pitch dark, and I kept one hand on the wall beside me and the other hand out in front of my face. I could feel the rock floor under my feet sloping downward, going deeper.

Suddenly there was nothing under my feet and I was falling—I don't know how far. I landed hard on my chest and for a minute I just lay there in the dark, afraid to breath. I could smell blood inside my nose and at the back of my throat. For a moment I thought I was going to faint, but I knew if I did, I might never get up again. *I could die*, I thought. *I could die right here.*

I pushed myself up on my hands and knees and felt a sharp pain in my side, but somehow I managed to stand up. I waited to see if my eyes could find some trace of light, but there was nothing, just cold and blackness.

I listened hard and thought I heard a noise. I called out Billy's name and the sound of my voice echoed all around me and kept going like it was never going to end. When it did, I could still hear that strange noise, and I realized what it was. Footsteps. But there was something different about them, not like the slap and squeak of Billy's tennis shoes on the wet rock floor. I listened hard then realized what was different about these footsteps. They were barefoot.

I wanted to run, but I didn't. Not because I was afraid of falling again, but because I felt like I wasn't meant to run.

The footsteps came closer, shuffling, unsteady, then they stopped. I couldn't see a thing, but I could *feel* someone standing right in front of my face in the dark. If I'd taken a half step forward, I would have touched him. Before I knew what I was doing, I knelt down on the rock. It was wet and freezing cold under my knees. Even though I couldn't see anything, I closed my eyes.

Take what you need, I thought.

I could hear a low, wet, rattling sound coming from above me like the sound my cats make when they're dreaming. Then I felt something touch my neck. It was a finger, I knew, but it felt ice-cold and wet and slippery like fish-skin. The low rattling sound was louder now. I felt the finger slide down my neck in a slow, straight line right down the center of my chest where it stopped. This time I bowed my head and said it out loud.

"Take what you need."

I could feel the cold, wet finger push harder and harder into my breastbone until I almost cried out. Then it stopped. I didn't feel the finger leave my skin. One moment it was there. Then it was gone.

o o o

TO: Maryanne Bishop
FROM: Kathryn James
DATE: 2–17–2016, 7:27 PM

RE: Request for interview

I told you I could only tell the rest of this story in the daytime. It's taken me longer than I thought.

You said you wanted the truth, and I promised to give it to you. Now I have.

Like I told you in the beginning, it wasn't Billy's fault. None of it.

There's one more thing I'd like to set straight.

The newspapers said I was disoriented when they found me down there, that I'd gotten myself lost trying to find my way back out. That's not true. I wasn't lost. I knew exactly where I was going. And it wasn't back to the surface. There was nothing left up there that I wanted to see anyway.

That's what I tried to tell the men who found me and brought me out, but they wouldn't listen. You've seen the photos. See how they have me strapped down to that stretcher? See all those scratches and bruises on my arms and my face? They didn't all come from tripping over rocks in the dark.

They burned candles outside that cave for weeks, like all those tragedies you see on TV. Fifty years later, nobody burns candles outside that cave anymore. But I keep the light going, every night. From dusk till dawn, you will never find a single light in my house that's not turned on. Even with all those lights blazing, I cannot make it bright enough.

We do what we can. That's what we say when we want to forgive ourselves for things we've done and things we've left undone. I'd like to believe that's true. I'd like to believe that we can't be blamed for mistakes we made when we were too young to understand. I'd like to believe that. But I know better. I know that even on the brightest day, there's a world of darkness just below us, and that one day it will open up and swallow us.

It's not the thought of leaving this body that keeps me awake at night—it's the thought of never leaving it, of being trapped in this body forever. What if that's what we have to look forward to?

I don't think I'll have to wait much longer to find out. That's what the doctors say, but they're liars. The X-rays they show me, all those bones and hazy white shapes floating around, my lungs, my liver, my heart, and this thing that's growing inside of me. They're not mine. I don't know whose they are, but they're not mine. Because when they cut me open, I know what they'll find. Nothing. Nothing but a hollow place, and something black and cold that goes on for miles and miles and never ends.

David Surface is the author of the collection Terrible Things *from Black Shuck Books. His stories have appeared in* Shadows & Tall Trees, Supernatural Tales, Nightscript, The Tenth Black Book of Horror, Phantom Drift, Morpheus Tales, Twisted Book of Shadows, Uncertainties III, *and* The Best Horror of the Year, Volume 13. *A YA supernatural suspense novel co-written with Julia Rust,* Angel Falls, *is now available from Haverhill House Publishing's YAP imprint. David is also the author of the newsletter* STRANGE LITTLE STORIES. *To learn more about David and his writing, visit davidsurface.net*

The boundaries which divide Life from Death are at best shadowy and vague. Who shall say where the one ends, and where the other begins? —*Edgar Allan Poe*

A SPECTER-HAUNTED PLACE DEDICATED TO THE CELEBRATION OF ALL THINGS LURKING WITHIN THE SUPERNATURAL HORROR REALM!

A TITAN OF THE TERROR TALE: AN INTERVIEW WITH PAUL FINCH

PAUL FINCH HAS DONE IT ALL. He's the editor of multiple anthologies, an award-winning short story author, a bestselling novelist and an accomplished television and film writer, for starters. He regularly updates his popular blog with book reviews, sneak peeks at projects, and even a free story or two from time-to-time. Needless to say, he's a very busy man.

I initially came across him through the Terror Tales series of horror anthologies he edits, with which I swiftly became obsessed. Those anthologies contained stories written by some of my favorite writers, such as Ramsey Campbell and Simon Kurt Unsworth, while introducing a host of new-to-me favorites, including Reggie Oliver, Anna Taborska, and Steve Duffy. The tales lurking within their pages felt as though Paul had tapped directly into my brain to curate the exact style of horror I most loved. I soon found he does more than just assemble enthralling, horrific stories—he creates them, as well, and they are superb indeed. I was

awed by his hauntingly beautiful ghost story "Devils of Lakeland," which starts off with a man investigating the recent death of his brother at a hotel they both stayed at as children. What brought his brother back there after so many years? And why had he been trying so hard to track down a used copy of a horror anthology they'd obsessed over back then? Seeking those answers, as well as trying to figure out what happened to him, leads to an even deeper mystery. I was literally holding my breath several times while reading Paul's intense story "Hell in the Cathedral." It follows a couple who are thrust into a life-or-death struggle against a bloodthirsty sea creature in the ocean. "The Old Traditions Are the Best" is another favorite

of mine wherein a young thief willfully defiles the traditions of a long-held local festival, bringing the wrath of a bizarre, ancient entity onto himself in the process. It's a top-notch folk horror tale.

If you are a fan of spooky Christmas fare, Paul has you covered there as well, with two darkly festive story collections, annual free stories on his website each December, and his excellent, gritty *Christmas Carol*-esque novella, *Sparrowhawk*.

I could continue singing his praises, but as he was gracious enough to grant me the opportunity to interview him, I think we'd be better served hearing from the man himself. So without further ado, here's my interview with the great Paul Finch!

AN INTERVIEW WITH PAUL FINCH:

Matt Cowan (MC): Welcome to the Abbey, Paul! When did you first discover an interest in horror and the supernatural? Can you tell us about some of the influences which spurred your creativity early on (books, television shows, movies, etc.)?

Paul Finch (PF): As a child in 1960s Britain, we didn't get much of what you would classify as horror or supernatural entertainment on mainstream TV. I remember getting my "telly scare-fare" about twice a week, and that was via *Dr Who* and *Star Trek*, both of which could certainly rise to the challenge. The Cybermen coming out of the ice petrified me as a child. And though I was a little bit older when I first saw the Autons breaking out of the shop windows and killing ordinary people in the street, I was stunned —for me, that's still one of the great moments of TV horror. There were horror movies on late, of course, mostly the old Universal and RKO pictures, but I wasn't allowed to watch them at that tender age. However, despite this, there were quite a few kids in my class at school who were interested in horror movies. Hammer were the biggest story in the business at that time, and I remember one classmate who regularly came in with cigarette cards, which he'd got from his older brothers, and which depicted scenes from the Hammer films. I found those fascinating. Christopher Lee as the Frankenstein monster and Oliver Reed as the werewolf seemed like the embodiment of horror.

That said, we occasionally got to see fantasy movies, which had monsters in them. Probably one of the most important moments in my entire life, in career terms at least, came when, still very young, my dad took me to the cinema to watch a double bill of *Jason and the Argonauts* and *The 7th Voyage of Sinbad*. The scene in *Jason* where Talos turns his head for the first time and looks down at Hercules and Hylas was a turning-point in my life. The thrill of that moment lingers even now, all these decades later.

However, my interest in all these things was really fueled by my dad, who always gave me bedtime stories that edged on the scary. Beowulf and Grendel, I remember vividly. But also Theseus and the Minotaur,

while the one that probably made the most lasting impact was the tale of Medusa, the Gorgon. Even though, as young and impressionable kids, we didn't have access to the mass monster-filled media of today, I think I was pretty-well primed for some kind of future in that world.

MC: When did you realize you wanted to start writing stories of your own?

PF: When I was at school. I always loved writing stories. I loved the English lessons at junior school because they were near enough all about creative writing, and I just used to let rip. This was probably an inheritance from my dad, who was a professional writer,

as I think you're aware. I recently met one of my old teachers, whom I literally hadn't seen since the early 1970s. He still remembered me, and he remembered the fact that I used to write pages-long stories for him, which he said he found amazing in a kid of that age. One thing he particularly recollected. We'd made a visit to the Catholic seminary at Upholland Hall, just outside Wigan, and we had to write an account of it. I'd found the whole thing tediously boring, so I wrote a story about Dr. Jekyll and Mr. Hyde instead. He recalled the incident well and said that he didn't know what to make of it at the time. I'm pretty sure I was disciplined for it, though not too severely. I like to think that was an indication at an early stage of a vivid imagination.

MC: I discovered you through the *Terror Tales* series of anthologies you edit, each of which include stories centered around a specific region of the UK. What inspired its creation?

PF: It was inspired by the Fontana *Tales of Terror* series of the 1970s, which I first

encountered on a family holiday around that time in the Lake District. Mary Danby (who I've since met and found delightful) was the genius behind that series, though Ron Chetwynd-Hayes was also involved and edited many of the books. They too interspersed the fiction with non-fiction, focusing heavily on folklore, legends, ghost stories and the like, rather than the slightly sleazier Pan Horror-type stories that were also very popular at that time. They also covered specific regions per volume, so for example, there was *Welsh Tales of Terror*, *Irish Tales of Terror*, *Scottish Tales of Terror*, and so on.

I was completely entranced by those books (I still own a full set of them), and they stayed in my mind for decades until I was old

Top: DOCTOR WHO, "The Tenth Planet" (BBC, 1966).
THE 7TH VOYAGE OF SINBAD and JASON AND THE ARGONAUTS (Columbia Pictures, 1958 and 1963)

SCOTTISH TALES OF TERROR

EDITED BY ANGUS CAMPBELL

WELSH TALES OF TERROR

EDITED BY R.CHETWYND-HAYES

and experienced enough and had sufficient pull in the industry to start a similar series of my own. As I've already said, I followed the same format, true horror interspersed with fictional horror, the fiction provided by some of the best talent around, but I wanted my catchment areas to be smaller, so the series could go on for longer. And, given that the whole thing was inspired by a trip to the Lake District, the very first one was inevitably *Terror Tales of the Lake District*. We've now done 14 in the series, boasting such titles as *Terror Tales of the Cotswolds*, *Terror Tales of Cornwall, the Home Counties, Northwest England, the Scottish Highlands, the Lowlands*, etc, with *Terror Tales of the Mediterranean* out later this year, which will hopefully indicate that we're not just focused on the British Isles.

MC: Alongside all the excellent horror fiction which appears in your *Terror Tales* anthologies, you also include essays about strange mysteries, legends, and folklore from each book's location. What have been some of

your favorite discoveries while researching these enigmas?

PF: It's very difficult to talk about all the things I've discovered in the limited space I've got here. I suppose every part of every country on Earth is planted thick with myths and legends, some of which are well known, some less so. However, when I set out to investigate the non-fiction that I'd be including in these books, I was staggered by how many spooky tales there were that I'd never heard of before.

In regard to supernatural stuff, for example, ghosts and haunted houses, there are plenty stories unknown outside their own localities, which would literally chill the blood. In *Terror Tales of the Lake District*, for example, we meet the Mad Clown of Muncaster Castle, the undead revenant of a murderous jester, still said to haunt the castle precincts and delight in playing deadly tricks on the unwary. In terms of spectacular cases of haunted houses, look no further than the Black Monk of Pontefract in *Terror*

CONTINUED ON PAGE 28

TERROR TALES
OF LONDON

Edited by Paul Finch

TERROR TALES
OF THE LAKE DISTRICT

Edited by Paul Finch

TERROR TALES
OF THE HOME COUNTIES

Edited by Paul Finch

TERROR TALES
OF WALES

Edited by Paul Finch

In addition, there is no end to the atrocities committed in the past, which, again, are not widely known about. I consider it a duty to include some of these in *Terror Tales*, because though these horrors were inflicted on humans by other humans, the terror factor is often beyond belief. Several can be found in *Terror Tales of the Scottish Lowlands*, where we learn about Blackness Castle, where there was a dungeon designed to flood at every high tide, Hermitage Castle, where evil Lord de Soules was immersed in a cauldron of molten lead, about Abbot Allan Stewart, who was cooked alive on a spit, and Cardinal Beaton, who after being hanged from a castle wall, was pickled for preservation so that his murderers could continue to abuse his corpse at their leisure.

Then of course, away from all this apparent insanity, there are those stories that are just plain weird and terrifying. For *Terror Tales of the Cotswolds*, I uncovered the story of a kennelman at Wychavon, who after going out late at night to see what had set his master's hounds barking, was never seen again—except for his legs, which were

Tales of Yorkshire, the ultra-violent poltergeist of Wallasea Island in *Terror Tales of East Anglia*, the infamous paranormal events at the Birkdale Palace Hotel, Southport, in *Terror Tales of the Seaside*, and possibly most frightening of all, the haunting at the isolated gatehouse on the outskirts of Preston in *Terror Tales of Northwest England*.

In terms of diabolism and demonic activity, there've been other very well-kept secrets, which we've enjoyed exposing. In *Terror Tales of London*, we discuss the fate of Lady Elizabeth Hatton, who supposedly kept a late-night assignation with the Devil, to repay the debt she owed him for her fantastical wealth, and who was found the following morning with her heart torn out. Then there was the case of the Bowen family of Llanellan, who were tormented by a truly fiendish doppelganger, as outlined in *Terror Tales of Wales*. Meanwhile, in *Terror Tales of the West Country*, we learn about the so-called Demon Drummer of Tedworth, a ferocious demonic entity unleashed upon a family by a vengeful gypsy.

found the following morning, having been ripped from his torso. No explanation was ever offered. For *Terror Tales of Yorkshire*, I found to my disbelief that the apocryphal story about the old woman on the moorland road who had a butcher knife in her handbag wasn't apocryphal at all and was actually investigated by West Yorkshire Police. In *Terror Tales of the Scottish Highlands*, you'll hear multiple accounts of a huge "grey figure" said to stalk after lone climbers in the highest peaks, while *Terror Tales of Cornwall* reveals the origin of the Hammer classic, *The Reptile*, by introducing you to the chilling tale of the Serpent of Pengersick...

There are many more I could talk about here, but it would get out of hand. It would literally go on indefinitely.

MC: You have published in multiple genres (horror, crime, science fiction, and historical fiction, to name a few) and formats (novels, short stories, screenplays, etc.). What adjustments do you have to make when switching between them?

PF: I'd like to say that adjusting between genres isn't that difficult, and that the things you want to say as a writer and the jeopardies you want to create are always going to be there, however you dress them up. But the truth is—at least, this is my experience —that if you are writing professionally, and a lot of that means writing to deadlines, you've got to be completely in the right zone for each individual project, which makes hopping from one to the next as if they were stepping-stones a very big ask. Not, if I'm honest, that I try to do this anyway. I often have more than one project on the go at the same time, but I would really struggle to write two books from scratch simultaneously. However, sometimes there are quick turnovers from one to the next, and while you may need to insert a fallow day between them in order to acclimatize from one to the other, you can't afford to sit around for too long. It helps, I think, to be very familiar with these different genres as a reader. Again, this is only my opinion, but I strongly believe that if you read widely across genre boundaries, you'll be able to write widely too, or at least it will come more naturally to you to attempt to do so.

Bouncing between formats is perhaps a tad more complex, because they are physically different disciplines. In my experience, if you can write a novel, you should certainly be able to write a novella or a short story, though you obviously need to be prepared to tighten everything up significantly, and that can be a real exercise if you're not used to it. In contrast, when it comes to writing a film or television script, it's very different technically, which can be a problem for some, but it's a different animal all-round. For example, film, and quite often television these days as well, is very much a visual

medium. Great movies rely hugely on the director and his cinematographer, to name but two of the many talents involved, but of course they can't do anything without a script. Even the auteurs tend to like to have a script handy at the start of the process (even if it's always their practice to completely rewrite it). But the point I'm getting at is that, when you're writing a script, you should only tell the director what he absolutely needs to hear. There's no point creating novel-type descriptive passages of landscape locations and so on, because ultimately, they'll go with the landscapes they can find. Describe a monster and while they might like it, 99 times out of a hundred they'll look to the costume and special effects

people to give them something even better and probably more affordable. Likewise, in a well-written scene, good actors will portray your characters effectively without requiring intricate notes from the writer. You don't even need to go heavy on the dialogue. Modern screenplays are remarkably dialogue-lite compared to those of yesteryear. So, it's really about adjusting to a completely different writing culture. I mean, you've still got to produce an intriguing story filled with compelling characters—those hard rules about creative fiction never change—but the adjustment from page to screen is a big one, in practice, a leap that not every author is able to make.

MC: You were able to adapt an unmade script your father Brian Finch initially wrote back in 1985, for season 22 of *Doctor Who* (*Leviathan*) and got it produced as an audio drama in 2010. How did it feel to bring your father's work to an audience?

PF: The main opportunity *Leviathan* gave me was to grab a shared credit with my dad, even though he'd been dead for three years by then. He'd always been a fan of *Dr Who*, and he particularly liked Colin Baker, as he'd written for him in *The Brothers* in the early 1970s. My dad's screenwriting career spanned four decades, so it wasn't as though he needed that kind of exposure, but for those reasons I've already mentioned, he was very disappointed when *Leviathan* was hacked from the schedule. It was not, as is commonly supposed, a casualty of the season cancellation that saw Colin Baker leave *Who*. Most likely, it was cut from the schedule, even though a shooting script had been produced, because it would have been a particularly expensive project. When I heard that Big Finish were looking to do the full-cast audio versions of these lost stories, with both Colin and Nicola Bryant back on board, it was a no-brainer to try and get *Leviathan* into the mix. It wasn't just about my dad's legacy. It would help me as well, as, having just left *The Bill*, my career was at a bit of a low ebb. I felt that if I could write the adaptation, it would get my name out and about again, and secure me an entranceway into *Dr Who*,

and that's exactly what happened. The story, which had a medieval setting, would certainly have been constrained by the budget available to the TV show in the mid-1980s, but when we did the audio version, there were no such limits. So, we had big crowd scenes, big battles and such, and were able to put a real epic sweep on what had originally been a very big idea from my dad. Thankfully, it all paid off. *Who* fandom circa 2010 seemed to like it. I was lauded at a few *Dr Who* conventions, which had never happened to me before, and I was chuffed to bits to get that all important shared credit, and of course, to finally get my dad's name on the roster of *Dr Who* writers, albeit posthumously.

MC: As someone who's worked professionally in both the film and television industry and given your love for the horror genre, what films or television shows have impressed you?

PF: That's a big question, to be honest. To avoid just giving you a list, I'll talk in vague terms.

Taking TV first, there's an awful lot to go at, though most of it dates back more than a few years. The 1970s and 1980s were particularly fertile periods for British TV horror, though obviously *Quatermass* and *Dr Who* predate that era. In the '70s, Nigel Kneale's *Beasts* set a very high bar, two particular episodes, "Baby" and "During Barty's Party," being memorably horrifying. At the same time, we had the BBC's *Ghost Stories for*

Christmas, which served up two especially spooky festive chillers in *The Signalman* and *Schalcken the Painter*. Less even delights were to be had from *Thriller* and *Supernatural*, though both were capable of hitting the fear switch. There were a number of TV plays around then that served a similar purpose—*Robin Redbreast* and *Penda's Fen* among the best known, but probably the scariest piece of TV horror from the whole of that decade was Graham Baker's half-hour play, *Leaving Lily*. It was an original WWI ghost story, and eerie as they come. Sadly, there doesn't seem to be any trace of it online, and barely even a reference to it. I dread to think that it may have been deleted from the archive, but I suspect that's what happened. Anyway, moving on to the '80s, with marginally bigger

budgets and slightly glossier production, we had Nigel Kneale's adaptation of *The Woman in Black* (the definitive version, in my view), *Tales of the Unexpected* and *Hammer House of Horror*, of which I only really remember "The House That Bled to Death," though the case of the Amityville haunting was big news at the time, so it worked very well. Quality TV horror was thin on the ground in later decades, though in the early '90s, *Ghostwatch* saw Stephen Volk make his

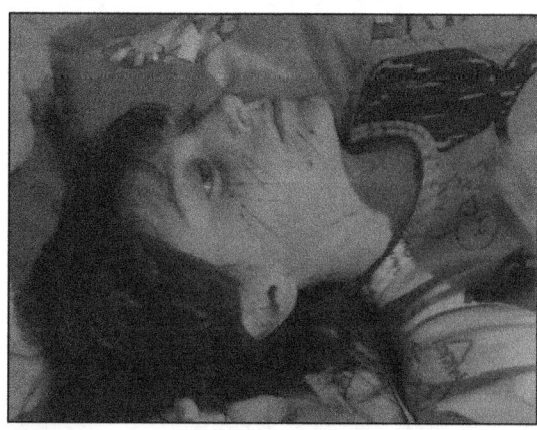

me, the two things, Christmas and scary stories, have always been joined at the hip. It's so steeped into me that it surprises me when people don't also make that connection. I remember when the late, great film critic, Alan Frank, told me how he got in trouble when choosing films for ITV's Christmas season sometime in the late '70s, because he inadvertently selected the Amicus classic, *Tales from the Crypt*, having forgotten that one segment of it, *All Through the House*, saw Joan Collins menaced and finally strangled one snowy Christmas Eve by a maniac Santa Claus. Alan felt he'd made a mistake and it was no use me trying to persuade him that Christmas-themed horror is one of the sweetest things in life; the same clearly applies to lots of other people even now.

ingenious foray into paranormal mockumentary long before anyone else thought of it, while in more recent times, *Black Mirror* has hit us with a number of chilling dystopian tales: "White Bear," "Men Against Fire" and "Hated in the Nation" are my favorites to date.

When it comes to horror movies, I'll just have to give you a list. I'm not going to be too original here, I'm afraid. They're all pretty well known and appreciated.

Night of the Demon, Hound of the Baskervilles (Hammer, 1959) *The Haunting* (1963), *Masque of the Red Death* ('64), *Quatermass and the Pit* ('67), *Blood on Satan's Claw* (1971), *The Abominable Dr Phibes* ('71), *Countess Dracula* ('71), *Tales from the Crypt* ('72), *The Exorcist* ('73), *Don't Look Now* ('73), *From Beyond the Grave* ('74), *The Omen* ('76), *The Tenant* ('76), *Alien* ('79), *The Shining* (1980), *The Thing* ('82), *Angel Heart* ('87), *Jacob's Ladder* (1990), *Event Horizon* ('97)...

And all the others. Sorry, but there are just too many to name.

Horror's a broad church, of course, and I suppose there's a world of difference between *All Through the House* and *A Christmas Carol*. But of course, MR James set many of his unashamedly terrifying ghost stories at Christmas, while Dickens brought out his scariest story of all, "The Signal-Man," in the Christmas edition of his magazine, *All the Year Round*. It's an age-old tradition, the spooky story at Christmas, and I seem to have latched onto it at quite an early stage in my writing career. You're correct that I produce numerous festive horror stories, posting one on my blog each December, but I've also brought out two Christmas collections, *The Christmas You*

MC: Every year you celebrate the Christmas season by crafting a new, festive-themed horror story. When did you begin this practice and how has it influenced your appreciation of the season?

PF: The moment I first fell in love with the concept of the Christmas-themed horror story is a difficult one to pin down. It must have been quite a while ago because for

of work on the off chance something more lucrative will show up in a few days' time.

In an ideal world, my daily routine involves me dictating in the morning and typing it up in the afternoon. I should add that I always dictate my first drafts onto a digital voice-recorder while I'm out walking. I don't have an app that then types them up. An app wouldn't work anyway, as the finished result is usually broken, disorderly, disorganized and so on, so it falls to me to make some sense of it, to refine it, to turn it into a coherent piece of text. It rarely works even that smoothly, of course. There are other things that need doing too. Editing, proof-reading, and that insufferable marketing and self-promotion thing that we are all required to do so much of these days. You simply must make time to write blogposts, give interviews, make use of social media and such, so that you have a presence and brand the world's readership can buy into.

To give you a shorter answer after all that longwindedness, the schedule varies every day. I guess it's up to me each morning to work out what needs to be done first,

Deserve and *In a Deep, Dark December*, and *Sparrowhawk*, a novella-length Victorian ghost story, which I still consider one of my best works, and which was short-listed for the British Fantasy Award. It's a definite ambition at some point to edit a *Terror Tales of Christmas* volume.

MC: Taking into account all the short stories, novels, screenplays and editing you do, what is your writing schedule like?

PF: It's pretty hectic. I'm not able to keep it nine-till-five or Monday-to-Friday, but I think most writers would probably agree that that was never part of the job description. I must always prioritize depending on whichever deadline is coming up next, or which is the biggest paying job. If that sounds very mercenary, well, this is my living. I sometimes find myself in the unenviable position of undertaking jobs that need to be done at roughly the same time as each other. As I mentioned in a previous answer, that's not something I seek or desire, and in fact will always try to avoid...but by the same token, it's a brave freelance who turns down offers

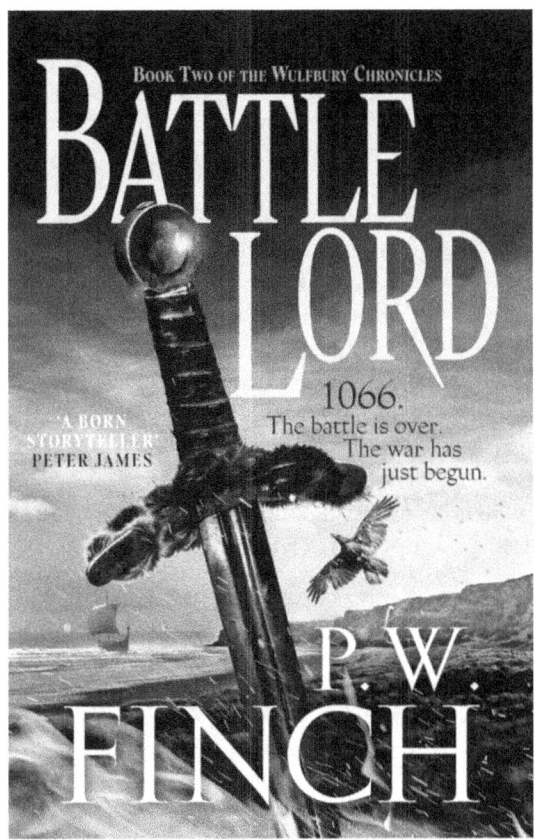

BOOK TWO OF THE WULFBURY CHRONICLES

BATTLE LORD

1066.
The battle is over.
The war has
just begun.

'A BORN
STORYTELLER'
PETER JAMES

P.W. FINCH

and how much time should be allocated to each project... and then I need to find the discipline to stick with those decisions.

MC: What advice would you offer new writers seeking to improve their craft?

PF: I've got two main planks of advice. Firstly, learn from your mistakes. Don't get uppity if you get rejected. We all get rejected. There isn't a writer working today who couldn't wallpaper a bedroom with their rejection slips. But don't just be stoical about it either. Make it work in your favor. If an editor or a broadcaster or a publisher takes the trouble to tell you why they've knocked you back, you might not agree with it but take note of it. Because if the same thing comes up again and again, the chances are they've got a point. So, don't just file it and move onto the next thing. Look at it, identify the problem, and fix it. That could be the difference between your next submission failing again... or hitting paydirt.

The second piece of advice is very simple. Keep going. It's a long, hard, rocky road to

becoming a successful writer. You will trip and fall dozens of times. You'll hit setback after setback. But you only fail the day you give up.

MC: Can you tell us about any projects you are currently working on?

PF: Putting my non-horror hat on for the moment, I'm making the final edits to *Battle Lord*, which is the sequel to *Usurper*, and the concluding part of my Norman Conquest era series of novels, as published by Canelo. That one will be out in January. I'm also doing the spadework for a further historical duology, which has now been commissioned. It's untitled as yet, but it's set during the Third Crusade. I have another crime thriller in the mix, which I can't talk about yet, while in horror terms, I'm putting the finishing touches to *Terror Tales of the Mediterranean*, which I hope will be published at Halloween. I've also got a couple of ideas for some horror short stories. I don't get invited to submit to this particular market as often these days because I assume that people think I'm too

TERROR TALES
OF THE MEDITERRANEAN

Edited by Paul Finch

to avoid snowmen. But there's something about unliving human figures brought to a semblance of animation, and it's usually a malign semblance, that plucks at my nerves. That must be the case because they've appeared throughout my fiction. And I'm not talking about zombies, rotting human carcasses roused through voodoo or weird science, because they once were alive naturally, or even robots, because they are supposed to walk around. I'm talking about things that are not supposed to. As I say, mannequins, statues and the like. No, I don't have nightmares about them, but because I write about them again and again, a latent fear of such abominations must reside deep within me.

Many thanks to Paul for taking the time to answer these questions. You can keep up with him over at his website:
http://paulfinch-writer.blogspot.com

busy. The truth is that, indeed, I often am too busy, but occasionally slots can be found. I've had two short stories published this year already, "No Such Place" and "Creatures of the Night" in *The Other Side of Never* and *An Unnecessary Assassin* respectively, and I've just sold another to a very prestigious anthology series, so if an editor invites me to participate, I'll always give it serious consideration, though I'll let them know there and then whether I can or can't. Of course, as the autumn moves on, I'll also have to think about my annual Christmas horror story. There's nothing in the barrel for that at present, but ideas can hit you at any time.

MC: Which horror element or creature in literature or films consistently gives you the chills? (Example: for me it's faceless creatures/specters.)

PF: I suspect the "horror being" that has most terrified me in my life is the inanimate figure given artificial life. Don't get me wrong. I'm not too scared to go into department stores filled with mannequins, and on winter days I don't go home the long way around

DEVILS OF LAKELAND

By Paul Finch

EVEN KILLINGTON LAKE SERVICES ON THE M6 MOTORWAY HAD AN AIR OF FAMILIARITY. As Graham locked his car and walked to the lodge, he looked up at the great hump of Brant Fell and saw it as he had that summer day all those years ago when he and Timmy had bought comics and sweets. Its great patchwork sides had been green and gold, dotted all over with sheep, its rounded summit misty and dappled with sunlight.

When he got back to his car, he sat behind the wheel to eat his sandwiches and looked up again at Brant, savoring the memory of that happiest holiday of all, even though now the fell was hidden in cloud and his windscreen spattered with February rain. There was still an atmosphere of peace. The Lake District would always have this effect on him, he supposed. Even here in its foothills. Even at a time of tragedy, like this.

After he'd eaten, he drove on, taking the A684 west to Kendal, then the A591 to Windermere. Everything he saw on the way, he recalled vividly: the pine-clad hills and deep river valleys littered with boulders, the quaint hamlets with their rock-built walls and slate cottages, the ever-distant mountains, and of course the lakes, dark and glimmering through the black trees—Windermere, Grasmere, Rydal Water, Thirlmere. There was no off-season in Lakeland, so even in this weather the lanes were lined with walkers in bright cagoules, the pub car parks full. Graham found it hard to believe he'd only been up here once before. Everything seemed so familiar.

He drove down into Keswick late afternoon, negotiating the complex, narrow streets with surprising ease despite the bustle of shoppers, and was soon out on the B5299, heading south along the wooded shore of Derwent Water. Folk seemed to agree this was the most scenic lake of them all, steel-grey and rolled out smooth as glass between the granite ridges of Catbells and High Seat.

However, as he followed the winding road, dark woods rose steeply on his left, hemming him to the water, and Graham felt his first pang of unease. Exactly what did he hope to achieve? Was it really worth taking unpaid absence from work and driving all the way here when the police had closed the case? Like so many men Graham knew, his brother Tim had bottled up most of his cares. Who could say what state he'd been in beneath that calm exterior? Who knew what could have caused him to do the thing he'd done?

Around the next bend, the shoreline trees gave out briefly to a shingle beach and timber jetty. Graham gazed at it as he cruised past, but then felt a sudden chill. Baffled, he braked and pulled up. This was the sort of place which in summer would be teeming, but now was quite dreary. The jetty looked unsafe; it was covered in green moss and leaned at an angle. The shadows of dusk were thick in the surrounding trees, and across the water an ebbing mist had blocked out the farther shore. Graham shivered and drove on. Five minutes later he had bypassed the Lodore Falls at the southern end of the lake and was heading towards Borrowdale village. The gigantic valley was still as bleak and grand as he remembered it. More so now, with the dark stains of evening creeping down the rugged flanks of the mountains.

The High View Hotel was off the road at the top of a steep drive, and enclosed by tall pines. As a structure it was very handsome, made from local slate and covered in green and purple ivy, but there didn't seem to be many lights shining out of it, and the parking area to the front was strangely empty.

Graham collected his sports bag from the boot and was about to go in, but first glanced up at the central window on the third floor. The "Tower Room," as the hotel management used to refer to it. Not in a tower as such, but the one with the best view. The one they'd taken all those years ago for that wonderful holiday. This too was in darkness.

Inside, the hotel was even less welcoming, all low beams, dark wood and sombre paintings. The one or two lamps switched on in Reception were heavily shaded and gave out minimal light. There was a smell of dust, as if renovation work was going on.

Nobody was on duty at the desk, so Graham rang the bell and waited. As he did, he glanced around. The layout was vaguely familiar. The staircase serving the upper floors was central, while to the right of that were the double-doors to the restaurant. At present they were closed and probably locked. Left of the staircase was the door to the bar. That too was closed.

A blonde receptionist slipped out from a back office. She wore an immaculate blue uniform and a practiced smile, which faltered badly when she saw Graham. For a moment she seemed stunned.

Graham understood. "I'm the brother. I booked yesterday."

The receptionist nodded, suddenly embarrassed. "Of course…it's just, well you look so similar."

"There was only a year between us," he said.

She seemed unable to reply, and handed over a room key as he filled in the register. Then, furtively, she crept away. There was some quiet conversation in the back office and a second later a man appeared in a pin-striped suit. He had wooden features, a beak-like nose and thinning grey hair. A gold tab pinned to his breast pocket revealed that he was "Mr. Summers, Manager."

He seemed awkward and unsure of himself, only coming to the counter when Graham finally looked up. "On behalf of the staff, Mr. Foster," he began. "I'd…I'd like to offer our deepest condolences. Such terrible news."

Graham closed the register and picked up his key. "I don't suppose any of your staff spoke to my brother?"

Mr. Summers shrugged helplessly. "Not that I know of. We had all this with the police, of course. Nobody remembers anything. Your brother was in very high spirits when he arrived here—that I do remember. He said it was a holiday he'd been looking forward to. It did seem odd that he suddenly cut it short like that. I mean he was due to be with us the whole week."

For the thousandth time, Graham mulled over what he knew about the incident. None of it made sense. Mr. Summers watched him unhappily. Clearly the manager was wondering why Graham had come up, and viewed the whole thing as an ordeal which he hoped would soon end. "Could it have been an accident?" he suddenly asked. "Perhaps your brother got lost and didn't realize the cliff was there?"

Graham shook his head. "I'd love to believe that, Mr. Summers. I really would."

When he went up to Room 22, he carried his own bag. There was no porter at the High View. Apparently there never had been, though Graham seemed to remember smiling, helpful staff everywhere when he'd been here as a child.

It would have been nice to think that Tim had died in an accident on the way home, but as the Cumbrian Traffic sergeant had said at the inquest, you can't drive off Black Sail Drop by accident. It's sixty yards from the road, and to get to it you've first got to crash through a perimeter fence, which Tim had done. As if that wasn't enough, the place was miles out of his way. He must have driven for hours to get there.

Room 22 stood alone on a dark landing on the second floor. There was a spiral stair opposite, leading up into shadow. Graham was puzzled. He had specifically asked for the Tower Room, the third-floor room where he'd stayed as a youngster. He sighed and let himself in. It would probably be the same design. Couldn't have half the same atmosphere though.

It didn't. And neither was it as cozy. Spartan would have been a better way to describe it. It was furnished with a single bed and side-table, a desk, a chest of drawers, a wardrobe and an armchair, but the walls were unimaginatively papered and the bathroom was cold. The fact that it was quite spacious made it feel emptier.

Graham dumped his bag and went to the window. Beyond it, through the trees, was the distant blue haze of the lake, at its far end the rolling black hummock of Skiddaw. The lights of Keswick twinkled at the mountain's feet. It was almost the same view he remembered, though not quite, because now he was one storey down and having to gaze *through* branches rather than over them. It still brought memories rushing back. Him and Timmy snug under their massive quilt while Dad went down to dinner; having pillow fights every evening; enjoying milk and sandwiches; reading comics and telling jokes.

After he'd unpacked, he called Reception and expressed mild disappointment that he hadn't been given the Tower Room. He was surprised however when the receptionist said that she didn't know of any Tower Room. When he explained which room he meant, she recognized it as No. 32, the one directly above him, but apologized and said that it was unavailable.

He hung up feeling disgruntled, but a minute later heard the scampering of tiny feet somewhere above his head. More than one pair too. It pricked his conscience. He'd been selfish, wanting that room for himself purely for nostalgic purposes. Why not let another young family enjoy it the way he and Timmy had?

After he'd put his things away, Graham lay down on the bed and glanced through the two paperbacks of Tim's that he'd brought along with him. They were collections of horror stories. Rare ones apparently, which his brother had sent for from abroad. Graham shook his head. He'd never been able to understand Tim's obsession with such garbage. It had been going on for as long as he could remember, easily since they'd been at school. First it had been the usual stuff, the popular titles gleaned from high street stores; then the works of antiquity found in second-hand shops; finally the really obscure material, purchased through literary fairs, specialist dealers or book-finding services. The collection had grown and grown over the years. The expenditure that had gone into it must have been phenomenal. But it had only really struck Graham how infatuated his brother had become a month before his death, when he'd unexpectedly announced that he was off to the Lakes to find the book that had originally sparked his interest. It was a special little tome called "Devils of Lakeland"; a collection of ghost stories with a Lake District atmosphere. He'd only thumbed through it, but even then he'd realized its value. Didn't Graham remember? They'd seen it in a poky little bookshop in Keswick all those years ago, during that wonderful holiday. At the time, Tim had wanted to buy it desperately, but Dad had said it wasn't suitable.

Graham hadn't remembered at all. How could he after three decades? Tim had been resolute though. He'd been determined to track it down, and Keswick was the obvious place to start. Only when he possessed that priceless book would his collection be complete.

Dinner that evening was not as pleasant an experience as Graham had anticipated. There were few other diners in the restaurant, and the windows were heavily draped in purple, which, along with the dark paneling, had a sombre effect. The food was of only average quality as well: the vegetables were dry, his steak bloody when he'd asked for it well-done. He ordered a bottle of house red with his meal, but found it vinegary, and ended up leaving it only half-drunk.

The restaurant staff were mostly young and seemed uninterested in the guests, bringing dishes and taking them away again with robotic indifference. There was one of them who Graham recognized, however: a Cockney waiter who on their previous visit they'd known affectionately as "Tel." Graham remembered him as a short cheerful man with cobalt blue eyes, sharp cheekbones and a head of ginger curls. Now he was bald, with grey wrinkled cheeks. His red tunic was crumpled and buttoned incorrectly, while he walked with a stoop and could only carry trays of food precariously. Graham

watched him sadly.

After dinner, he went over to the bar, but halfway there noticed a long corridor which he didn't remember. He stopped to look at it. It was located behind the staircase, thus hidden from the main vestibule, and ran off into darkness. It was clearly for public use; there was no "Private" or "Staff Only" notice above it, and closer inspection revealed that it was decorated all the way down with paintings and display cases containing Lake District crafts. Graham presumed it had been added since his last visit. It probably connected with the hotel gardens or a walk to the fells. He put it from his mind and went into the bar, ordering himself a scotch and soda.

"I was sorry to hear about your brother, sir," the barman said, as he attended to it.

Graham glanced up. The man was quite young, but very smart in a shirt and bowtie. He nodded politely as Graham handed him the money.

"You didn't have any conversation with him, I don't suppose?" Graham wondered.

"None at all, I'm afraid," the barman said. "Neither him nor the young lady."

It took a moment for the words to sink in. Graham looked up again. "Excuse me... young lady?"

"That's right, sir. The young lady he was in here with. Brunette, she was." Graham gazed at him, and suddenly the barman blushed. "Oh dear sir, I hope I haven't compromised somebody."

"No, it's alright. Tim wasn't married. It's just that... he never said anything."

The barman was now pouring drinks for the next customer. "Perhaps he met her here, sir?"

"And she was a brunette, you say?"

The barman thought about it. "That's right. But you know, it's a bit funny. She had this white dress on. Looked a bit formal, it did. Knee-length. Like a uniform. Like she was a nurse or something."

"A nurse?"

"That's right. Couldn't have been though. I mean she was in here at the bar with him."

Graham puzzled over it for the next hour or so, downing one scotch and soda after another. It was possible that Tim had met a woman here, but it seemed out of character. Graham's brother had never been particularly interested in women or sex. His obsessive hobby had taken up most of his spare time. It could have been that there was a secret side to him, but Graham was sure that he'd have known about it.

Later, close on one o'clock, when he stumbled out of the bar, he glanced back into the darkened corridor—and went rigid with surprise. Just for a split-second then, he'd fancied he'd seen a woman walking away down it. A woman in a knee-length white dress. He stared into the shadows at the far end. Finally, he took a tentative step towards them. Then another. A moment later he was making his way unsteadily down the passage. It grew dark quickly, and almost immediately he blundered into a glass display case, rocking it noisily. He moved back, cursing. The darkness had gripped him completely. Briefly, he didn't know where he was or what he was doing.

"'Scuse me, sir," someone said.

Graham turned. A silhouette was approaching from a blur of light, which he supposed must have been the bar area. "'Scuse me, sir," the figure said again, in a distinct Cockney accent.

Fuddled as he was, Graham recognized the chalky tones. He wondered if the old Londoner would recognize him. "Tel...how are you, mate?"

"'Fraid you must have got me mistaken for somebody else, sir."

Graham's eyes attuned to the half-light as the waiter came up close—it was clearly Tel.

"I'm John," he added.

Graham slurred as he spoke. "You...you were called Tel, though."

The waiter shook his head. "Not as I recall, sir."

Graham was baffled. Why should the man lie? "You are that London bloke who was here thirty years ago?"

The waiter eyed him curiously. "Well yes, I am, sir. But I've never been called Tel."

Graham pondered this, and as he did, the waiter took him gently by the elbow. "Thing is, sir...there's nothing down this passage. This wing's being renovated. I was wondering if you might be lost or something?"

Graham glanced over his shoulder as he was steered back towards the light. "I thought I saw someone go down there."

"Couldn't have, sir. It's all boarded up down there. Leads nowhere."

Graham allowed himself to be led back to the stairs and then up to his room. Inside it, the walls began to spin around him. He toppled over as he stripped off his shirt and tie, and fell onto the bedclothes. Sleep stole over him with astonishing speed, but before it took him completely, he heard the youngsters upstairs again—two pairs of scampering feet and muffled giggling.

HE DREAMED ABOUT Timmy and himself as they had been on their first arrival at the High View, tearing out of Dad's green Morris 1100, dashing to the main doors in a frenzy of excitement. Behind them, framed on an azure sky, Dad was getting luggage out from the boot. Not Dad as he was now: hairless, gammy-eyed and drooling in his wheelchair; but Dad as he had been then, looking like Elvis with his quiff and laughing eyes, shouting at them not to knock anyone down. Finally out of his shell again, after the months and months of mourning for Mum.

When Graham woke up, his head was splitting and he was sick to the pit of his stomach. He lay helpless, dazed and shivering in the milky light of dawn. His cheeks were wet with tears.

It took hours to get himself together, though he had no plans to even attempt to eat breakfast. By ten he'd dressed in jeans, trainers and a thick sweater, and was ready to face the world. He closed the door behind him and was just locking it when he thought about the Tower Room and the youngsters. He glanced at the narrow stair spiraling upwards. A pale light was shining down it. He considered, and then, deciding that it couldn't do any harm, crept up to have a look. When he reached the top, he found the door to the Tower Room standing ajar and daylight streaming through.

Graham peeped in. Then, perplexed, he opened the door properly and entered. The room was bare of carpet and furniture, and thickly layered in dust. The wallpaper, faded and brownish, hung off in strips. Not only was room 32 not in use, it had not been in use for what looked like years. He strode aimlessly around it, finally moving to the window and gazing out. At least the stunning vista was still the same, though at present it was buried in rainclouds. Below, a car was pulling away down the hotel drive. Within a second it vanished, but Graham had the distinct impression it had been a green Morris 1100.

He went downstairs. Inevitably, his feet led him back to the corridor where he thought he had seen the woman in the white dress. Now he wasn't sure what he remembered from the previous night, but the passage still stood empty and in darkness. As old John had said, it was awaiting restoration. There wasn't a lot in the High View that wasn't, Graham thought sourly. He wondered if they'd bothered telling this to Tim when he'd booked himself in so excitedly a few weeks ago.

LATER THAT MORNING, he drove to Keswick. As he followed the lakeside road, he thought again about the woman in white and puzzled over who she might be. If she was local and he could get to speak to her, it might at least help in his understanding of what Tim had done. It wouldn't bring him back, but there was a mystery here and this woman was the only lead.

The local police were as helpful as they had been previously but seemed bewildered that Graham had come up to see them. He spoke to a uniformed inspector in a side office in the station, and, over several cups of tea, had it reiterated to him that Tim had driven his car off Black Sail Drop in Copeland Forest, a point only accessible by the most primitive back roads. And in broad daylight, too. An accident was out of the question. It had to have been suicide. They'd even found a road map beside the body, folded open on that page.

When Graham mentioned the woman in white and wondered if anyone had reported her to them, the inspector simply shrugged. As gently as he was able, he reminded Graham that the case was now closed. Tim

Foster had committed suicide. Only new evidence of ground-breaking significance could change that verdict. The fact that Tim had been seen talking to a woman in a bar did not alter anything.

Outside the station, Graham found the weather changing for the worse. The temperature had plummeted and the spitting rain was turning to sleet. Beyond the high roofs of the town, the mountaintops were capped with snow. He huddled into his thin jacket. He couldn't have prepared less for February in the Lakes if he'd consciously tried. A spot of lunch in a fish and chip bar didn't help, so he called in to the boutique next door and bought himself a scarf and a pair of suede gloves.

While he was in there, he asked about local bookshops. How many were there? Were there any particularly good second-hand ones? The proprietor was delighted to tell him that they had lots of bookshops in their town, and some especially good second-'anders. Graham thanked him, then went to search for them.

As always, the centre of Keswick, around its information bureau and medieval moot-hall, was thronging with people, but away from it, out of view, its various narrow courts were quieter than Graham had expected. They ran back and forth between jumbled buildings of grey slate, winding up and down from one level to the next. Many were cobbled and now greasy with rain.

Graham traversed them for an hour, and found plenty of "poky little shops," to use Tim's own description, but invariably they sold either antiques or cream teas. He didn't seriously expect to stumble across that little bookshop from so long ago, but felt certain that Tim would have looked for it. Five minutes later however, he came upon an arch clustered with ivy and, inexplicably, he felt that he knew it.

As he walked towards it, he remembered running under the arch as a child. Timmy had been in front and shouting something about "the cyclops' cave," because it reminded them of a Sinbad movie that Dad had taken them to see.

Now Graham passed under the arch again, followed a curved tunnel and came out at a crossroads of passages. Instinctively he went left, and to his surprise began to feel a tingle of excitement. It became a positive surge when he rounded the next bend and saw, tucked away at the end of the alley, a poky little shop that was undeniably familiar. It was "olde worlde" in style, with mullioned windows and a shield hanging over its front door.

Graham hurried towards it, almost breathless with anticipation—*only to stop in his tracks*. The windows were not filled with books, as he'd expected, but with old toys. He went slowly forward and pressed his face against the glass. Stuffed teddy bears were propped up in heaps, all ragged and filthy. In the middle stood a decrepit rocking-horse, without a flake of paint left on it and only wisps of string for a mane. Graham gazed at it, recalling how its eyes had once flashed sapphire blue, how its scarlet lips had drawn back on a set of strong white teeth, how its flanks had been a brilliant orange with large green polka-dots on them.

Then he wondered how he remembered all that, and he stepped back, alarmed. He was touched by something cold, the way he had been at the jetty on the lake, and briefly he was mesmerized. Slowly, he came round and looked up.

Above his head, the shield read:

Second Hand - Bought & Sold

The wrong shop. That was all. Probably the wrong side of town. He turned to walk away—but was immediately confronted by another shop directly behind him. He hadn't noticed it before, but it hit him full force now. This one was equally as dingy as the other, and equally poky. And its sign read:

Books Books Books

Graham approached it warily. Again, he felt a tingle of anticipation. A moment later he was inside. A thousand memories swam back: the dark cave-like interior, racked on every wall with old volumes; the musty smell; the thick carpet under his feet. The shop was manned by a red-haired man in tweeds. He was reading a book himself and

smoking a pipe. On Graham's entry, he looked up from behind his till in surprise as if this was a startling event.

"Anything I can help you with, sir?" he asked cheerfully.

Still entranced, Graham waved him into silence and drifted through the foyer into the back room, where he knew he would find various passages leading off into the rabbit warren of a building, each one lined with books.

For minutes on end, Graham searched, going spine by spine along the creaking shelves, emptying boxes onto the floor, working his way through one untidy pile after another. It seemed that every book ever printed was to be found there, most stiff and cracking and assembled in no logical order. However, Graham knew that he would find what he was looking for. And he did. In a narrow space at the back of the shop—a type of conservatory in fact, with a roof of stained glass—he crouched down and placed his finger on a single dusty volume. On its spine, in gold leaf, it was inscribed:

Devils of Lakeland

Almost giddy, he drew it out and opened it. He expected it to be ludicrously expensive but could find no price-tag. Puzzled, he flipped through several pages.

Then he flipped through several more.

It was impossible to believe what he was seeing. A feeling of dismay grew steadily inside him. Frantically, he raced through the rest of the book, but it was the same from beginning to end: a collection of creepy stories with a local flavor, just as Tim had described. *But they were stories for children!* Printed in a large typeface and interspersed with nursery rhyme-type pictures. Graham's brow beaded with sweat as he stared down at the yellow pages, from which pixies, elves and sprites gazed innocently back.

Only then did he hear the feet scraping somewhere above his head.

He glanced up sharply. To his astonishment, he saw two misted shapes through the stained glass, clambering over it like spiders and with no great care. Heavy boots came down hard on the glass panels, dust trickling from the leaden joists. Graham supposed they were workmen involved in some job or other, though surely they'd be more careful than this?

He wondered why he hadn't heard them before.

And then, with a shock, he realized.

At first, they'd been silent because they'd been watching him. As in fact, they were still watching him. Their faces were blurred and misshapen through the glass but were clearly fixed on him. And now they were making a noise because they were trying to find a way down. *A way down to him!*

Graham dashed out, stumbling along darkening passages filled with books but twisting back and forth, constantly returning him to the conservatory. On several occasions he passed under skylights, and imagined dark shapes above them, peering through. At last, he made it to the front of the shop and stood there quaking, ears straining. From above, there was still a faint scraping of feet. It was muffled and distant but getting closer.

"That'll be two pounds fifty, please, sir," a voice said.

Graham started. It was the shopkeeper, sitting up behind his till, smiling.

Graham glared at him. "Are you mad? I don't want this! Why the hell would I want this?"

He thrust the book into the startled man's hands and fled outside, hurrying down the nearest alley and not stopping or looking back until he was in the town centre.

He crossed it quickly and took another entry down to the car park. The sweat was now cooling on his brow, and he felt a little more relaxed. As he dug into his pocket for his keys, he glanced over his shoulder—and saw two men slouching down the alley about forty yards behind. Workmen, in fact, clad in heavy coats and dust-caked boots. Their hands were stuffed into their pockets, and they were staring at him hard, from livid red faces.

Graham began to run. He crossed the slip-road without looking and vaulted the barrier into the car park. Again, he glanced around. The workmen were still coming, but only slowly. He started to run again,

staggering down the lanes of parked cars, at first unable to find his Ford Fiesta. When at last he did, his hands were shaking so badly that he dropped the key twice before he could insert it.

He leaped into the vehicle and drove out of the car park in a rush, swerving onto the slip-road. Only when it was too late did he remember that this road would actually take him back around the perimeter of the car park before feeding him into the main traffic. Which meant that he'd pass right by the two workmen. Within touching distance.

Graham felt his blood freeze, but then he swore and jammed his foot down hard. He'd get past them! Damn right he would! But what if they were blocking the road?

They weren't, however. As he bore round one curve after another, the passage remained clear. There was no sign of anyone at all. Even the car park was deserted. Gasping with relief, Graham reached the next junction and cut out sharply into the traffic.

THE FIRST THING he did when he got back to the hotel was totter into the bar and order himself a stiff whisky. He drank it in a gulp and ordered another. The young barman watched him with faint alarm. Graham swallowed only half of the second one, then stood erect, breathing hard, eyes tightly closed. He could still feel the sweat on his neck and shoulders.

Eventually, the barman asked him if he was alright. Graham wasn't sure himself. He opened his eyes, glanced round, and was just about to answer when he saw two diminutive shapes walk past the door. It rooted him to the spot.

Two young boys, they'd been.

In T-shirts and short pants.

Walking hand in hand.

He laid the whisky on the bar and crossed to the door. There was no sign of the youngsters now, but he knew where they'd gone. Across the hall from him, the black mouth to the unused corridor gaped invitingly. Graham could imagine them, innocent and happy, toddling hand-in-hand towards the shadows at its deepest end.

He walked over and gazed down it, seeing only darkness. Then he realized that somebody was standing at his shoulder. He turned—it was old John, uniformed up for another evening of duty. The waiter was watching Graham with a kindly but concerned expression. "A bit fascinated with that corridor, aren't we, sir?"

Graham wiped the sweat from his brow. "I know where it leads to now. It goes down to the old nursery, doesn't it? Where the parents used to leave their children while they went off gallivanting."

John seemed surprised that Graham knew. "We haven't used it as a nursery for a very long time," he said.

Graham gazed into its depths. "What… what happened to that rather attractive young nanny you used to have working there?"

The old waiter seemed even more surprised. "Miss Anne…well, there's an old story. And a sad one. Almost finished us off, that did."

"How?"

John frowned. "Well, nice young girl she was, but I guess she didn't have the dedication. Terrible, what happened. Absolutely terrible. I think she was more interested in the young men than their nippers, sir. After what happened, it was no wonder she threw herself off that jetty into the lake."

But Graham was no longer listening. At least, not to old John. Because behind him, in the bar, he could hear the loud drunken laughter of a man and a woman. Hysterical drunken laughter, in fact. It was ridiculous to get so pissed at this early hour. Ridiculous and shameless. If only their voices didn't sound so familiar. *Dear God…*

Without looking back, Graham turned and ran. He took the stairs three at a time and reached his room in seconds. It was filled with late afternoon shadows, and he had to fumble for the light switch before finding it. He flung his belongings into his bag haphazardly, all the time singing to himself. Singing as loudly as possible so that he wouldn't hear any more sounds from above, any more sounds that might suddenly move out from the Tower Room and come hurriedly down the spiral stair.

He scrambled down to Reception without even checking that he'd got everything. The woman on duty was astonished. She asked him if everything was alright. But he told her to hurry up please, just hurry up. He had to go!

She didn't seem particularly upset by this, but still took ages totting up his bill and processing his credit card, almost as if she was deliberately delaying him. And as she did, Graham became aware of the figure approaching down the darkened corridor from the old nursery. A figure in a white dress. Coming right towards him.

He clenched his teeth, unwilling to look round, and the second the receptionist handed him his receipt, left the hotel at a staggering run, crossing the drive and throwing himself into his car. He gunned the engine furiously and, before he knew what was happening, he was speeding down the narrow drive and onto the winding lane to Keswick. He had to put *the High View* behind him.

Behind him.

Behind him…

Graham stiffened. The hair prickled on his neck.

There hadn't been a nanny called Miss Anne in that nursery, of course. Not that afternoon, at least, when she'd found a liquid lunch with Dad preferable to tedious hours watching Graham and Timmy kick around the teddy bears and play on the rocking horse. That glorious holiday afternoon, when the two workmen, who'd been watching them through the window all morning, had finally come in.

There *was* a nanny now though. Graham didn't need to glance into the rear-view mirror and see who was sitting in the back seat, to know that. There was a nanny now. And she'd never make the mistake of leaving him alone again. Not ever again.

He wondered how long he'd be able to take it, before he headed for the nearest cliff.

"Devils of Lakeland" first appeared in the September 1998 issue of Enigmatic Tales.

Paul Finch is an ex-cop and journalist turned best-selling author. He first cut his literary teeth penning episodes of the British

CONTINUED NEXT PAGE

cop show, The Bill, *has written extensively in horror and fantasy, including for* Doctor Who, *and is a two-time winner of the British Fantasy Award and a one-time winner of the International Horror Guild Award.*

He is best known for his crime/thriller novels, of which there are fourteen to date, one of which, Strangers, *made* The Sunday Times *Top 10 bestseller list.*

As well as what he calls his "dark fiction," Paul also writes historical action-adventures.

His latest novel in that line, Battle Lord, *is due on the bookshelves in January 2024.*

Paul created and still edits the geography-specific horror anthology series, Terror Tales. *The fifteenth in that line,* Terror Tales of the Mediterranean, *is due for publication this autumn.*

Paul lives in Lancashire, England, with his wife and business-partner, Cathy.

INVASIVE SPECIES

By HELEN GRANT

ELSPETH'S MOBILE RANG WHEN SHE WAS PASSING FALKIRK. She knew what it was, but she couldn't stop until she got to the next services. When she got there, she parked up and went inside to get herself a strong coffee before she called back.

Afterwards, as she slid her phone into the little space under the dashboard, she wondered whether there hadn't been a slight edge of reproach in the voice at the other end, a little tang of bitterness under the crust of sympathy. She was going to arrive too late. She was *already* too late. Elspeth sipped the coffee and tried to analyse how she felt about that. Upset? Distraught? *Relieved?* She honestly wasn't sure. Something had changed seismically in the landscape of her life; that ought to hurt, surely? But she couldn't imagine a reconciliation with her father after all this time.

Eventually she set off again. There wasn't much traffic and she was making decent time; it was just a *very* long way. She'd chosen to live in the very south of England, near the sea, and that was about as far as you could get from the place she was supposed to call home. It was mid evening by the time she got to Inverness, and there she broke the journey with a night in a cheap

motel. There was not much point in hurrying now, after all.

The following morning she took the early ferry. She was grateful to get a place; she'd turned up prepared to explain the situation, to plead if necessary, but it seemed there was plenty of space. That was unexpected; it wasn't too late in the season for tourists. Perhaps it was the wrong weekday. When she'd left the island, they hadn't yet started running ferries on Sundays, since the church forbade it and nobody wanted to be seen taking one. It was a surprise to Elspeth that they were even doing it now; in her sporadic communications with her father she had never had the impression that religion was losing its grip on the place.

After she had parked her car behind a supermarket lorry she went upstairs to the passenger deck and ate a huge breakfast: eggs, bacon, sausages, mushrooms, tomatoes and potato scones. Later she went up on deck and watched for the long grey bulk of the island coming into view. It always seemed to have cloud hanging over it, Elspeth remembered.

Probably the odor of sanctity, she thought grimly.

THREE QUARTERS of an hour after docking, she was looking at her father's body.

The nurse told her they'd have moved it by now, except there wasn't anyone else on the ward, so they'd waited for her. The woman said this in an impassive way, and Elspeth wasn't sure whether she was a little deficient in empathy, downright disapproving, or simply very reserved.

"Thank you," she said, with an equal lack of fervor. She looked down at her father. It was odd seeing him in a hospital gown; his natural costume was a stiff dark suit. His eyes were almost—but not quite—closed and his mouth was wide open. His hair, which was still abundant in spite of his age, was flattened at one side where he'd lain on it.

Elspeth had never seen death before, but there was no mistaking it. The utter inertness, the gaping mouth. She was struck forcefully by the idea that her father had simply been the instrument through which divine disapproval had been funnelled towards her mother, herself, and others. Now it had ceased to resound. To her surprise, she felt pity. She looked at him for a little longer, and then she turned away.

THERE WAS ONLY ONE undertaker on the island, so there was no decision to be made about that. Elspeth took their number from the phlegmatic nurse, and then she left. She had a handful of his things in her pocket, including his house key; she'd had one of her own, long ago, but she hadn't been able to find it.

She got into her car and sat there for a while without starting the engine.

How do I feel about this? she asked herself. She wasn't sure. Not *sad*, exactly. *Shocked* was perhaps nearer the mark. She felt as if she had been in an accident, and was checking herself gingerly for some terrible wound that she was not yet able to feel.

Is it normal to feel this calm?

Eventually she did start the car, and she set off for her parents' place, turning automatically onto the modern road, which was wide and metalled and had a broken white stripe down the middle. There was an old road, which was shorter, but less well-maintained, and narrower, with passing places. This one was faster, in spite of the greater distance. It was also pretty quiet, although she supposed it simply seemed that way because of the contrast with the south of England. Down there, in summertime, you could sit in traffic jams that stretched for miles.

In spite of the comparative quietness, the island seemed to be thriving. Elspeth drove past a number of new or half-built houses, some of them in rather unpromising spots—huddled into curves in the road, or set a long way back in what looked like boggy ground. Perhaps those were intended for holiday homes, she thought. You could get people to stay in nearly anything: caravans, glamping pods, even converted horseboxes. A little further on, she passed the shell of an abandoned croft, weeds growing up around its walls, and considered the irony of new places springing up while old ones crumbled away. Everything was changing, that was for certain. She wondered whether she'd even recognize the hamlet where her parents had lived.

In fact, when she got there she only knew it from the battered metal sign. Elspeth pulled in to the side of the road and sat there staring.

This much development, she thought. It didn't seem possible. Houses crammed against houses, with barely an alley in between, and seemingly little regard for aesthetic principles. Island architecture always tended towards the functional: tacked-on extensions and ugly dormer loft conversions. Still, this went several steps further; in places the buildings looked downright haphazard, squeezed into narrow plots and sprawling out into any available open space. The nearest one didn't even have its front door facing the road, presenting instead three opaque windows like cataracts.

That must be a pain for the postie, she thought.

Elspeth pulled out into the road again

and continued a little further, looking out for her parents' house. There was nothing to distinguish it, because her father disapproved of ostentatious individuality, but she picked it out easily anyway because it was one of the few with a good space around it. The gates were closed; she'd have to get out and open them if she wanted to park the car on the little drive.

When she got out of the car she could hear the rise and fall of the wind like ragged breaths. Somewhere a little way off there was an unidentifiable sound—perhaps someone driving slowly over gravel. Otherwise, the village seemed very quiet. Well, it was a Sunday. Elspeth looked around her and could see very little moving either. On a rooftop a large bird seemed to be flapping vigorously but its movements rapidly subsided. She opened the gates.

A couple of minutes later she was fitting her father's key into the front door. When it swung open she was almost surprised not to see her parents there in the hallway—her father looming over her mother, who was skinny and shriveled, like a baby bird. The house exhaled the familiar smell of furniture polish and dejection. There was also an underlying odor of decay—vegetables abandoned in the rack when her father went into hospital, Elspeth guessed.

She carried her cases inside and went back for the small box of groceries. Supermarkets on the island had traditionally been closed on a Sunday and she suspected it was the same now. Also, there was no shop in the village itself. After she had put the food in the kitchen, she went to look at her old room, since she could not under any circumstances imagine sleeping in her parents'. The door was closed, shutting the room off from the rest of the house, but when she opened it there was that same scent—clean but somehow stale. Her parents had not maintained her room as it had been when she lived at home—the posters, soft toys and scattered art materials had all gone. It could have been a room in a bed-and-breakfast. Elspeth sat on the bed and bounced; it felt comfortable enough.

She realised that she didn't really know what to do. She could call the undertaker, she supposed, but would anyone even answer on a Sunday? The funeral would have to be arranged too, and the church was presumably the same as ever, but who was the minister now? Her mother's funeral was sufficiently long ago that it might not be the same person anymore. It occurred to Elspeth that she could answer that question pretty easily by wandering down to the church at the end of the village and looking at the board outside. Other questions were more difficult to answer, though. Was the house now hers? That wasn't a given, since she was cast as the prodigal child. Even if it was, what would she do with it?

After some deliberation she went into the little dining room that also served as her father's study. In the far corner was an oak bureau with the lid down and an upright chair in front of it. Elspeth went over intending to search the pigeonholes for the will, but before she started looking she saw that there was a letter lying on the green leather insert. Well, half a letter; she saw the words ran out partway down the page.

Dear Elspeth, it began.

She picked it up, wrinkling her nose at her father's handwriting, which was full of loops and spikes.

Dear Elspeth,

I do not believe you received my last letter as it seems unlikely that you would ignore it. At least, I hope not. I must ask you to come home. Since your mother died things have become considerably more difficult here and alone I am not equal to the task of

That was where it ended. Elspeth frowned. The task of what? Not running the house, surely? It was small, and although it was old-fashioned it wasn't badly maintained. The garden? She drifted over to the back window and looked out.

There were vegetables growing in neat rows on both sides of the little path and some kind of berries on the wall at the far end, which caught the sunshine (when there was any). It looked as though it was all pretty much under control. A section of wall at the right-hand corner had subsided a bit, scattering bricks onto the earth, but that was all.

Perhaps, Elspeth thought, *it was just ... everything. He felt old.*

She dug into herself again, searching for regret, and only came up with pity again.

My father, she thought. He was never *Dad,* never anything half so cosy.

She went back to the bureau, put the letter down and began to explore the pigeon-holes. It didn't take long to find the will, which was in an unsealed envelope. Elspeth perused it briefly and saw that everything was hers.

THAT AFTERNOON Elspeth went down to the beach, a little curve of white sand between buttresses of rugged grey rock. She sat a little above the high tide mark, where the sand was dry, and let handfuls of it sift between her fingers as she watched the breakers rolling in. The water was an amazing shade of turquoise. It looked like something from a holiday brochure, although she knew it was freezing cold.

What will I do? she wondered. She couldn't see herself living in the house; she couldn't have stood it without a complete makeover, and she didn't have the money for that. It would be equally impossible to rent it out without refurbishment: she'd seen the adverts for holiday cottages and they all looked like something out of a magazine— white walls and rolled-up towels and LOVE spelled out in giant letters on top of the mantelpiece. That left two options. She could put it on the market as a "fixer-upper" and hope someone fell in love with the ancient range and the wooden window frames. Or she could lock it up and walk away. Quite a few people did that, out here on the islands.

Eventually Elspeth got up and walked back to the house, the wind ruffling her hair. Once again she picked it out before she got there, because it stood a little apart. That made her feel hopeful; someone might go for that, for the peace and quiet.

THE FOLLOWING MORNING Elspeth woke early, feeling disoriented. Without all her teenage things, the room was so anonymous that it took her a few moments to realize where she was.

Coffee, she thought blearily. She threw back the covers, stood up and ambled down to the kitchen. Something struck her as a little off, but she couldn't identify it until she was standing at the sink, listening to water running into the kettle. Then she leaned forward, and stared out of the window, round-eyed.

A wall. There was a wall out there. It was to the right, almost out of sight, but it was sufficiently tall that it cast shade on this side of the house.

Elspeth put down the kettle, turned off the tap and went out through the back door, wincing at the cold paving stones under her bare feet. She stared at the wall.

It seemed impossible that she wouldn't have noticed a construction of that height the day before, and yet clearly she had. Even if someone were building in the next plot, they couldn't have put up something that high and that wide overnight. It was rather an ugly thing too, monolithic, unpunctured by windows or any other features. It looked very new, and in the morning sunlight it gleamed damply, as though the rendering were not quite dry.

Elspeth's gaze dropped and she saw that her parents' garden wall, considerably smaller, was crumbling in this part of the garden too, as though the weight of the edifice looming over it were crushing it.

Damn, she thought. This would almost certainly mean a dispute with whoever had constructed the wall next door. She went back into the house to finish making her coffee; she felt she needed it, and besides, it was far too early to go out and confront anyone.

After breakfast, the issue still untackled, she wandered down to the church to see if the current minister's name was on the board outside. It was a dry, though breezy morning, but nobody was about. It was not all that easy to tell which of the older houses were occupied and which not: unkempt shrubberies and lawns run wild suggested abandonment, but perhaps the inhabitants were simply too old to do the work. Elspeth saw one house that was startling in its modernity, combining sections of wood and stone in an almost organic way. It made her think of the old black houses, if one of them had grown wrongly, like a tumour.

Trendy, she thought. The flat roof was probably wildly impractical.

The church, she now saw, was flanked by low, ugly little bungalows. She crossed the road to look at the noticeboard, alive to the possibility of busybodies watching her from behind the net curtains. *Morrison*, that was the minister's name. There was no telephone number. Elspeth sighed. She tried the church door, but it was locked. She'd have to hope the number was in her parents' address book, or the directory, if they had one. Everything felt difficult. Could she ask at one of the houses? It seemed that there was someone at home in the nearest of the bungalows; through the veiled window a shape was vaguely visible. It was very still, though, and she was fairly sure the person was watching her. The idea of going and explaining the situation to them was faintly off-putting—she'd probably have to endure avid eyes and prurient questions in exchange for the information she wanted. In the end she decided to go back to her parents' place and look for it. Probably the undertaker would have the number.

When Elspeth got back to the house she called the number the nurse had given her, and had a business-like conversation with the lilting voice on the other end. She agreed to drive over that afternoon with things for them to dress her father in: a favorite suit, shirt, tie, as though she would know which those were. It took her a while to find suitable things, and when she had packed them all up she drove into the town, taking the metalled road again.

The meeting with the undertaker felt somehow aseptic. The man was polite, offering condolences and practical information, and in fact she wondered what more she could have expected, but there wasn't real warmth. Everything about being back seemed to be conspiring to remind her that she was a stranger now, an outsider. Well, she had chosen that.

Afterwards, on impulse, she decided to drive back via the old road, across the miles of bleak peatland that formed the heart of the island. She remembered it as having a kind of grim beauty: there were few trees, but there were rocky outcrops and tiny lochans gleaming amongst the heather, and no signs of human activity other than the road itself and occasional little stacks of cut peat. It took her a little time to find the beginning of it, because the outskirts of the town had changed so much over the years, but eventually she came to a place where the rash of little houses petered out and there was the road, stretching off into the distance.

Elspeth drove slowly, savoring the experience. This was wild, genuine solitude—not like the solitude she felt in her parents' house, where the atmosphere was heavy with decades of stale memories. The sun came out from behind a cloud and suddenly the landscape looked really beautiful. Once, she actually pulled into a passing place just so that she could spend a few moments contemplating it before setting off again.

As she crested the next rise, however, she saw something that made her brake hard, and stare in disbelief.

Houses. Out here, there were *houses*. They had sprung up with all the charm of boils on previously unblemished skin. It was outrageous, and incomprehensible. Wasn't this protected land?

There were two houses that looked complete, but they were set some distance from the road, so the fine details could not really be picked out. Large windows reflected the sunshine, and they had those eco-friendly turf roofs sprouting with vegetation, as though the buildings had just reared up from the earth by themselves. That didn't compensate for the desecration of building in this spot, though. There were also several other houses in the very early stages of construction—bare foundation walls protruding from the heather. She was so incensed about this that she would have driven over there, or even got out of the car and walked over, to ask what was going on, but there was no visible route. Doubtless access to the houses was on the other side, which meant that further injury had been done to the peatland—a track laid across virgin ground. Elspeth fumed, but in the end she had to drive on. There was nothing else to do. There was no movement around any of the buildings, and no vehicles visible. There wasn't even anyone she could gesticulate at from a distance.

She eventually arrived back at her parents' house with the evils of unrestrained development still on her mind, and went straight into the back garden to re-evaluate the crumbling wall.

The garden wall had—improbably—subsided further; there were bricks scattered on the vegetable patch. That wasn't the thing that made her stare, though. It was the encroaching wall next door. There was a *window* in it. It was high up, too high for her to see into, and unmistakably new—it appeared slightly convex and it had such a high gloss on it that it looked wet, like a great eye waiting to blink.

Elspeth gazed at it open-mouthed. The window had absolutely, definitely, one hundred percent *not* been there that morning. She couldn't account for it now: it didn't seem possible for a window to simply *appear* in a wall, nor did it seem a practicable construction technique to punch windows into a wall after building it.

Am I going off my head? she thought.

With an ill-defined feeling of trepidation she went back into the house, climbed the stairs and went into her parents' room. Was it her imagination, or was it a little gloomier, a little more overshadowed than it had been that morning, when she had gone in there to find clothes for her father's body? She opened the window and leaned out as far as she dared, looking at the wall next door.

The window was at the same height as she was, but it was like looking into a fisheye lens. Elspeth couldn't clearly make out what was on the other side, although perhaps that was the point, because who would place a window such that it allowed people to stare straight into their house? There was something to one side of it—a dark streak that might have been a person—but it was impossible to say. She stared at it, waiting for it to move, but it didn't. After a few moments she drew her head in, and closed the window, feeling more unsettled than before.

It occurred to her that she hadn't seen the whole edifice; when she had driven in from the town, she'd approached from the other side.

No time like the present, she said to herself briskly, although she wasn't sure what she was hoping for. If she saw the owners or builders, what would she say? Complaints about the subsiding garden wall were unlikely to be received sympathetically. All the same, she was curious, in a not entirely pleasant way. There were of course the practical implications of nearby construction impinging on her parents' property, but it wasn't entirely that; the presence of the wall felt in some way *hostile*, as though it were a physically imposing person standing far too close to her in a public space.

Elspeth made herself go downstairs, and out into the front garden. Peering towards the next plot, she saw that the building to which the wall belonged was set further back than her parents' house. She went out through the front gates for a better look.

There was a whole house next door.

Elspeth searched her memories and it seemed to her that there had been space all around her parents' house when she first saw it, *and* when she walked up from the beach. But there *was* a house there, in the neighboring plot.

It was an odd-looking house. It was a little too tall for its width, and there was only one window on the front façade, so that it presented itself largely as a featureless slab facing the road. The window was on one side of the front door, which was painted a very shiny black. The ground in front of the house was rough and unpaved, suggesting the drive had not yet been laid. Elspeth picked her way between weeds and chunks of rubble, aiming for the door.

There were three steps leading up to it, which she ascended, and then she hesitated.

Knock, she urged herself. *If there's someone home you can introduce yourself—say you've taken over the house next door. If they're friendly, you can work your way round to the topic of the garden wall.*

She raised her hand.

The surface of the door was so lustrous she found herself thinking of tar: glossy, sticky, scalding. Touch something like that and you would stick to it, like fly paper... She let her hand fall to her side. For a moment she hesitated, and then she stepped to one side and looked through the window instead. The glass had a mildly distorting effect, like the side window, but at close quarters she could see through it more clearly. The house wasn't fully furnished. She could pick out the shapes of furniture—a table, a chair—but none of the paraphernalia of living. There were no pictures or knick-knacks or soft furnishings that she could see—no sprays of flowers or stacks of books. So it was empty, awaiting occupancy?

No, she realized. *It's not empty.*

Towards the back of the room there was a figure, standing perfectly still.

Elspeth stepped back, away from the window. There was a cold, slithery feeling in the pit of her stomach. She went back down the steps, back across the rough ground to the pavement. All the time she had her back turned she was acutely aware of the house behind her, of the window. She went back into her own garden, latched the front gates shut, went into the house and closed the door. Then she locked it, and drew the bolts across. Her hands were trembling.

She went to the back door, and checked that it was locked. Then she went upstairs, to her parents' room, and closed the curtains. She felt a little sick. All the time she was doing these things she was telling herself that she had had a bereavement; illogical reactions to things, forgetfulness, misconceptions, even outright hallucinations—all those things might be normal for all she knew. But still she kept thinking about that silent, still figure, and the fact that, like the house, it had seemed to be *unfinished*. It was a simulacrum of a human being, she thought—something raw and clumsy, like unfired clay. But it had been watching, she felt sure of that.

Elspeth fetched her bag, and searched through it until she found the scrap of paper on which the undertaker had jotted down the minister's telephone number for her. The landline was in the hall, so she called from that, and then she tried with her mobile. The phone at the other end rang and rang, but nobody answered. There was no answering machine either.

—Since your mother died things have become considerably more difficult here and alone I am not equal to the task of

—things have become considerably more difficult here—

—alone I am not equal to the task—

Elspeth buried her face in her hands. *Dad*, she thought. She remembered his almost closed eyes, his mouth yawning wide. It had seemed like the dregs of disapproval at the time, but now she thought of a silent scream.

I'll go, she said to herself. *Tomorrow, first thing.* It didn't matter that it was irrational. She'd lock the place up and leave, like other people did when it was all too much to deal with. There'd be somewhere she could stay in the town—a hotel, a cheap rental, anything. From there she could make the necessary arrangements, and when she was finally on the ferry, heading back to the mainland, she'd throw the key as far out into the water as she possibly could.

Tomorrow, first thing, she promised herself.

But at half past two in the morning she awoke with a start to a long drawn out creaking, the sound of a structure under great strain. A tremor ran through the entire house, followed by a distinct rupture.

Elspeth sat up in bed, her heart thumping, and reached for the bedside lamp. She could *feel* that something was happening; there was a change in the quality of the air, an increased pressure. A *pushing*. In the low light she belted her dressing gown around herself and crossed the room, moving swiftly but stealthily. Her mouth was very dry. Her fingers closed around the doorknob and slowly, making as little sound as possible, she turned it and opened the door.

Half the breadth of the landing had gone. Instead there was *wall*, glistening wall, and it was protruding into the space like a great lung inflating. Very soon, she saw, it would engulf the entire space, trapping her inside her room. The heaving, wet quality of it revolted her, but that was not the worst thing. Something was budding off from it: a shape that was vaguely human, but blunt and unfinished. The thought of seeing the face at close quarters filled Elspeth with dread. Already it had both feet on the landing floor; as she watched, it pulled its

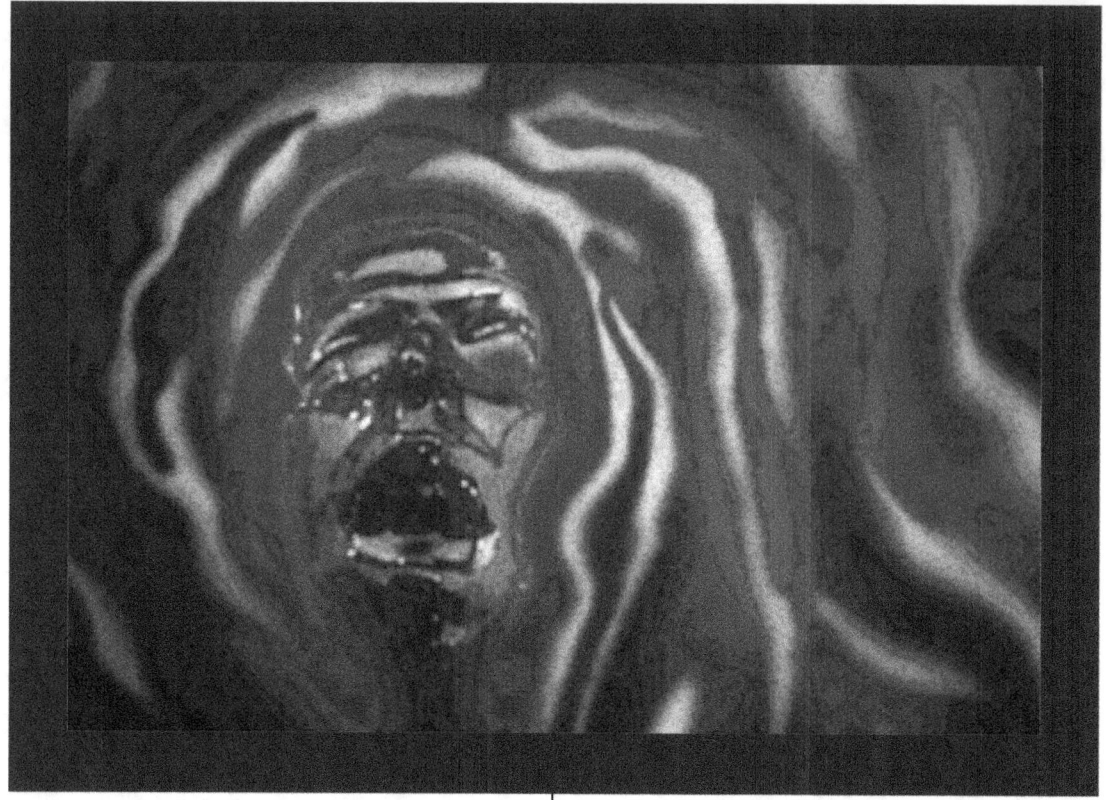

second arm free and stood there, looking at her.

Elspeth had one chance, and she took it. She lunged for the head of the stairs and went downstairs at full tilt, cringing away from the encroaching wall. To touch it would be bad, very bad—she knew that instinctively. In the downstairs hallway the space had narrowed to a pulsating sliver, so she ran for the kitchen. Her handbag was on the table and she grabbed it in passing, then she unlocked the back door and burst out into the garden.

The night air was unpleasantly cold, but it had a sobering effect. Elspeth took a moment to think about where she should go, then went around the opposite side of the house from the invading wall. She was barefoot, and it was impossible to see where she was treading. The gravel cut into her feet, so that she hobbled and swore. When she got to the front of the house she saw with relief that her car still stood apart from whatever was consuming the house. She opened the gates, got into the car and drove out.

The outskirts of the village in the rear view mirror dwindled to a distant speck.

It was uncomfortable driving with bare feet, but Elspeth kept going. The headlights were the only lights in the landscape for a long time. They picked out the road ahead, but nothing on either side; she could have been anywhere. All the same, she took the metalled road, even though it was longer. Nothing could have induced her to drive across the darkened peatland, where those houses were growing like fungi.

When she got to the town Elspeth parked in a large empty car park, where there were no buildings of any kind nearby. Then she folded her arms and waited for the sun to come up. Sleep was impossible. She kept going over and over it in her mind. What was the meaning of it all? The buildings seemed to be growing almost organically over large areas of the island, like invasive plants, though where it had started she couldn't imagine. She suspected that like Nepenthaceae, they derived their nutrients from live things. There was the bird struggling on the roof, that first day... Supposing she, too, had touched one of them—that glossy black door, for example? She shuddered.

What really troubled her, though, were those crude human forms. What was the purpose of *those?*

Perhaps, she thought, *they are lures.* That made a kind of sense. An empty property is melancholy, lonely—even slightly sinister. A house with a person in it is cosier. It is *approachable.* By the time you got close enough to realize that it wasn't a proper person you were seeing, it would be far too late.

There was another possibility, however. Perhaps those things truly were *unfinished*, and at some later point they were *finished*, becoming indistinguishable from the beings they simulated. The final form might be so sophisticated that it would be hard to tell it apart from the real thing, except that it might be a little lacking in animation. It might resemble a dispassionate nurse, or an impassive undertaker.

Elspeth thought about the ferry on the way over, and the hospital, both of which had been unusually quiet. And she wondered.

The sun came up at last, and as expected she did not find it difficult to get a ferry ticket. Nobody even looked askance at her pyjamas and grubby bare feet. She didn't go to the cafeteria this time, and she kept well away from the few other passengers. At the other end she drove off the boat with relief and put as many miles as she could between herself and the terminal.

She would not say anything to anyone about this, Elspeth knew. They'd think she was delusional, unhinged by grief. She very much hoped that whatever the infestation was, it would be confined to the island. If it wasn't, at least she'd be far away.

It was true what they said, she thought, as she drove south: you can never, ever go home again.

Helen Grant writes Gothic novels and short supernatural fiction. Her new novel, Jump Cut, *about a notorious lost movie, was published in September 2023 by Fledgling Press. Film maker and novelist Jack Jewers describes it as "phenomenally creepy." Helen's short stories have appeared in* Weird Tales, Supernatural Tales, All Hallows *and anthologies including Egaeus Press's acclaimed* Crooked Houses, *Swan River Press's* Uncertainties 2 *and Black Shuck Books'* Ars Gratia Sanguis *(Great British Horror 6). Joyce Carol Oates has described her as "a brilliant chronicler of the uncanny as only those who dwell in places of dripping, graylit beauty can be." A lifelong fan of M.R. James, she has spoken at two M.R. James conferences.*

"Invasive Species" was inspired by Helen's visit to the Hebridean Isle of Lewis, where she pondered the coexistence of ruined blackhouses, deserted crofts and modern new build homes.

JILL LOOKED AT HER REFLECTION IN THE GLASS AND SAW A STRANGER. THE STRANGER HAD A NAME—BETH SAMUELS. She also had a driver's license, a Visa credit card, and a passport. The documents hadn't been cheap. Jill had spent the last of her "gitout money" on them. Normally she would have been using this time to scope out a new site and start planning another job. All while building up another stake for the next inevitable escape.

But none of it was necessary anymore. She wasn't looking for a new site and she wasn't planning another job. The next escape would be her last, and she wouldn't need money where she was going.

Strange, she thought, to be so mesmerized by her reflection when there was a much more interesting sight on the other side of the glass.

She looked down the row of stasis tubes, six of them in all. Each one the size of a phone booth. Each one containing a monster. Dead monsters. Preserved in solution that, combined with the internal lighting within each tube, gave them a pale violet glow.

No two creatures were alike and none could be found on earth.

The one Jill was currently staring at looked like a six-foot-long silver eel with milky eyes, a lower jaw that protruded to accommodate a set of long curved teeth, and a pair of vestigial arms ending in long, floppy feelers.

Speaking of feelers, Jill thought as Ted came up behind her and wrapped his hands around her waist, hooking his thumbs into her Sam Browne belt.

"So what do you think?" He kissed the side of her neck, his moustache tickling her skin. "A regular house of horrors, eh?"

"Frightening," Jill agreed. "And fascinating."

"These aren't even the best ones," Ted said. "Those get shipped off to Florida."

Jill turned her head slightly without taking her eyes off the creature in the tube. "What's in Florida?"

"PIA Headquarters," Ted said. "You know, your employer?"

He laughed and gave his head a little shake. *Women. Aren't they a hoot?*

Jill bit her lip. Technically they were employed by the Department of Homeland Security, or rather a joint U.S.-Canadian offshoot of DHS called the North American Portal Border Authority, which was itself a component of the Paranormal Intelligence Agency. But there was no point splitting hairs, not with someone like Ted. Subtlety was as lost on him as all the ships and planes that had vanished in the Bermuda Triangle. Besides, saying anything would only draw attention to herself, anyway.

Play your part, Jill told herself. *Always ask yourself: what would Beth Samuels do?*

Jill tapped the glass, then recoiled with a nervous giggle as the eel-thing revolved slowly in the tube. She looked over her shoulder at Ted, putting on a cute, vulnerable grin.

"Sorry," she said. "I thought it moved."

Ted tightened his grip around her waist. "Nothing alive in here, babe," he said.

Jill turned around in his arms so she was facing him. Ted was tall and broad and handsome. At a glance, he seemed like the kind of guy whose good looks had probably worked like a skeleton key on all of life's trickiest locks. But if you looked a little closer a different picture came into focus. Suddenly the suave, easygoing smile became a cocky grin; the deep blue eyes of an introspective thinker turned into the cool gaze of a callous bully. Ted wasn't the brightest bulb in the pack, but he was charming and cunning, two traits that Jill knew could be dangerous in the same package.

Still, he was awfully trusting for someone with his security clearance.

"Has anything ever come through alive?" Jill asked him.

"That's classified," Ted said. His mouth curved in a sly grin, but Jill knew he was dead serious. That was Ted to a tee. One moment he was breaking the rules, the next he was enforcing them with an iron fist.

As the head of security he could sneak Jill into this place, the most secure area in the entire facility, but the moment she tried to work it to her own advantage, the walls went up again. Getting access to this section—where they kept all of the creatures that washed over from the Black Lands—was the reason she had started sleeping with Ted in the first place. Well, one of the reasons.

"Who decided to call this place the Plutonian Shore?" Jill asked.

"That's not the official name," Ted said in his supercilious tone. "It's just something one of the guys came up with."

"Another guard?"

"Yeah," Ted said. He slid his hands back into her belt and pulled her toward him. "But he wasn't as pretty as you."

"Few are." Jill wrapped her arms around his neck and kissed him. He tasted like stale coffee and cigarettes. She broke the kiss and grinned at him. "You want to do it in here?"

Ted flushed. "Yeah," he said, "but it's against about a dozen regs."

Jill knew he would say that, which was why she had suggested it. She put on a pouty face and said, "Oh, pooh on the regs. Being in here makes me hot."

She pressed her body into his. He reached up and gently removed Jill's arms from around his neck. "That would be awesome, but we're on duty, and there are cameras everywhere."

Jill let out a theatrical sigh. "Okay," she said. "You're the boss."

"I am," Ted said, regaining his composure. "You should probably get back on your rounds."

It took Jill a moment to realize he wasn't being flirty, that he was actually telling her to go back to work. Ted to a tee.

Before she followed him out of the room—it took a pass-card and a handprint scan to open the pressure door into the Plutonian Shore—Jill took one last look at the creature in the tube. Then she unfocused her eyes and stared again at her reflection in the polished glass. She understood now why she was as transfixed by her own face as that of the demonic visage within.

They were both monsters.

JILL USED TO DREAM about the Black Lands.

It started when she was a child, before she even knew what the Black Lands were.

In the dreams, she was submerged in deep, dark water, arms and legs moving as if in slow-motion as she struggled to reach the surface. She could feel the fear mounting inside her, filling her up as the oxygen was slowly squeezed out of her lungs. No matter how much she thrashed and kicked, she was never able to reach the surface before her air ran out.

Jill didn't so much awaken from these dreams as she was ejected from them, bathed in sweat, bedsheets twisted around her body, sometimes with a scream still echoing in her ears.

Jill didn't realize it was the Black Lands she was dreaming of until she was older.

When she discovered she wasn't alone in those dark depths.

THE BUILDING looked like a prison.

It was a concrete block with slit windows squatting behind an electrified fence topped with a double row of razor wire. The sign out front, next to the security checkpoint, said PORTAL 34 CONTAINMENT AND RESEARCH FACILITY, but no one ever called it that. From the very beginning, everyone—even the people who worked there—referred to the place by its nickname.

Old Frightful.

The portal was discovered in August of 1973 by a Kitchener farmer named Ross Traynor. That summer, Southern Ontario was experiencing a record-breaking heatwave that had everyone, not just the farmers, praying for rain. Traynor had gone out to one of his cornfields to see how his crop was faring. Better than it should have been, it turned out. Traynor was surprised to discover that while the majority of the field was bone dry, one large section of ground was wet. More than wet, it was *flooded*. Seeing as how there hadn't been any rain for weeks, not even a mild shower, Traynor was at a complete loss to explain where the water had come from. The answer came a few days later when Traynor was back in the same field and witnessed a great gush of water appear seemingly out of thin air. Traynor told a local newspaper: "It looked like someone poked a hole in a giant invisible bucket and water came pouring out." Despite his initial shock, Traynor soon realized what he was looking at, when, in addition to the water, half a dozen creatures that looked like crabs but definitely weren't crabs landed in his cornfield and started scuttling around on the muddy ground. Traynor used the garden rake he'd been carrying to bash the creatures to death, then ran back to his house and made a phone call.

The following day, the feds arrived and set up a cordon around the cornfield.

They could have simply taken Traynor's land—they were perfectly within their rights under the Portal Proximity Relocation Act—but they did him one better and bought it from him instead, paying considerably more than the market value. Over the following months, a facility was hastily constructed around the portal, which continued to expel random amounts of water from the Black Lands on an equally random basis.

One of the scientists who worked at the facility remarked that the portal reminded him of Old Faithful, the geyser at Yellowstone National Park. Except Old Faithful didn't spew water from another dimension. Or dump out the occasional sea monster.

After that, it didn't take long for someone to come up with the nickname.

JILL PRESSED A BUTTON on the remote control and the DVD started playing again.

The screen was divided into four squares that displayed the video feeds of the closed-circuit cameras monitoring the containment chamber at Old Frightful. The chamber was a large, cavernous room with concrete walls and viewing windows made of thick shatter-proof glass. The floor slanted at a forty-five degree angle on all four sides to a recessed steel grate in the center that looked exactly like what it was—an enormous drain. When the water poured out of the portal, it was funnelled down to the grate and then through a series of pipes to a storage tank underneath the facility. There it was tested for contaminants before a tanker truck came to pump it out and transport it to an off-site storage facility. (Ted said the location of the facility was classified, but Jill suspected he didn't know where it was.)

The DVD was a compilation of footage taken over the years of Old Frightful expelling water from the Black Lands—or "shooting its wad," as Ted so eloquently put it. Jill had been shown the footage during her orientation, back when "Beth Samuels" was first hired on. Later, she filched the DVD from the audio-visual room, made a copy for herself, and returned it with no one the wiser.

Jill picked up her beer and took a swig. On the screen—the timestamp in the lower right corner said 14 NOV 1998 – 13:21—water began to pour into the containment chamber from a spot in mid-air about ten feet above the drainage grate. Like all portals, Old Frightful was invisible to the human eye, but when it was open and discharging water, its general size and shape could be discerned. Currently it was small, with a bore no wider than that of a garden hose. But as Jill continued to watch, the flow of water increased from a steady trickle to a heavy stream. When it reached full blast, the portal was about six feet in diameter.

During her orientation, Jill had also been shown archival footage of scientists trying to send small probes through the portal. The first few attempts didn't work. The water pressure was too strong for anything to get past it to the other side.

At least not at first.

On the screen, the water flow was starting to slow down. Right before it stopped entirely, the flow abruptly changed direction and the water was sucked back into the portal.

Jill pressed pause on the remote, freezing the water in mid-reversal. In the ten months she had been working at the facility, Old Frightful had shot its wad seven times. She had been present on only two of those occasions, and both times she had seen this unusual effect in the moments right before the portal closed.

The scientists called it the backwash.

For Jill, it was her ticket to the Black Lands.

IT CAME AS NO SURPRISE to anyone that the dreams Jill had as a kid—dreams of drowning in a deep, dark sea—ended up resulting in a lifelong fear of the water.

Bathtubs and swimming pools were okay. So were creeks and rivers as long as they weren't too deep. But ponds and lakes were out. And the ocean? No way, Jose.

Jill wasn't so much afraid of the water as the things lurking within it. Her policy when it came to bodies of water was that if she couldn't see the bottom, then she wouldn't even dip in a toe. Anything could be in there, she reasoned. *Any thing.*

When Jill was eight, her parents made the mistake of letting her watch *Jaws*. If she wasn't getting in the water before, she definitely wasn't after that. For years afterwards—on family vacations and camping trips with friends—whenever Jill encountered a large body of water, she would invariably ask the question: "Do you think there are sharks in there?"

She knew it was silly, but it didn't make the fear go away.

Sharks weren't even the scariest things in the water. There were other creatures out there, bigger and deadlier, lurking in the deep, dark depths.

Jill knew this. She had seen them in her dreams.

ON HER NEXT DAY OFF, Jill went to Toronto.

It was a two-hour drive from Kitchener, which she felt was a safe enough distance away. Being careful and discreet had become second nature to her; she didn't even think about it anymore. Her natural instinct the past few years was to keep moving, always stay under the radar, and never leave a trail for anyone to follow.

She went to a coffeehouse on the Danforth called Jet Fuel. The last time she came to the city, she had gone to a place called Java Paradiso. She never went to the same place twice.

She bought a large black coffee and sat down at one of the computer workstations in the back. As always, the first thing she did was download the Tor browser. The computer she was using had Internet Explorer and Google Chrome, but Tor would allow her to cruise the internet anonymously.

Once Tor was installed, she went to the PIA's website. Like the FBI, the Paranormal Intelligence Agency maintained a public list of most-wanted fugitives. Unlike the FBI, the PIA didn't limit their list to ten individuals. There were dozens of people on it, all of them wanted for various paranormal-related crimes.

Jill scanned the list—as she had done every few weeks since she arrived in Kitchener—but her name still wasn't on it. She was surprised.

Even though Duncan had told her and the others to keep their mouths shut if they were ever arrested, she didn't think any of them would actually follow through on it.

While other government agencies might use "enhanced interrogation techniques" such as beatings, hooding, and sleep deprivation, the PIA was said to have more unusual and insidious methods to extract information. It was rumoured they had psychics in their employ who could invade a subject's mind and convince them they were experiencing any number of horrible, painful acts—burning, drowning, bodily dismemberment. This technique was known as "ouijaboarding."

But if the PIA was looking for Jill, they weren't advertising that fact.

She supposed it made sense. None of the news networks had reported on the incident in Montana. There should have been major press coverage—a portal border had been breached and people had died—but it was like the whole thing had never happened. Which meant the PIA had covered it up.

This placed Jill in one of two possible scenarios.

One, Duncan and the others hadn't given her up, so the PIA really wasn't looking for her.

Two, Duncan or one of the others—or all of them together—had squealed like little piggies and the PIA was on the hunt for her, but they were doing so quietly.

Jill had no way to confirm either scenario without exposing herself. But she knew that even if Duncan and the others had managed to keep their mouths shut, their minds were completely open to the PIA's psychics. Therefore it was only a matter of time before the feds started looking for her. They could be on her trail right now—a thought that left her feeling sick and anxious.

She needed to get away, but the decision was out of her hands.

Old Frightful was on its own schedule.

THINGS STARTED GOING BAD soon after Jill joined Black Dawn.

They were one of the Black Lands activist groups that sprung up after the portals started appearing in the late 1940s. While most people saw the portals as an international crisis, there was a small but vocal few who believed this was a natural condition of the planet, or possibly karmic retribution for all the death and destruction humanity had inflicted upon the earth.

The typical Black Lands activist often started out as an animal rights supporter who had become bitter and disenchanted with the movement. They'd come to believe the fight to protect the planet's wildlife was over, that the number of species becoming endangered or outright extinct had reached critical mass, and it was too late to turn the tide. The planet was doomed. Noah's Ark was sinking.

In the Black Lands, these people saw their chance to start fresh with a whole new world. Perhaps less an Eden than a dark, primeval wood, but still a place with creatures that needed their protection.

Jill was one of those born-again activists —starting out with animal rights in high school, then, when her enthusiasm began to wane, shifting her efforts to the supernatural fauna of the Black Lands.

After graduation, she joined a group called the Dark Lighters. She marched in rallies and spread petitions to protest the capture and extermination of Black Lands entities. She picketed outside PIA headquarters in Boca Sombra, handing out leaflets that said things like NOT ALL MONSTERS ARE MONSTERS and DON'T LET MANKIND MURDER ANOTHER WORLD.

It wasn't easy to advocate on behalf of vampires, shifters, and other paranormal predators. There were no cuddly panda bears they could use as a symbol to illicit sympathy or support for their cause. They were on the fringe of all fringe groups. All they had was their belief that what they were doing was right.

It was an uphill battle, to say the least.

The way Jill saw it, great white sharks and black widow spiders killed people, too, but no one was calling for their complete and total eradication. The creatures of the Black Lands may be dangerous, but they had as much a right to live as any other animal, supernatural or otherwise.

Jill lasted two years with the Dark Lighters before ennui began to seep in. It was like what happened with the animal rights groups she worked with back in high school, only this time she couldn't tell herself the fight was over and simply move on to the next crusade. As long as the portals continued to pop up all over the globe, the battle would never be over. She couldn't quit. She had to do something.

The operative word was "do." Jill realized that for all their energy and enthusiasm, the Dark Lighters didn't actually *do* anything. Like other organizations that rallied against human trafficking or climate change, most Black Lands activist groups used peaceful and largely non-confrontational methods to express their message of interdimensional unity.

But then, as with other protest movements, there were other groups that took a decidedly more active approach.

Black Dawn was one such group, and Jill noticed the difference almost immediately.

One week after she joined, she went from designing newsletters to building bombs.

It was an intense time in her life, startling and thrilling in equal measure.

She took to it like a duck to water.

Jill stopped at a hardware store on her way back to Kitchener.

It was one of those big-box megastores she usually avoided because she found them too overwhelming. Now she was glad for the crowds of people and the screaming children. It made it easier to stay anonymous.

After wandering around for twenty minutes, she managed to find the section devoted to dive gear. She also found a young man who worked there, a smooth-cheeked surfer-looking kid with shaggy blond hair who said "awesome" a lot. His name tag said Devon and he was able—and eager—to answer all of her questions. Like what the difference was between a wetsuit and a dry suit.

"Temperature mostly," he said. "Wetsuits are usually for warmer dives, because they let water in. Dry suits are more heavily insulated and have seals to keep water out. Where are you diving?"

Jill was ready for this question. "Tobermory," she said. "I hear they've got some decent dive sites up there."

"Oh yeah, awesome," Devon said. "I've been there a few times, you'll love it. You should check out the Tugs. Some really cool wrecks you can explore."

Jill smiled. "Thanks. I'll do that."

Devon rubbed his chin thoughtfully.

"Tobermory, eh? The water isn't that cold up there. You'd probably be okay with a wetsuit."

"I was thinking a dry suit," Jill said. "Just to be on the safe side." She smiled again. "I get cold easily."

Devon nodded. "Always be prepared. That's, like, rule number one when it comes to diving."

He helped Jill find a dry suit that fit her, as well as a full-face mask, fins, gloves, a web belt, a dive computer, an underwater flashlight, a Luxfer scuba tank, a regulator, half a dozen bolt snaps, and a titanium knife with a strap-on sheath.

"You know," Devon said, after he had rung up all of her purchases, "you could probably rent most of this stuff at the place where you're diving."

"I know," Jill said, "but when it comes to a new hobby, I like to go all-in."

"New hobby?" Devon said. "So you've never gone diving before?"

"No," Jill said, relishing the look of surprise on the young man's face. "I'm afraid of the water."

The leader of Black Dawn was a man named Duncan Norris.

Duncan had a history with the Black Lands and he would happily share it with anyone willing to listen—especially if it netted him a new recruit. It was a story he had told so many times it came off sounding a little rehearsed when he told it to Jill the first time they met.

When Duncan was a boy, his father went hunting with his brother, Duncan's uncle Chet, and they came upon a bear. Not an unusual sight in the deep woods of northern Maine, only the brothers could tell right off that this was no ordinary bear. Besides the unusual color of its fur—a deep rusty red streaked with silver—the animal stood over fifteen feet tall. The biggest bear on earth, Duncan told Jill, was the polar bear, and it never grew taller than eleven feet.

This made sense because the creature the two brothers had come upon wasn't from earth. It was a shifter from the Black Lands —a werebear that had crossed over through a portal located somewhere in the woods.

Although the men were armed with rifles, neither of them took a shot at the creature. They were both scared, but that wasn't the reason. There was no point shooting at the animal because their guns weren't loaded with silver rounds, which were the only things that could kill a shifter. Instead, they attempted to leave the area quietly without drawing the beast's attention. In this they were unsuccessful, and the shifter attacked the two men.

Duncan's father was killed outright with a single swipe of the creature's claws that nearly decapitated him. Duncan's uncle Chet managed to escape with only a single bite wound to his arm, but died six hours later in the hospital, shackled to a gurney in the ER's paranormal bio-containment chamber. While he might have survived the trauma of the wound, there was no cure for the infection that came along with it. If he hadn't been administered a lethal injection of potassium chloride and silver nitrate, Chet would have eventually transformed into a werecreature himself.

Despite losing his father and his uncle, Duncan said he didn't hate supernaturals, and he never entertained any thoughts of vengeance against them. *You can't get revenge on an animal*, he said to Jill. *And that's all these things are. Animals from a place we don't fully understand.*

The real monsters, he said, were the people in government—the PIA, the Portal Border Authority, and the rest of the bureaucrats—who heartlessly slaughtered supernatural creatures, even the ones that posed no threat to humanity. They put up walls and fences around the portals—not only to contain them, but to keep people from crossing over into the Black Lands.

Duncan created Black Dawn for the expressed purpose of bringing down those borders—by any means necessary. Leaflets and petitions wouldn't do the job. Duncan had spent years trying to get the government to listen, to change their attitudes toward supernaturals and the Black Lands, but it was like talking to a brick wall.

That's fine, Duncan said. *Walls fall down all the time. And if they don't fall on their own, we can* make *them fall.*

Jill was captivated, both by Duncan's story and his compassion, his conviction. Here was a man who had every right to hate the creatures that had taken so much from him, but instead he fought for their survival. She found herself drawn to him—in part because of his rugged good looks, but mostly because of his devotion to the cause. She was concerned when the talk turned to bombing portal border sites, but Duncan assured her no one would be harmed. Black Dawn didn't want to kill anyone, he said. Not even the government pigs who deserved it. They only wanted to tear down the walls and set the portals free.

Jill didn't need much convincing. Duncan's story went hand-in-hand with her own need to do something about the government's oppression of the Black Lands and the creatures that lived there.

Looking back on her time with Black Dawn, Jill realized something else as well.

People often do crazy things when they're in love.

OVER THE WEEKS and months she spent working at Old Frightful, Jill prepared as best she could for her trip to the Black Lands. It was a bit like waiting for a bolt of lightning to strike a specific location. She knew where the portal would open, but she didn't know when it would happen next.

After studying the security footage of Old Frightful, Jill realized her task was made even more difficult for two reasons.

One, the portal opened at completely random times.

Two, the portal remained open for anywhere between five minutes to five hours.

Since there was nothing she could do about either of these things, Jill decided to focus on those that were within her control.

The key to carrying out her plan was to minimize the risk while maximizing what little time she might have to pull it off. Which meant being prepared.

She started by scoping out the women's locker room at work. Since there weren't very many female guards at Old Frightful, the majority of the lockers were empty and unused. Jill commandeered two of them and spent the next few weeks bringing her equipment to work piece by piece, hiding each item in the large hockey bag she used to carry her uniform and other personal belongings. During one of these trips, Ted had asked her why such a little girl needs such a big bag. Jill replied, *For all my shoes,* and Ted had laughed and laughed and laughed.

Since Jill had no way of knowing when the portal would next open, or for how long, she considered the idea of wearing the dry suit under her uniform while she was at work. It took a long time to put the suit on, and once the plan was set in motion, every second would count. She eventually decided against it, figuring there was always the chance Ted might decide to take her out to his pickup truck for a quickie, and if that happened she wouldn't be able to explain the dry suit under her clothes.

In addition to her dive gear, Jill also smuggled in some camping equipment and wilderness survival supplies. The kinds of things designed to break down into their smallest components for easier storage and lighter travel. She put a pair of heavy Yale padlocks on the two lockers containing all of her equipment and went back to waiting for Old Frightful to open.

It was another four months before she got her chance.

JILL DID FOUR JOBS with Black Dawn before the incident in Montana.

Four jobs over six years. It didn't sound like much, but each one required a great deal of planning—from the selection of the site, to the construction of the bombs, to the execution of the act. And it didn't include all the jobs that had to be aborted for one reason or another before they could be carried out. The members of Black Dawn were committed, but they were also careful.

Although the locations were spread out across the United States, the jobs themselves were basically the same. They always selected a border portal site in a remote location, one that didn't have a security detail. They went in fast, under cover of darkness, planted their bombs on the fences or walls or whatever the feds were using to contain the portal, and then they got the hell out.

Duncan knew the bombings weren't a solution to the problem—it never took the government long to repair the damage Black Dawn had done—but he said their actions would inspire others to do the same thing, and if enough people pushed against the walls…well, look what happened in Berlin.

Things went smoothly for a time—or as smoothly as it could go for a group of militant activists who were committing acts of domestic terrorism on a semi-regular basis.

Then, Montana.

The job should have gone off without a hitch, as all the others had, but instead it went completely to hell. Afterward, Duncan told Jill it was inevitable. They had been lucky before, he said, but luck always runs out. Jill felt no consolation in his words. It wasn't their luck that had run out.

The site was located outside of Red Lodge ("Gateway to Yellowstone National Park!") in a densely wooded area at the foot of the Beartooth Mountains. According to the PIA's website, it was considered a low-risk portal in that, while it was still an open doorway to the Black Lands, there had never been any reports of supernaturals crossing over. As was the case with all "benign" portals, the government felt an electric fence topped with razor wire was all the security required to contain it.

What the feds didn't say on their website—but what Duncan, Jill, and the others knew from past experience—was that a border patrol team visited the site once a month to confirm the integrity of the fence and carry out routine maintenance.

Jill asked herself later: was it fate or simple bad luck the patrol team arrived on the same night Black Dawn came to plant their bombs?

She didn't know. What she did know was she was one of the people who physically handled the bombs and assisted in placing them around the fence when they heard the sound of a truck grumbling up the service road.

She and the others scrambled into the woods as the truck came through a break in the trees, headlights blazing. Half a dozen men in khaki uniforms hopped out and immediately began moving along the perimeter of the fence. Watching from the trees, Jill couldn't tell if they had somehow been alerted to their presence or if the men were only going about their usual work.

She determined it was the latter a few moments later when one of the men suddenly called out, "Hey! Come take a look at this!"

Jill knew what he had found and what was about to happen. The timers on the bombs had been set for ten minutes—enough time for her and the others to get to a safe distance and watch the fireworks before they skedaddled.

Jill was about to break cover so she could warn the guards away when she felt Duncan's hand clamp tightly around her arm. "It's too late," he said.

Jill didn't believe that, they still had time, it couldn't possibly have been ten...

The bombs exploded.

Jill couldn't tell in the conflagration that followed how many of the border guards had been killed in the initial blasts. Some of them, surely, but not all. Amid the flames and the roiling smoke and the sprays of electric sparks, she could hear two men, maybe three, screaming in pain. In the clearing where only moments ago a seemingly empty patch of ground had been fenced off, there was now a hellish landscape of burning debris, twisted, blackened wire, and things that looked like mangled, ruptured sandbags but were in fact the smoldering remains of dismembered human beings.

As Jill and the others wandered about like sleepwalking children, she noticed some of these singed and smoking shapes were still moving. One of them was a man with his legs missing below the knees and one of his arms torn off at the shoulder. Jill could see the white nub of bone protruding from the socket of burnt-black flesh. The man's face was bright red, the skin on his cheeks and forehead peeled back in crispy patches like he'd gotten the mother of all sunburns. He was still alive. Jill thought this was a miracle, then quickly reconsidered.

The man looked pleadingly at Jill with eyes that were melting out his head like runny eggs. "Puh-puh-please..." he sputtered. His lips had been burned off, so the word came out slick and sibilant. "Pleasssssse... hurtsssss..."

Jill started to reach for him, then Duncan had her by the arm again, pulling her back, and this time she didn't resist. She let him drag her away. Back to the jeeps they had hidden in the woods. Back down the service road to the highway. Back to the motel in Red Lodge where they were staying.

Only she never really left that place of blood and fiery ruin. No matter how far she ran, she always ended up back in that clearing in the woods.

When she was a kid, she used to dream of drowning.

Now she dreamed of fire.

She dreamed she was the one burning.

JILL WAS WORKING the late shift—midnight to eight—on the night she made her attempt.

Part of the reason she was sleeping with Ted was so he would keep her on this shift instead of making her move along the usual schedule rotation with the other guards. There was no evidence to suggest Old Frightful was more likely to go active during those particular eight hours, but it was the best time for Jill because it was the shift with the fewest number of people in the facility. None of the scientists worked that late, and there were only ever three guards on duty. On this night, those guards were Jill, Ted, and a soft-spoken Indian man named Vihaan.

It started out like any other shift, with Jill and Vihaan taking turns strolling through the facility corridors while Ted sat in the security suite and watched the banks of surveillance monitors (or, more likely, read the latest issue of *Field & Stream* with his feet up on the console).

At 3:34 a.m., as Jill was pouring her third coffee of the night, the klaxon went off.

She let out a yelp of surprise and, while she managed to hold onto the carafe in her one hand, the other one, holding her Styrofoam cup, went flying into the air. The cup landed on the break room floor, spilling hot coffee across the scuffed linoleum.

It took her a second to realize what that sound meant.

Old Frightful was open. And then: *This is my chance!*

Jill had spent the past few weeks in a state of near-constant readiness, and now that the time had finally come she found herself unable to move. Like a race-car driver who has been revving his engine harder and harder only to have it suddenly stall out the moment the race has begun.

She left the break room without cleaning up the spilled coffee and went sprinting down the hallway. The klaxon blasted off the walls, rising and falling, pressing in on her like a physical force. Mercifully, it cut off in mid-blare as she reached the security suite.

Vihaan was already there, standing behind Ted, who was seated at the console. Both men were staring at the four large monitors displaying the video feeds from inside the containment chamber.

"She's gushing," Ted said, sounding bored. "Whoop-de-do."

He swivelled around in his chair to face Jill. She recognized the look in his eye. Old Frightful was shooting its wad, and now Ted wanted to do the same.

"Hey, Apu," he said to Vihaan without taking his eyes off Jill. "We're going on our break. Keep an eye on the store."

Vihaan looked at him with concern. "Is it safe to go while the portal is active?"

"Don't wet yourself." Ted slapped Vihaan on the shoulder hard enough to knock him off balance. "If you see any big scary monsters, just slap the panic button."

The red button on the control panel said SEAL, and that was what it did—seal the doors into the containment chamber so nothing could get in or out. Once upon a time it also summoned a STAR team from Toronto, but not anymore. Not since the facility's directors realized the creatures that washed over from the Black Lands always ended up dying, even if they got them into a water tank before they expired. So what did it matter if they left them in the chamber to be scooped up in the morning?

Vihaan sat down in Ted's chair and stared fixedly at the monitors while Ted took Jill's hand and led her out of the room. In the hallway, when she realized Ted was leading her to the parking lot, she gave his hand a sharp tug to get his attention. Ted stopped and looked at her.

"Ladies locker room," Jill said.

Ted's lips spread in a slow grin. "Cool," he said. "No one'll be in there."

Exactly, Jill thought.

Ted tightened his grip on her hand and pulled her down the hallway in the other direction.

In the locker room, Jill went over to her locker, spun the combination on the lock, and cracked the door open. Then she turned to Ted and said, "Strip."

Ted looked confused for a moment, then he grinned and started unbuckling his belt "This is great," he said. "We've never done it in here before."

And we never will, Jill thought as she reached into her locker and picked up the Taser sitting on the top shelf.

Taking a quick look over her shoulder, she saw Ted had his uniform shirt off and was currently struggling with his undershirt. In his rush to pull it off, he had gotten it stuck on his head.

Boy, I sure know how to pick 'em.

Jill strolled leisurely over, taking her time, and when Ted finally managed to get his undershirt off, she held up the Taser and waggled it at him.

Ted looked confused again. His hair standing up in springs and corkscrews only added to the effect. "Where'd you get that?" he said. "Those things are illegal, you know. You shouldn't have brought it to work."

"Take it up with human resources," Jill said.

Then she zapped him.

THIS WAS A BAD ONE, Jill knew, and she had the bad feeling to go along with it.

While Duncan and the others retreated to the motel where they were staying, Jill took one of the jeeps and went to a bar. She had a drink. Then she had another. And another. And another. At some point she stumbled out of the bar, threw up next to an old rusting trash barrel, and fell asleep in the jeep. She woke up sometime before dawn with a roseate glow rising up behind the mountains.

The bad feeling she had tried to drink away was still there. At first she thought it was a hangover, but she was pretty sure she was still drunk. Driving back to the motel she realized what it was—the sixth sense she had developed for danger. The one that had kept her out of trouble—and out of jail—for the entirety of her career as a Black Lands activist. It was trying to tell her something was wrong.

The motel was surrounded by cops.

In addition to the half dozen Montana Highway Patrol cruisers, she also saw a couple of unmarked sedans with flashing lights on their roofs, and a black armored truck with STAR printed on the side in white block letters. This was no ordinary police raid. This was the feds, and they had come down on Black Dawn with both feet.

She wondered how the PIA had caught up with them so fast. The bombing had only happened last night, and no one had seen them leave. Did someone in the group tip them off? If she managed to avoid getting picked up, would Duncan think it was her?

Staring at all those flashing lights was hurting her eyes. Jill squinted to cut the glare and almost drove into a police cruiser angled sideways across the entrance to the parking lot. A state trooper wearing mirrored sunglasses tapped on her window. Jill rolled it down.

"What's going on?" she asked.

The trooper wrinkled his nose, and Jill realized he probably smelled vodka and vomit on her breath. Then she thought: *If he busts you for a DUI, that'll be the least of your problems.*

"That's none of your business," the trooper said. "Move along." He made a twirling gesture with his finger.

Jill rolled up her window and moved along.

The trooper was right. It wasn't her business.

Not anymore.

Jill dragged Ted over to the long bench in front of the lockers, laid him face down on top of it, then used his own handcuffs to lock his hands around one of the pedestal legs bolted to the floor. She took his keys and his radio and tossed them into the shower room. Then she jogged back to the security suite.

Vihaan was still watching the monitors when Jill came up behind him.

"Old Frightful still gushing?"

Vihaan nodded. "Looks like it's gonna be a long one."

Jill stared at the pouring water on the screens. "Do you think there are sharks in there?"

"What?" Vihaan started to turn around, and Jill pressed the Taser against his side. Vihaan bolted upright in his chair, then slithered bonelessly to the floor. The Taser didn't pack as strong a charge since she'd just used it on Ted, but Jill still felt bad about having to use it at all. She liked Vihaan. She had considered drugging the two men, putting Rohypnol in their coffee or something, but she didn't have time to wait for it to take effect. She had a very narrow window and it was getting smaller with each passing moment.

Jill used Vihaan's handcuffs to lock his hands behind his back, then used her own set of cuffs to lock his feet together. Then she dragged him over to the closet, shoved him inside next to a stack of plastic storage bins, and shut the door.

Back in the women's locker room, Jill checked on Ted—he was still unconscious—then went over to the two lockers she had requisitioned and unloaded her equipment. After stripping out of her uniform, she struggled into the dry suit. This was the part she figured would take the most time, and she was right. She had practiced putting the suit on at home, but still managed to get her arm stuck in one of the sleeves. She had to force herself to slow down and do it right, even though every impulse in her body was telling her to *hurry hurry hurry*.

When she finally had the suit on and all the seals properly secured, Jill shouldered the big duffel bag containing the rest of her gear, picked up her scuba tank by its straps, and jogged as fast as she could to the containment chamber.

At the main pressure door, she slapped the fat red release button and waited. There was a loud hiss of escaping air, then the door slid open.

The containment chamber always reminded Jill of a theatre. In the place where a stage would be, a heavy stream of water was pouring apparently out of thin air. The water struck the slanted floor and ran down to the large grate in the center of the chamber.

Jill stood there for a moment, staring at the falling water. *It's still open,* she thought. *The luck is still with me.*

Then she heard Duncan's voice in her head: *Luck always runs out.*

She set the scuba tank and duffel bag on the floor, then went over to the cantilever rolling ladder in the corner of the chamber. The scientists used the ladder to send in their probes and drones. Jill pushed it down the ramp and positioned it as close to the portal as she could get without putting it directly under the flow of water.

She went back over to her pile of equipment, started to sling the duffel bag onto her shoulder, then remembered she had to take something out first. Something she would need close to hand once she was on the other side.

It looked like a small orange sack, the kind a windbreaker folds into, with a plastic ripcord attached to a lanyard. Jill clipped it onto her web belt with one of the bolt snaps, then picked up the duffel and her scuba tank, and carried them up the ladder steps.

Now that she stood facing the portal, Jill experienced her first real doubts about her plan. Not the execution but the intent.

There was a reason why Jill decided to go to the Black Lands, and why she was using Old Frightful to get there.

It wasn't about avoiding legal prosecution and jail time. She might have been able to evade the feds for years, maybe even forever, but she couldn't get away from the feelings of guilt and shame that were constantly bubbling up inside her, like lava in a volcano that could blow at any moment.

And then there were the dreams. Dreams of drowning from a fear of water that had turned into dreams of burning as the men in Montana had burned.

Someone might have seen Jill using Old Frightful to get to the Black Lands as ironic, maybe even poetic, but that wasn't why she was doing it.

Even though Jill would pass through water, this was not a cleansing. There was nothing in this world—or in the Black Lands—that could remove the stain from her soul. She had taken lives, and nothing, not even taking her own life, would restore that balance.

This was about atonement.

Jill was going to the Black Lands to be judged. She would accept whatever fate came to her on the other side. If she was ripped apart by sea monsters, then so be it. If she drowned before she could make it to the surface, then so be it.

And if she lived?

Well ... she didn't know. She hadn't thought that far ahead.

She glanced down at the dive computer on her wrist. It looked like a watch, only instead of the time it showed dive depth. She wasn't sure if it would work on the other side—electronics were notorious for crapping out after going through a portal— but it didn't really matter. If she was too deep to make it to the surface, having the information relayed to her wouldn't help her anyway. And if she was really, *really* deep, then the pressure deferential would crush her like a beer can before she even had time to look at her wrist. Like much of her prep work over the past few months, it fell under the category of "No Sense Worrying About It Until I'm Over There."

Blood was beating in her temples as she stood on the elevated platform. Spray from the pouring water tickled her nose. She picked up the scuba tank, slipped her arms through the straps, and pulled it up onto her back. Her mask dangled around her neck on its strap. She pulled it up onto her face and adjusted the straps so they were tight and secure.

She was ready.

Now all she had to do was wait, and hope the portal closed sooner rather than later. Before Ted or Vihaan woke up or the next shift of guards came on duty. This, she knew, was the most difficult part of her plan, because it was the one over which she had absolutely no control. Either the portal would close and she would hitch a ride on the backwash, or the pressure door would open and a STAR team would come in and arrest her. The last member of Black Dawn finally taken into custody. Or maybe they'd simply shoot her on sight.

Jill didn't know how long she stood there, staring at the pouring water. Minutes? A full hour? Somewhere in between, she guessed.

Then the water changed.

She didn't notice it with her eyes; they had glazed over from staring at the same place for so long. She heard it—the sound of the rushing water lowering in volume.

Jill gripped the railings on both sides of the platform, ready to propel herself forward at the right moment. She was hauling so much gear she would have only one chance at this. If she mistimed her jump, she'd end up sprawled on the drain below.

The flow was tapering off, like she'd seen on the security footage. As if someone was slowly turning an invisible tap.

The water continued to pour out for a few moments more, then the sound of it splashing on the drain below stopped. Jill had time for one final, frantic thought—*I missed it! I was watching it the whole time but somehow I missed it!*—and then the water suddenly changed direction and started getting sucked back into the portal.

She thought of the dreams she had as a child. She thought of drowning. She thought of men burning.

"I'm sorry," she said.

Then she jumped.

SHE THOUGHT IT would be like splashing into a deep pool.

It wasn't.

There was no feeling she could compare it to. One moment she was flying through the air. The next she was suspended in water. Dark cold water.

She could feel it even through her dry suit, a chill that spread through her entire body, turning her fingers and toes instantly numb. With it came fear, enveloping her as completely as the water, holding her tight and paralyzing her while it squeezed the air out of her lungs. She was back in her childhood nightmares. Only this time it was real.

She fumbled around for the regulator hose, followed it down to the mouthpiece, and jammed it between her lips. She sucked

in a breath…but there was no breath to take.

Her thoughts turned frantic, but then she realized her mistake.

She had put on the scuba tank, but she'd forgotten to open the air valve.

She reached back blindly, slapping her hands against the tank in search of the valve, but couldn't find it. Which only caused her to flail around even more frantically.

Panic and die, a voice told her. *Be calm. Be calm.*

Easy for you to say, Jill thought, but she forced herself to slow down. She didn't have the time or the air to make any more mistakes.

After a few seconds that felt like minutes she found the valve and opened it. She took a breath and tasted the metallic tang of canned air. She took another breath, slow and easy, and the coolness of the air seemed to put out the fire in her lungs.

She began to calm down—or as much as her fear of water would allow. She tried to reassure herself further by pointing out the pressure hadn't killed her outright, which meant she wasn't miles below the surface. Of course, if she was down deep enough, she could still end up getting pressure sickness. If that happened, she was well and truly screwed. She was pretty sure there were no hyperbaric chambers in the Black Lands.

I knew the risks, Jill thought. *I considered them all when I…*

Something bumped her.

Jill would have screamed if the regulator wasn't wedged in her mouth. Instead she sucked in a big gulp of air and tried to push herself away from whatever it was that had struck her.

She couldn't see it—she couldn't see *anything*—so she had no way of telling if she was moving away from whatever it was or only bringing herself closer. A faint warmth seeped through her dry suit, and Jill realized she had pissed herself.

There was a flashlight in her bag, and for a moment she considered getting it out. But then she thought of the marine life in her own world, specifically the creatures that lived in the deepest, darkest depths. The ones attracted to light. Whatever had struck her seemed to have done so in passing, rather than out of aggression—did she really want to tempt it back by shining a light at it?

Jill was starting to regain her composure when a light pulsed below her. She thought it was from her flashlight, then remembered she hadn't taken it out of her bag. The cold water was messing with her mind, frazzling her thoughts. That had to be it, she decided. She couldn't think straight, and now she was seeing things...

The light flashed again. At some indeterminate distance below her. Too quick to tell exactly how far down.

Jill maneuvered herself around so she was facing the direction of the light and waited for it to go off again. Just when she thought it was over, the light flashed, still below her but further ahead now, moving away from her.

Jill was ready this time and looking directly at it, although she immediately wished she hadn't.

In that split-second burst of light she saw the shape of the thing moving through the water below. Or at least part of it. The creature was too big to be completely illuminated, but Jill could make out a long, cylindrical body, segmented like a worm rather than the smooth skin of an eel. It wasn't as big as a blue whale, but it was large enough to swallow her whole, should it have a mind to do so. The pulsing light came from a node at the end of a long, tapering stalk protruding from what she guessed was the creature's head. Similar, she thought, to the esca on an anglerfish. Only the light from the creature below seemed artificial, like a slowly pulsing strobe light, rather than one powered by bioluminescence.

The light went off again, quick and intense like a camera flash, and Jill could tell it was indeed moving away from her. But that didn't mean it wouldn't come back. Or that something else wouldn't come along and take more of an interest in her.

The oxygen tank and duffel bag were heavy, and it was a struggle to keep from sinking deeper into the dark water. She was losing body heat at a much faster rate than expected. She had to remind herself this was water that had never been heated by any sun. And since there was no sun, she couldn't look up to see how far it was to the surface.

Her fins were in her duffel bag. She hadn't bothered to put them on because she knew her life depended on getting to the surface as quickly as possible, and she couldn't do that simply by swimming. Instead she reached down and unclipped the small orange pack from her belt. She wrapped the lanyard around her forearm, gripped the ripcord tightly, and gave it a sharp pull.

A burst of bubbles exploded out of the pack as the compressed gas in the canister was released. Jill held onto the lanyard with both hands as the pack suddenly shot upward through the water, dragging her along with it like a fish being reeled in on a line. Looking upward through the flurry of bubbles, she could see the pack unfolding into an inflatable life raft.

This was the final test. She had survived the trip through the portal, and so far managed to avoid getting eaten by a sea monster. Now it was time to see if she could make it to the surface without her air running out or the raft failing to inflate properly.

So far as she could tell, the water never changed. She was cutting through it pretty fast, but it seemed as dark as it had been when she first crossed over. There was no indication she was getting closer to the surface. She wouldn't know until she got there. If she did.

The raft continued to drag her upward. It had fully inflated, making it look as though she was being pulled through the dark water by a large orange hexagonal balloon.

She worried the strain of the raft pulling her and all of her gear might cause the lanyard to break. If that happened, she'd be left floating in the water while the raft continued on without her. Then it would only be a matter of time before her air ran out and she drowned.

One more thing that isn't worth worrying about, Jill thought. *Not now.*

When she finally did reach the surface it was much like crossing through the portal: It happened suddenly and unexpectedly, with no sense of transition. One moment Jill was rushing through the water, the next she was flying through the air like a leaping trout.

Something bumped her, like when she was down below, but this time she knew it was only the raft. It was bobbing gently on the water, the canvas canopy making it look like a tent or one of those bouncy kid castles. The canopy was designed as protection against sunburn. That wouldn't be a problem over here, Jill reflected, as she hauled herself up over the side and into the raft.

After slipping off the straps of the scuba tank and the duffel bag, she took the regulator out of her mouth and pulled the mask off her face. She took a breath of the air. Black Lands air. She expected it to taste different, and while it seemed a bit fresher, perhaps because it was unpolluted by climate change and a degrading ozone layer, it wasn't much different from the salty sea air back home.

She crawled over to the opening in the canopy and peered out. The water was almost perfectly still. The sky was clear and dusted with stars, allowing her to see for some distance. She went back to her duffel bag and dug around until she found the collapsible oar. She unfolded it and crawled back to the opening, slipped the oar into the water, and paddled around in a slow circle, straining her eyes as hard as she could, searching for any sign of land.

She couldn't see a thing. And it wouldn't get any better. No sun was going to rise here in the Black Lands. With the sky clear and the stars out, this was, in fact, as good as it was going to get.

Jill sighed, picked a direction at random, and started paddling.

LAND CAME LIKE A DREAM. At first she thought it *was* a dream.

She had spent three days at sea—or what she guessed were three days. Without the rising and setting of the sun, it was hard to tell for certain. She was wearing a watch in addition to her dive computer, but as she suspected, going through the portal had damaged its fragile electronics.

She might have been able to navigate by the stars, but she didn't know how, and besides, those weren't *her* stars up there.

Her days—it was weird calling them days in a place of forever night—were all the same. She would paddle until her muscles burned and her arms felt like mush, then she'd take a break. Then she'd paddle some more until she couldn't feel her arms at all. When her body was completely exhausted, she'd lay down in the raft and let the gentle rocking of the water lull her to sleep. *Is there a current?* she wondered in the moment before she drifted off. *Is it leading me closer to land or taking me further out to sea?* When she woke up—how many hours later? who knew?—she would have something to eat, something to drink, and then start paddling again.

It was after she had awoken from one of these exhaustion-induced sleep sessions that Jill noticed something was different. For a moment she thought she was back at home, lying in her own bed, and all of this had been a dream. There was precedence for such a thought, considering how long she had lived with those dreams of swimming in dark waters. It wasn't until she rolled over onto her side that she realized what was wrong.

The raft was no longer moving.

She crawled over to the opening in the canopy and peered out.

The first thing she noticed was the stars were gone. They were hidden behind thick banks of clouds veined with silver filigree like clumps of steel wool.

The second thing she noticed was the beach.

The raft was sitting on it, a few feet up from the slow, steady shush of the tide.

Jill blinked her eyes a few times, not quite believing what she was seeing. When she was sure it wasn't a mirage or a hallucination, she lifted her leg over the side of the raft and climbed out. She stumbled forward and almost fell. She hadn't walked on solid ground in a few days and her legs had momentarily forgotten how. Her muscles tingled from lack of use.

Once she reached the water, she dropped to her knees with a splash. She ran her hands through the churning foam, then brought them up to her face and licked her fingers. The water tasted cold and salty, with a tangy medicinal undertone. She turned her head to the left, then the right, her eyes following the full length of the beach. The sand was a dull matte black above the tide line, and a glistening onyx where the water lapped at it.

This is it, Jill thought. *This is the* real *Plutonian Shore.*

Was she on an island or was she in the Black Lands proper? Did it really matter? No, she decided. It didn't. She was here and she was alive.

But for how long?

She had brought enough field rations and bottled water to last about four weeks. After that she'd have to find new sources of food and fresh water. Local sources.

She turned away from the sand and sea and stared into the woods spread out beyond the shore. Was there a creek or a stream somewhere in there, and if so, would she be able to drink the water without getting sick? Were there any edible plants and berries? She didn't know. There were no guidebooks for wilderness survival in the Black Lands. Every day she spent here, every action she took, would be fraught with risk. The smallest mistake could result in her death. The creatures she had fought for so passionately as an activist would have no qualms about making her their next meal. There was no denying it. This was going to be a very hard life. But it would still be a life. It was, Jill thought, more than she deserved.

First thing's first.

She went back to the life raft and dragged it up to the edge of the treeline. It would make a suitable shelter until she could construct something more permanent. And not one moment too soon, Jill thought, as a rumble of thunder rolled across the dark sky.

She looked back out to sea. Lightning flared within the steel-wool clouds. Not just a flash or two, but a prolonged series of silent explosions that left an afterimage on Jill's eyes. She was raising her hand to rub them when she noticed something. She held her hand in front of her face, staring at it until the white blobs flowing across her vision went away...then kept on staring.

Something was wrong.

No, not wrong—different.

A translucent membrane extended between her thumb and index finger. She raised her other hand and saw the same thin fleshy webbing. She tugged on them but they were firmly attached to her skin. Like they'd always been there.

Jill had heard the Black Lands could cause changes in a person, like mutations from some kind of supernatural radiation. It was called the Influence. The changes manifested differently for everyone—physical, mental, or psychical—and sometimes they didn't happen at all. It seemed to be happening to her. But why? Because she had been in the water? Was it something as simple as that? The rest of her fingers appeared to be normal, at least for now. But maybe in a few days or weeks she wouldn't need her fins to go swimming.

It was a small change, but maybe it would be enough to help her survive in this place. She remembered something her mother used to say. *A change is as good as a rest.* It might be true, but at that moment Jill didn't feel like resting.

She looked toward the sea as a wave crashed on the shore. Silver foam splashed across the black sand. The water came rushing toward her.

Jill ran to embrace to it.

Ian Rogers is the author of the award-winning collection, Every House Is Haunted. *His novelette "The House on Ashley Avenue" was a finalist for the Shirley Jackson Award and is currently being adapted into a feature film produced by Sam Raimi and directed by Corin Hardy. His debut novel,* Sycamore, *the first book in the Black Lands series, is forthcoming from Cemetery Dance Publications in Fall 2024. Ian lives with his wife in Peterborough, Ontario. For more information, visit ianrogers.ca*

ZERO

BY

GREGORY L. NORRIS

ART BY ALLEN KOSZOWSI

A WEEK BEFORE IT HAPPENED, I'D SENSED THE WRONGNESS. It hung like a damp fog above the city of Boston. Winter had been in no hurry to leave and was still holding on in early April. A brief spring greeted the middle of the month. On its heels was summer heat, oily and unforgiving. It beat down on the new flowers and greenery of the Common and turned the start of the baseball season into the dog days of August. Everywhere around me, the city's residents complained and scowled. But that was only a preview of the creeping hopelessness to follow.

THE WINDOWS HAD BEEN OPENED—for fresh air, sure, not that what oozed in off the street refreshed us. I sat with the bow in my grasp, the violin positioned under my chin. Around me, my fellow students readied to play. Outside the open windows, heat sat thick above the asphalt and drifted up in waves. The traffic noise distorted as, for the latest round, I beat myself up in silence. Violin? What kind of future was there in music? I was a former band geek, not some concert protégé who'd coast from one big city symphony to another, lured like a secret agent to the enemy side. Yes, I could play. But the sidewalks were littered with buskers who thought they belonged at major orchestras and record labels.

The familiar leaden weight returned to my gut as the class performed—though what emerged in that miserable heat in the College of Music in Boston the week before it happened sounded more like a dirge than the happy exultation and lifting melody of Mahler's Fourth.

The music didn't float—it seemed to *clot* and hang suspended over the performance room. From the cut of my eye, I noticed my fellow musicians and future buskers all frowning as they played. Not one face beamed with the joy of the music or its creation, which had led us all to this place and point. That love of music, to each of our parents' chagrin, all of whom wanted us to focus on tech, medicine, or law, where the real money was to be made, was gone. The most any of us would earn was coins or a few small bills in our instrument cases.

We all loved music and, in our naivety, it was easy to fall on the sword of that love, to be all-in, do or die for art. By the time we reached thirty, we'd have another opinion. By forty, we'd curse our choices, be bitter, and yearn for that innocent, lost love.

My hand stilled. The bow dragged to a stop. Forty? Looking around, I had the sudden belief that none of the musicians with me needed to worry about finances—or lack thereof—or reaching those distant, disappointing years. As the dirge clawed at my ear and the hot air boiled in my lungs, terror so intense filled me that I screamed without understanding why.

The music shorted out, as jarring in pitch as my shriek. The temperature in the room doubled. I lowered my bow in one hand and violin in the other to see all eyes trained upon me.

An awkward silence followed. I told myself it didn't matter—none of those eyes would be around much longer and, soon, they'd have far bigger concerns than my outburst, which I could easily have explained away as worries over the future.

Sure, the future—I was a violinist with no job prospects other than the sidewalks outside the bus station.

The future.

I didn't know for certain then but suspected it at the time that something worse than performing on the streets for my next meal waited.

In that silence, the air still and stagnant, I excused myself, returned my instrument to its case, and casually walked out of the performance room, the cadence of my steps across the ancient hardwood floor striking my ear like heartbeats. Or thunder.

I WALKED TO THE COMMON, where the grass had just greened and would likely brown in the blast furnace of an early summer in late April. The duck pond exuded a fetor of swamps, and the new bulb flowers sagged. The daffodils and tulips, which had slept through the winter and burst forth to new life in what had passed for a spring, wore the same defeated frowns as the people walking around the paths.

I sat on a bench beneath a shade tree with drooping new leaves and tried to slow my galloping heart. What was wrong with me? What was wrong with the world?

Eventually, my racing pulse calmed. I choked down a dry swallow and looked around me. The sound of traffic beyond the oasis of the Common waned. The background chirrup of insects evaporated. The heavy silence was back.

I tipped a glance up at the horizon, where city buildings lurked like gray ghosts in the brutal humidity. Rising above them was a shard of the waxing moon. It seemed to study me like a narrowed eye. No other sounds marked my surroundings apart from the resumed quickening of my heartbeat.

The moon, inching its way up from the horizon of buildings into the muddied, gray sky... the eye wasn't aimed at Boston, it saw only the person on the bench, a wannabe musician frozen in fright.

I SAT BY THE WINDOW of the room I rented in an apartment with four other students, two of them a couple, and waited for a sudden breeze to stir the old gingham curtains. No relief came. Outside was the same uninspired view of the alley two stories below and the back end of another brick building without windows—one of those storage units people paid for monthly that was heated in the winter and kept cool in the summer. Somewhere up there, hidden by the city's construction, was that wedge of moon.

Since the Common, I'd sold myself on the lie that all was fine; that the undercurrent of wrongness I'd convinced myself was real was, in fact, only a kind of reality check—fear for my future. I was a starving college music student. I had willingly chosen to be a starving adult with a useless degree and trade. Only whenever I thought about the tech industry, nursing, law, or anything other than music, my insides knotted in misery—better to give up three square meals a day for the body than my soul for something I hated. Sure, I could commit to another line of work with a bigger profit margin, retire my violin to the back of a closet, pull it out for the amusement of family members each Christmas or on special occasions, make money, live a perfectly normal and hopelessly boring life, drink or develop a drug habit as a result of not feeding and being fed by the creativity within, go mad—

A knock sounded on the door. I roused. The wrongness I'd convinced myself wasn't real surged back, tangible despite its invisibility.

A voice spoke my name. "Can I come in?" Chauncey asked.

I untangled from my position at the windowsill to answer the door. "Yeah, just a sec."

Armand Chauncey stood outside. Chauncey—with a last name like that, I just couldn't bring myself to call him 'Armand'— smelled of the day's warmth, like clean male sweat and the dregs of deodorant. He hadn't shaved. I tried to not think of how attractive I found my third roommate despite the way his T-shirt and cargo shorts fit his lanky physique in a way that suggested his clothes loved him. Wide-eyed, he radiated nervous energy.

Chauncey marched into the tiny room, stirred its airlessness with a hint of his attractive scent, and circled in place.

"Something's happened," he said. "Something *huge.*"

His nervousness made breathing difficult. Hands shaking, Chauncey reached into the right pocket of his cargo shorts and withdrew his phone. He nearly dropped it but caught the cell with a backhand grab.

"What is it?"

He flashed a crooked smile, one I normally would have found appealing, but in the wrongness, Chauncey's expression struck me as that of a lunatic. "You're gonna hear about it soon enough. All of the big telescopes are trained on it."

While Chauncey fumbled with his phone, I held my breath. Armand Chauncey was a student at MIT and an amateur astronomer. Like me, unless he landed a government contract job after graduation, he was staring at a life of stargazing from the street corner through a telescope of cupped hands.

"Even the little guys are looking at it. After it transited Mars, it was inevitable. This one's from a dude in New Mexico. They haven't released any of the images from the Puerto Rico super-telescope or the James Webb in orbit."

He showed me a static capture—something gray set against a black backdrop dotted by what I assumed were stars.

"What—?" I asked.

The anxious waves vibrated off him. "We don't know, but it's heading straight toward us. It's traveling at incredible speed, and here's the thing—it *decelerated* at Mars and then *accelerated* after it cleared the red planet, which means it isn't random space junk like an asteroid! They don't slow down and speed up! Do you hear what I'm saying?"

I did and solemnly nodded.

Chauncey turned the phone screen up to his face, and his smile widened.

"Isn't it wonderful? Proof—*finally*, real proof of something else alive out there! A message from another civilization, and it's coming here! I mean, I can hardly wait. I want to run through the streets shouting like those idiots every time a sports team wins a championship!"

He let forth with a manly hoot and raised his hand for me to high-five, but by then the tears were spilling out of my eyes, unable to be stemmed, and the unnamed wrongness I'd sensed coming closer, closer, had a face.

"What's the matter?" Chauncey asked.

II

THE NEXT DAY, it was everywhere—in the news, the headline of every paper, and spread through social media. Someone labeled it *O.U.R.O.*: Oncoming Unidentified Reflective Object, and the name stuck. And, of course, the world reacted as the world usually reacted.

Some attempted to be dignified as transmissions were beamed in human and computerized languages, even music. Not that anyone in O.U.R.O.—if there was anyone in O.U.R.O.—responded. Churches, temples, synagogues, mosques, and halls of worship filled. There, certain flocks sang joyously of the event. Others took a more fire-and-brimstone approach. Concerts were planned to coincide with the object's arrival. Quick fingers designed merch—T-shirts and coffee mugs to capitalize and make a fast buck. Two days before O.U.R.O. reached Earth, lootings and riots broke out. By then, most grocery store shelves had been picked clean, and a gallon of gas had tripled in price.

I called home.

"Are you all right?" my mother asked.

"Sure am," I lied.

"Exciting, isn't it?"

I didn't answer. "What's the weather like there?"

EVEN AS TRANSMISSIONS were sent at the object, and O.U.R.O. ignored them, the military readied a response.

I DON'T REMEMBER passing out in my room, only that, as the afternoon wore on humid and strangulating, the black spots before my eyes all linked together, and I was falling, falling.

From what sounded like a thousand miles away, I heard Chauncey calling to me. I stirred out of the fog and came back. His face hovered over mine. I spoke his name.

"Come on," he said.

"Where?"

Mad excitement filled his eyes. My pulse, which hadn't slowed since that afternoon at the Common, thrummed in my ear.

"It's here."

I knew what he meant. "*It?*"

"It used the moon's gravity to slow its approach, assumed a close orbit, and vanished behind the far side. They expect it to circle back out to the near side in just over an hour."

Something jagged bloomed in my gut. "An hour?"

"If we hurry, we should be able to see it with the naked eye when it transits around. There's a full moon tonight. It'll be like it's right over Boston!"

He said this excitedly like a kid on Christmas morning eager to tear into presents. Still, that look in his eyes—it could have been wonder but struck me as insanity.

"Do you know how big a thing this is? We can't miss it," he said.

"*We?*" And with that one word, I surrendered. I liked the illusion that Chauncey and I were a *we*. We never had been before. I doubted we would be again after that night.

I eased off the bed, aware of my sweat and the awkward fit of my clothes. And then, before I could talk myself out of it, I followed Chauncey out of the apartment and into that balmy late afternoon right as the sun was to set, and O.U.R.O. swung out of hiding from the far side of the full moon hanging over the city.

A STIFF BREEZE BLEW along the sidewalks, which grew more crowded the deeper we moved into the heart of Boston. Numerous police cars were out and present. Some corners had been blocked off.

"We urge you to return to your homes and vacate the streets so that emergency response vehicles and personnel can be present to assist without delay," a woman's voice broadcast from somewhere up ahead.

A man shouted something about infringing on the personal right to be out and about. Others held signs—

Is Mary Up There With You?

It Ain't Fun Being an Illegal Alien!

All You Can Eat During O.U.R.O., $9.95 at the Last Kitchen Buffet!

We made it to Boylston Street. Our goal was to reach the Prudential Plaza, but the foot traffic on the sidewalks jammed, and it was clear that the way ahead had been cordoned off against pedestrians.

The sun had set behind the buildings. It was still April, and that meant early twilights. But between the city's glare and that of the moon, a counterfeit daytime surrounded us.

"This way," Chauncey called over the noise. "We can get to a better viewing spot than this."

He turned right at the next street corner, and he was correct in his pledge. We'd reached a kind of canyon between the metal mountains of the city's tallest buildings. Above us, in clear sight, was Earth's moon, its cratered face peering down. I noticed that none of the usual contrails of jumbo jets from the city's airport strafed the sky. No planes soared up there. The world had become one gigantic no-fly zone. The moon gazed down, its expression sad, its eyes unblinking. At my side, Chauncey chuckled. The sound struck me as the laugh of a madman.

Like so many others, he had his phone out to record the transit. He checked the time.

"Any second now," he hooted and then swore.

I didn't realize I'd held my breath until the last sip of air sucked into my lungs began to boil. I expelled it. Breathing after that was no easier. I stared at the moon—like it, I'd forgotten how to blink. My eyes burned. There, at the very edge of the lunar horizon—

The object appeared, flat and gray and gargantuan! I recalled what I'd read or seen or gleaned from phone screen or TV or overhead in conversations—*the size of ten football fields at its longest point.* It drifted soundlessly up there in the vacuum of space, rounded the curve of the moon, and then, though I knew this wasn't the case, appeared to grow.

It's coming closer, I thought right before someone on the street looking up stated the same thing.

O.U.R.O. continued to near, laid flat on its side, and the jagged spike in my gut drilled deeper. A foul taste ignited on my tongue. Closer. Closer yet. Around us, an airless silence shrouded the city. Even the usual traffic noises flatlined. It was as though the entire world held its breath.

Then the object flipped upright. Floating in front of the moon, I saw it clearly—round nd reflective, strangely familiar despite its foreign design and origin. The silence shattered in a deafening surge of voices, Chauncey's among them and the loudest in my ear.

"No way!" he shouted.

Round, perfectly so, O.U.R.O. loomed over us and in front of the moon, which glowed full and silver behind it. Then the analogy struck me, and I nailed what seemed so familiar about it. *An eyepiece or monocle... no,* a magnifying glass!

Even as I thought this, the moon's silver light streamed through the alien object and down, down, across Boston. An opaque glow infused the air and created shadows where none had been. Once when I was little, we experienced an eclipse in the middle of a summer afternoon. The world went both bright and dark in a similar manner, and I recall fighting the urge to look up at the black center of the sun.

"*You'll go blind,*" my mother had warned.

The same conflict plagued me at that moment as O.U.R.O.'s transparent mass beamed the moon's light down. I resisted until someone in the crowd shrieked, "*What is that?*"

And I looked up.

I faced O.U.R.O. and saw *it* there, staring back through the moon's corrupted glare.

Then somebody screamed.

III

THE AIRLESSNESS erupted with an unfamiliar roar and a rush of invisible current. Something stirred. At first, I only saw it from the cut of my eye, the giant made of silver light. To face it directly would be to lose it altogether. Even indistinct, the horror manifested on the street challenged what remained of my sanity. Two stories or taller, the vague red orbs glowing across that main mass of silver-tinged malevolence suggested numerous eyes. It swung either a trunk or tentacle down from the main stalk of its body. When it snapped back its trunk or tentacle, a dozen of the night's onlookers lifted off the street, impaled on sharp hooks or barbs or teeth, all screaming, all already dead as they were whipped into that main body and vanished from sight.

Chauncey stood paralyzed beside me. The alien roar sounded again and, once more, the hook-covered limb swung out, passing over our heads to grab at the poor souls frozen in place on the other side of the street. As its motion sent the hot air into a cyclone, I saw it clearly—saw that it seemed to be made of moonlight; saw the crenulated hide and sharp burrs that ripped people off the sidewalk and swept them back to the horror that only appeared half there, a reflection made possible by the moon's glow through the mechanism of the alien construct.

I pushed both hands against Chauncey and shouted, "Run!"

He woke. We didn't get far in the sudden chaos of the panicked crowds around us. At the corner, I looked up. A nightmare identical to the one behind us was positioned ahead and engaged in the same wide scale devouring of lives as the thing we sought to escape.

I didn't need to see the entirety of the city to understand there were more than two. The sharp squawk of police sirens and the report of gunshots confirmed it.

Chauncey grabbed my hand and made for the other side of the street. Not far from us, a car collided against another. The alien roar pulsed louder through the new night, and this time, I heard that the one bellow owed to numerous callers, all of them crying out to their kind in unison.

We ran.

And ran.

DETAILS BLURRED like that moment in general anesthesia when they tell you to count backward from ten and you never make it to nine, or that instant after surgery when you wake up in your hospital bed with no recollection of how you got there.

The city passed by, silvery around the edges of shadows. Screams and sirens, alien roars and the mad cacophony of buildings being ripped open, thundered in my ear, creating a nightmarish white noise. On the corner of West Boylston, we passed the Counterpoint Café, where I sometimes went for coffee and to sell myself on the lie that music was all I needed in life to be happy, truly happy. But the college beyond was in pieces, and one of *them* lurked silver and indistinct in the new rubble.

Chauncey sobbed something unintelligible. We darted across the street and into a vacant lot where, in the sane world before that night, drivers risked tickets if they parked there. A scraggly green space spread between the lot and the Mass Turnpike. The Turnpike's lanes were jammed full of gridlock. Honking car horns blasted through the air. One of those things—I saw it, a tall, silver wraith, tearing open vehicles and extracting passengers from their rides.

They're here, but not really, the voice in my skull mused. *Here, yes, but only in reflection, beamed down in moonlight. Not entirely physical…but physical enough!*

We reached the chain link fence that wreathed the vacant lot. Chauncey grabbed at it with his hands and shook it. I heard him whimper. I wanted to ask him where next? Or would we climb the fence, drop over the other side, pivot away from the danger in front of us and the one at our backs? But the words refused to emerge, and then, as though blessed with wings, Chauncey was flying, flying.

I heard his scream when I whirled to see the alien colossus standing there, not really there, but there enough, with the young man I liked a lot and maybe even loved hooked through his chest.

I froze. Of course, I'd be next. There was nowhere left to go. For a terrible second, I faced the horror, and though it didn't have a recognizable expression, it seemed to face me. Though not there, I smelled its fetor, a mix of burned motor oil and upturned graves. I saw the details of its physical anatomy, something so alien it had no terrestrial comparison. I sensed its hunger, its gluttony, its giddiness at having cornered me.

And above it, I also saw the streak of a contrail tearing through the night sky as my would-be killer readied to grab at me.

Then there came the blinding flash. I looked when I shouldn't have and instantly recoiled. Just above the stratosphere, the object they'd named O.U.R.O. came apart in a powerful detonation, and the gigantic horror reaching toward me evaporated.

That missile the military had secretly readied for liftoff and response…its payload was capable of forty megatons.

IV

THEY DON'T KNOW the exact numbers yet in total lives lost, though early guesses are staggering.

The after image, the damage to my sight, they say it's permanent. It won't stop me from playing the violin. I can't read sheet music, but I'm intimate enough with the classics to continue on memory.

Which is what I'm doing now. What I'm

doing in my rented room. What I'll be doing until...

My two other roommates survived O.U.R.O. They tell me all of the major telescopes turned on the sky have detected them coming in from numerous different directions...hundreds of identical O.U.R.O. objects, all headed our way. They're expected to arrive in time for the next full moon.

So I play my violin and lose myself in the dream of a future in music.

Raised on a healthy diet of creature double features and classic SF TV, Gregory L. Norris writes regularly for numerous short story anthologies, national magazines, novels, and the occasional episode for TV or film. Gregory novelized the NBC Made-for-TV classic by Gerry Anderson, The Day After Tomorrow: Into Infinity *(as well as a sequel and a forthcoming third entry into the franchise for Anderson Entertainment in the U.K.), a movie he watched as an eleven-year-old sitting cross-legged on the living room floor of the enchanted cottage where he grew up. Gregory won HM in the 2016 Roswell Awards in Short SF Writing. He once worked as a screenwriter on two episodes of Paramount's* Star Trek: Voyager. *Kate Mulgrew,* Voyager's *"Captain Janeway," blurbed his book of short stories and novellas,* The Fierce and Unforgiving Muse, *stating, "In my seven years on* Voyager, *I don't think I've met a writer more capable of writing such a book—and writing it so beautifully."*

In late 2019, Gregory sold an option on his modern Noir feature film screenplay, Amandine, *to the new Hollywood production company Snarkhunter LLC, owned by actor Dan Lench, a devotee of Gregory's writing. In late 2020, Snarkhunter optioned Gregory's tetralogy Horror film based upon four of his short stories,* Ride Along. *That same month, his short story "Water Whispers" was nominated for the Pushcart Prize.*

Gregory lives and writes at Xanadu, a century-old house perched on a hill in New Hampshire's North Country with spectacular mountain views, with his rescue cat and emerald-eyed muse. Follow his further literary adventures at:
www.gregorylnorris.blogspot.com

AVAILABLE FROM
CENTIPEDE PRESS
CentipedePress.com

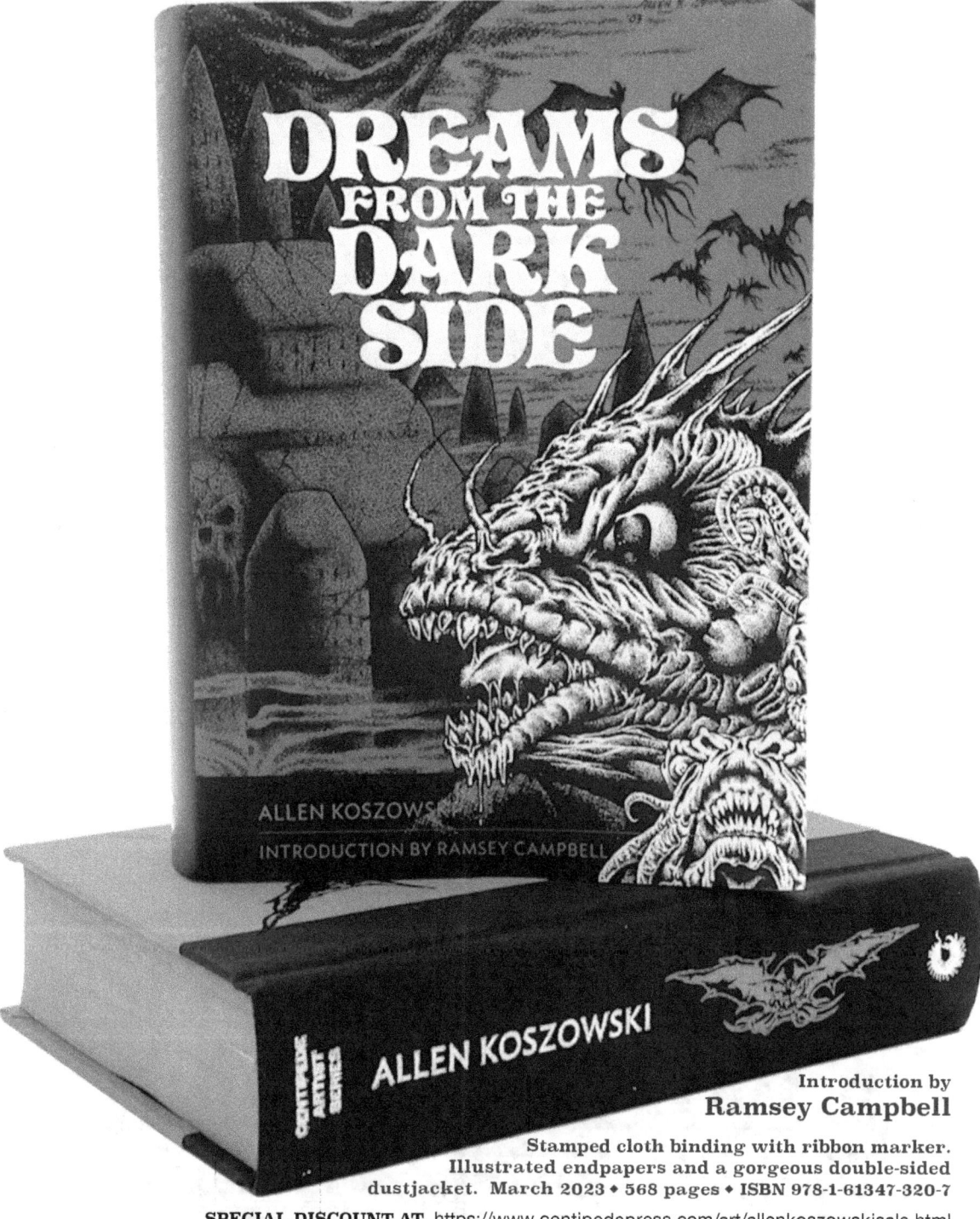

Introduction by
Ramsey Campbell

Stamped cloth binding with ribbon marker.
Illustrated endpapers and a gorgeous double-sided
dustjacket. March 2023 ◆ 568 pages ◆ ISBN 978-1-61347-320-7

SPECIAL DISCOUNT AT https://www.centipedepress.com/art/allenkoszowskisale.html

THE ORIGINAL SWAMP THING: THEODORE STURGEON'S "IT"

NIGHTMARE ABBEY

WINTER SOLSTICE 2022

2

STEVE DUFFY

HELEN GRANT

DAVID SURFACE

ALLEN KOSZOWSKI

GREGORY L. NORRIS

EDWARD LUCAS WHITE

GARY FRY ☠ JAMES DORR

JOHN LLEWELLYN PROBERT

KURT NEWTON ☠ MATT COWAN

GARY GERANI REMEMBERS
BORIS KARLOFF'S *THRILLER*

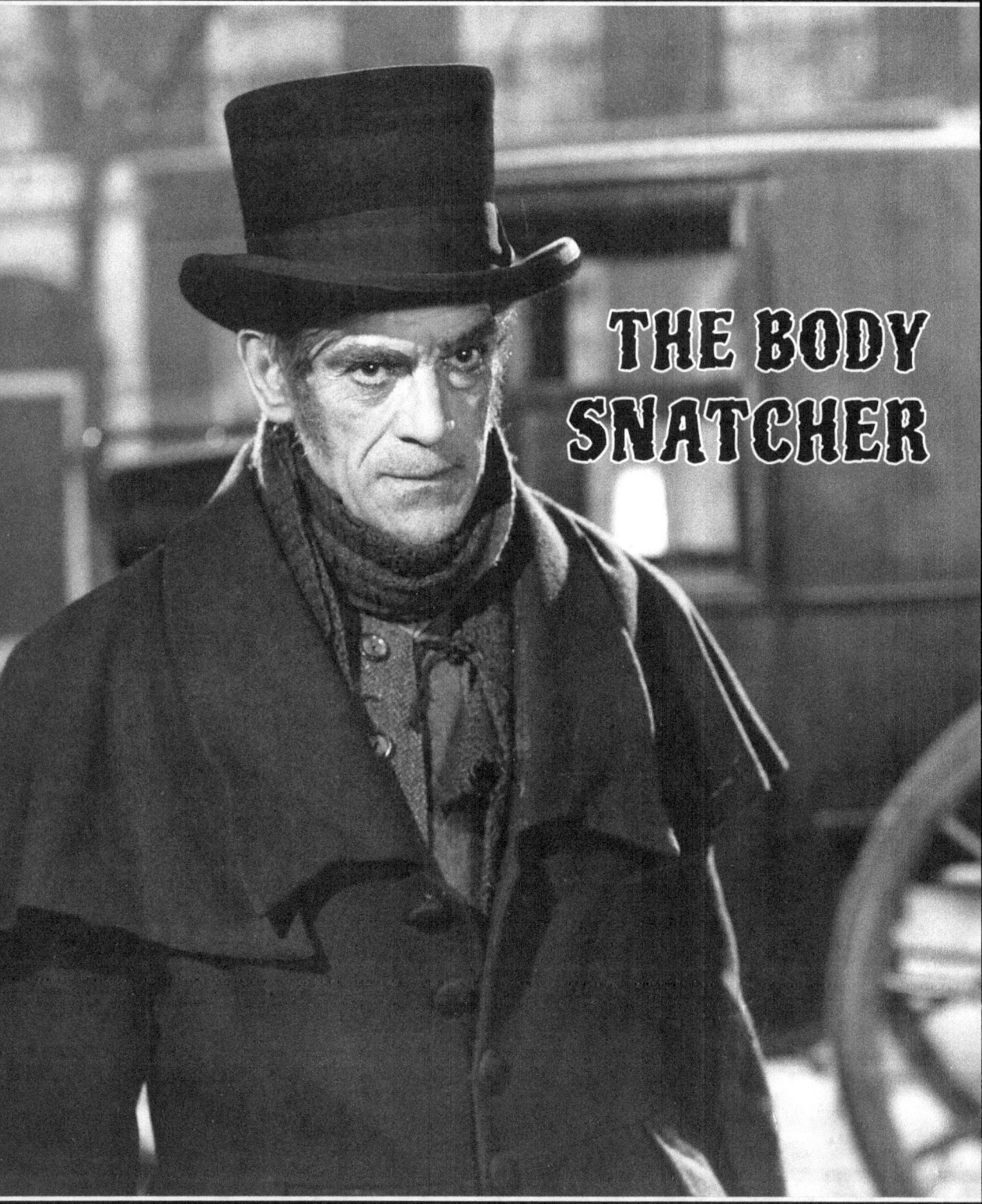

RESURRECTING A CLASSIC:

THE BODY SNATCHER

BY JOHN LLEWELLYN PROBERT

By 1945, Val Lewton's B-movie production house at RKO was considered a huge (and to some, unexpected) success. Conceived by the studio as a unit that would churn out unassuming low-budget B pictures, it had been obvious from the off that Lewton had other ideas, and the success of his first production, Jacques Tourneur's *Cat People* (1942), had paved the way for a string of subtle, thoughtful horror films that belied their studio-imposed exploitative (although admittedly eye-catching) titles. Lewton quickly followed up his highly profitable first production by making Jane Eyre in the Caribbean (*I Walked with a Zombie*), adapting Cornell Woolrich's novel *Black Alibi* (*The Leopard Man*), giving the world the tale of a cult of satanists in New York (*The Seventh Victim*) and a tale of death at sea (*The Ghost Ship*), all released in 1943. The studio-imposed sequel *Curse of the Cat People* followed in 1944, after which the next Lewton production to see release was *The Body Snatcher*.

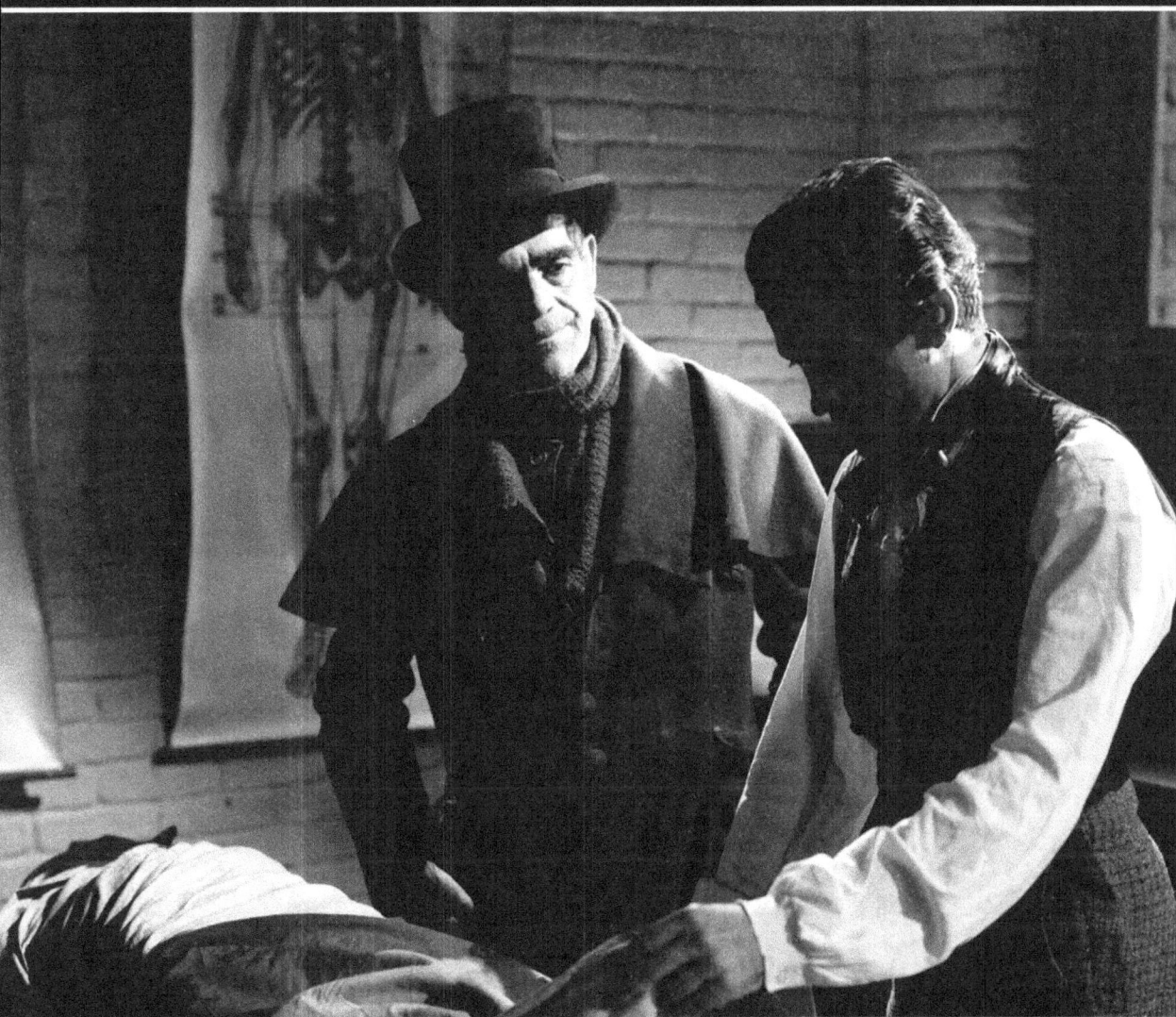

During Robert Louis Stevenson's short life (he died at the age of 44 of a cerebral hemorrhage), he created a body of work so memorable and so skillfully written that both he and many of his stories remain justifiably famous to this day. Born and raised in Edinburgh, where he attended the university to study engineering but ultimately switched to law, Stevenson was plagued throughout his life with respiratory problems. In 1881 he spent some time convalescing in Pitlochry (about 70 miles north of Edinburgh). While there, he planned to write a book of supernatural tales. Sadly, that never happened, but he did leave the place having written

three stories, "The Merry Men," "Thrawn Janet," and "The Body Snatcher." "The Merry Men" was about the sea and shipwrecks, and reading it one can see how it led to *Treasure Island* (1883). "The Strange Case of Dr Jekyll and Mr Hyde" came later in 1886 and all three stories are not without their influence upon it, especially "The Body Snatcher." Lewton was doubtless well aware of this in preparing his screen adaptation, as we shall see.

So let's take a closer look at the movie version of *The Body Snatcher*, directed in 1945 by Robert Wise, a man of such versatility he achieved colossal success in almost every genre he turned his hand to, from science fiction (*The Day the Earth Stood Still*) to musicals (*West Side Story* and *The Sound of Music*), from epics (*Helen of Troy*) to horror (*The Haunting*).

The opening gives us Boris Karloff's name above the title, with Bela Lugosi second billed despite his participation in this film being sadly minimal. How times had changed since the two of them were billed equally in Edgar G Ulmer's classic 1934 *The Black Cat*. By the mid 1940s Karloff was still a huge star and box office draw, whereas Lugosi had not fared quite so well. Even so, and even after top-lining a string of movies for ultra low-budget outfit Monogram (later Allied Artists), he had starred in *The Return of the Vampire* in 1943 for Columbia, and it's a great shame he is not used to better effect in *The Body Snatcher*. Far more prevalent in the film is Henry Daniell, also known for playing Sherlock Holmes' arch nemesis Professor Moriarty in Universal's *The Woman in Green* (1945) as well as the villainous Dr Emil Zurich in the quirky fan favorite *The Four Skulls of Jonathan Drake* (1959). Also of note here is the screenplay, credited to Philip MacDonald and "Carlos Keith," which was actually a pseudonym for Lewton himself.

We open with a card informing us that we are in Edinburgh in 1831. Unfortunately, this is immediately followed by a brief piece of stock footage of Edinburgh Castle that, while the location is correct, shows parked cars in the background and people in contemporary 1940s dress. Perhaps the horse and carriage we see was supposed to distract the viewer. We cut to a street singer (Donna Lee, who also appeared in Lewton's *Bedlam* the following year, but not much else at all) who will be important later, followed by a few more stock shots before things settle, appropriately, in a cemetery where medical student Donald Fettes (Russell Wade) is eating lunch sitting on a gravestone. This scene of a medical man eating amongst the dead is certainly significant, even if we don't yet know his profession. Fettes is trying to convince a little dog to take some food but the animal isn't keen. It takes the arrival of Mrs. McBride (Mary Gordon, who at the time was still busy playing Mrs. Hudson in Universal's Sherlock Holmes film series) to explain that the dog belonged to the boy buried

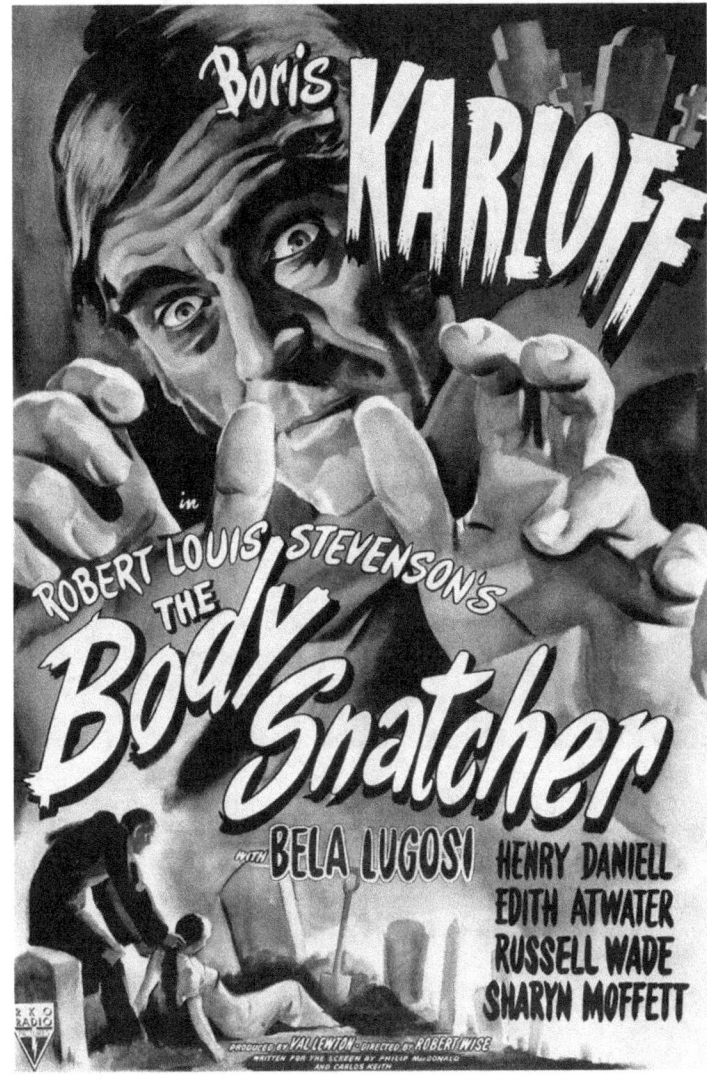

where the dog is sitting and now refuses to move. She remarks that she's actually grateful, as they do not have the money to hire a grave watcher.

The scene segues to a coach being driven by none other than Boris Karloff, here playing cabman John Gray. He is dropping off rich young Mrs. Marsh (Rita Corday) and her little girl Georgina (Sharyn Moffett) at the house and consulting rooms of Dr. Todd "Toddy" MacFarlane (Henry Daniell). The little girl is unable to walk and has been

brought to the doctor for a consultation. Gray, all smiles, allows her to pet his horse. This brightly lit, pleasant scene is going to allow for even more of a contrast as things get considerably darker both in terms of the general mood and especially Gray's persona later on. For now, however, all we get is a subtle exchange of glances between Gray and MacFarlane's housekeeper Meg (Edith Atwater).

Here and opposite: Sweet and sour; a gentle Gray initially contrasted to a very disagreeable Dr. MacFarlane.

Always listening: Bela Lugosi as Joseph.

It's established that Dr. MacFarlane is a man of great reputation. Even so, and despite Mrs. Marsh's pleas, he refuses to treat Georgina as he claims he is too busy teaching the medical students for whom he is responsible. It's also established that Fettes is one of these students, and that he is considering quitting as he can no longer keep up with the fees. To "help him out" MacFarlane employs him as his assistant, even though Meg advises against it. MacFarlane reveals that he was assistant to Dr. Robert Knox. Knox was the real-life Scottish anatomist infamous for employing Burke and Hare, the grave robbers responsible for a series of sixteen murders committed in 1828, just a couple of years prior to the events unfolding here. It seems that MacFarlane uses the basement of his own house both for teaching and for the receiving and preparation of his anatomical specimens. We meet servant Joseph (Bela Lugosi) briefly, as MacFarlane laments that there are never enough bodies for medical study.

That night, Gray enters the churchyard we saw at the beginning and, to cement his role in this film as a blackhearted villain, he kills the dog that has been keeping watch over its master's grave before he begins to dig. Almost all of this action is rendered by director Wise in silhouette, and it's a scene that is both more effective for this technique while also handily avoiding (or at least minimizing) any concerns the censor at the time might have had. Gray takes the corpse to MacFarlane's house and Fettes gets to receive a body "as bright and lively as a thrush not a week long gone." Fettes is shaken but MacFarlane describes it as a milestone in Fettes' medical career.

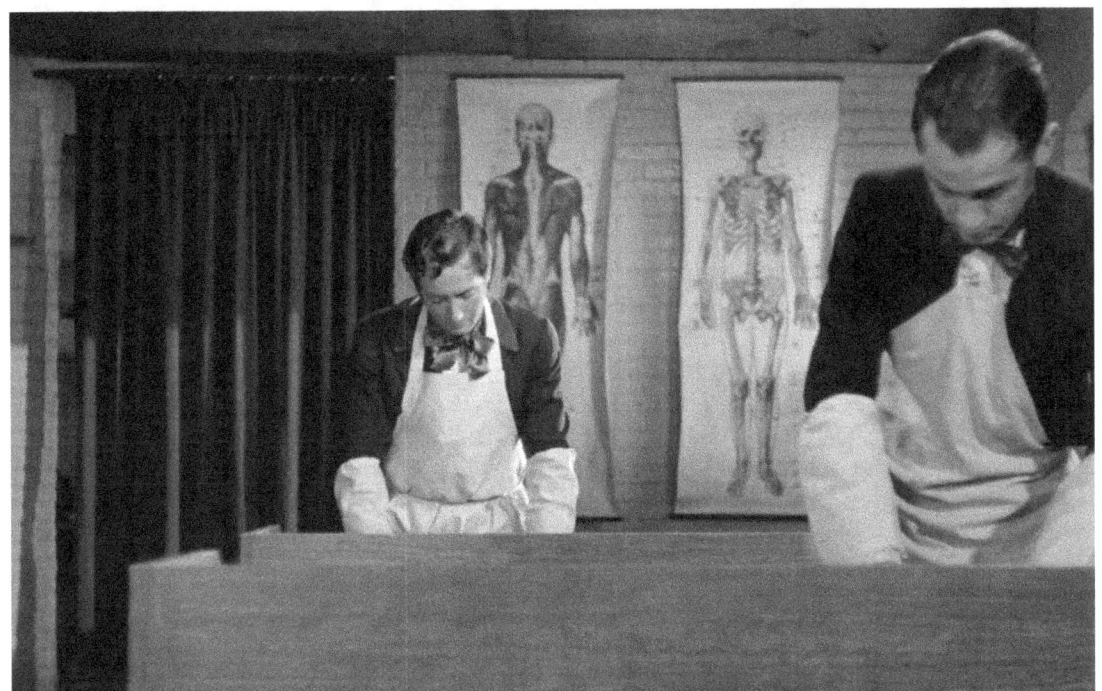

The next day Mrs. Marsh calls and asks Fettes to try and convince MacFarlane to operate on her little girl. Downstairs the students are busy dissecting, and one commits the *faux pas* of actually mentioning the names Burke and Hare. Gray's activity of the night before has been discovered, including the murder of the dog, something which convinces Fettes he no longer wishes to continue in his post. In an attempt to convince him otherwise, MacFarlane takes Fettes to a remarkably spacious pub with a fireplace large enough to roast a pig on a spit. There they encounter Gray who insists they sit

with him despite MacFarlane's insistence they have a medical matter to discuss. The matter in question is of course the operation on Georgina, one which MacFarlane is still reticent to perform.

"Maybe you're afraid of being a doctor," Gray says to MacFarlane, convincing him to perform the surgery because of the, at the moment unexplained, history between them. "We're closer than if we were in the same skin," he adds for emphasis, and this won't be the only suggestion of MacFarlane and Gray's Jekyll and Hyde relationship.

However, the next day MacFarlane claims he was drunk when he agreed to the procedure. This is unfortunate, as Fettes has already told Mrs. Marsh that his employer intends to go ahead. MacFarlane's excuse is that they have no female spines to practice on, and Fettes foolishly believes he knows how to solve that problem. Gray is reticent about obtaining another graveyard specimen so quickly, especially in view of what he had to do last time. "People are so concerned about...dogs," he says in a bit of delicious line delivery from Karloff.

Gray's acquiescing to Fettes' request provides one of the highlights of *The Body*

Snatcher's brief 78-minute running time. The victim is the street singer whom we have already seen a couple of times (most importantly just before Fettes visits Gray), and thus whom we feel even more sympathetic towards than if she was introduced here for the first time purely for the purposes of being dispatched by Gray. In a scene that's almost Hitchcockian in style and tone, the singer passes beneath an arch and into the blackness of the rain-drenched night, shortly followed by Gray's carriage which soon, too, disappears. The camera stays fixed on the empty archway, and all we hear is the girl singing. Singing, that is, until her voice is abruptly cut off. It's not surprising to learn that this scene had a major effect

on cinema audiences of the time, and there are more horrors to come.

When the girl's body is delivered, Fettes recognizes who it is and tells MacFarlane that Gray must have killed her, exclaiming "It's like Burke and Hare all over again." MacFarlane constructs a story to explain her injuries while also reminding Fettes that the student was the one who ordered the subject, received it, and paid for it. The body is dissected, and MacFarlane then operates on Georgina. Unfortunately, and despite her rapid recovery from the surgery itself, Georgina is still unable to walk (or perhaps refuses to) and MacFarlane goes to the pub to find solace in alcohol.

"You can't build life the way you put blocks together," the ever-present Gray tells him before forcing MacFarlane to confront his own visage in a mirror, Gray peering over his shoulder like an evil alter ego, one that is sometimes subdued but never fully absent, never completely got rid of. Did MacFarlane create Gray? He's certainly responsible for how Gray makes his living. But Gray is also responsible for MacFarlane's current position in society, having shielded the surgeon from blame

in on significant previous conversations and threatens to blackmail him. This was the final time Karloff and Lugosi were to act together on screen and this scene is as poignant as it is memorable. Indeed, it is a great shame that their time together in this film is so brief, and that Lugosi's role is so minimal. Henry Daniell is superb as Dr MacFarlane but just imagine for a moment if, with the aid of movie magic and a bit of rewriting to accommodate him, Lugosi had played the role of the persecuted surgeon, how much more of a duel of the titans this film might have been. Gray gets Joseph drunk and kills him. As with the death of the street singer the actual act is performed offscreen, in this case behind a curtain, so that once again the audience is forced to imagine the scene that accompanies the sounds of the murder.

during a court case. It would seem the two have each other to blame (or thank) for how they have ended up, and perhaps therefore they do indeed "exist in the same skin." MacFarlane is still desperate to end his relationship with the resurrectionist despite their historical connection, reminding him that "they hanged Burke, they mobbed Hare, but Knox is living like a gentleman in London."

When Gray returns home he is confronted by Joseph, who has been listening

Joseph's body is delivered to MacFarlane as "a little present, in very good condition." Fettes is ordered to dissect it to render it unrecognizable. Meanwhile it turns out Meg the housekeeper is actually MacFarlane's

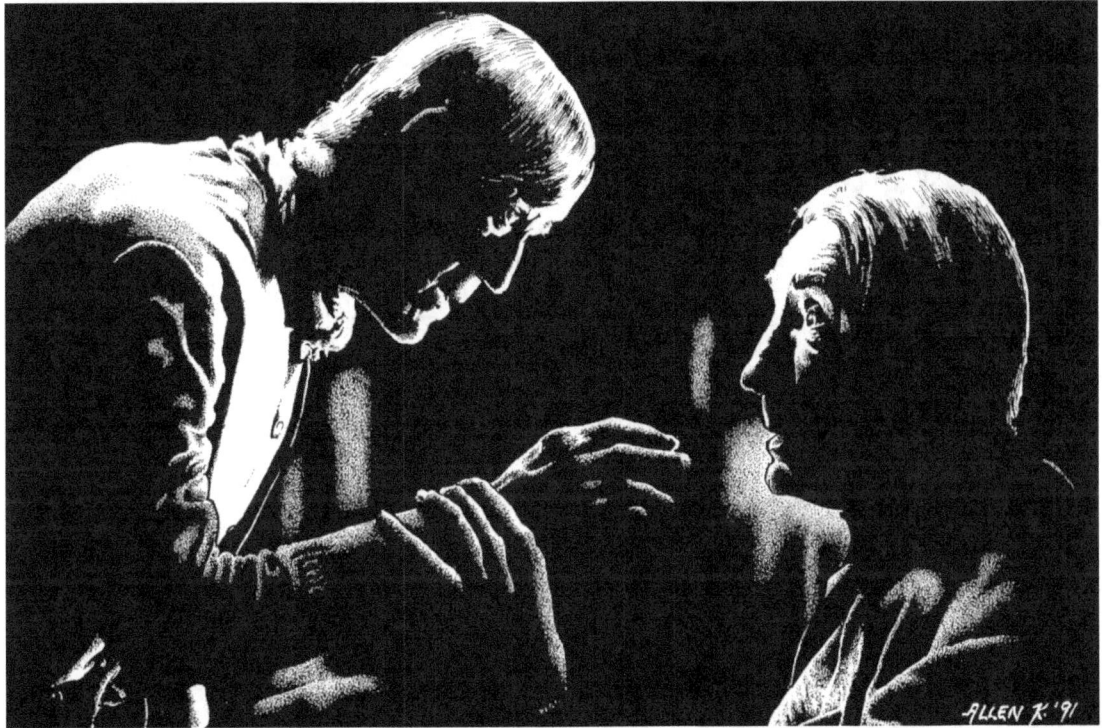

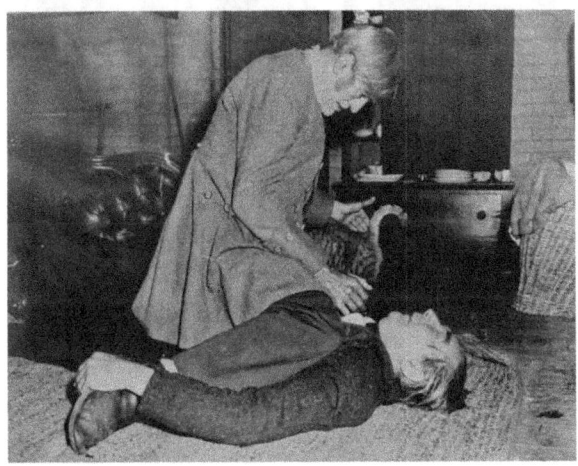

wife, and she has a story to tell Fettes about the relationship between her husband and Gray, who at the trial of Burke and Hare refused to name MacFarlane as being involved even though he was Knox's right hand man. She also claims to have some degree of second sight, claiming that "the pit yawns" for the two of them.

When Gray gets home MacFarlane is waiting for him. It's time to be properly rid of the man. "You'll never be rid of me," Gray growls, admitting that he believes

he would be nothing without his control over the doctor—yet another connotation to the Jekyll and Hyde story.

The two of them fight, Wise segueing the action into silhouettes so that when one murders the other by beating him to death, we are not quite sure who has killed whom for a few moments, not until MacFarlane reveals himself to be alive as he carries Gray's body in to be the latest specimen for his dissection table.

GEORGINA CAN WALK! Fettes witnesses it and rushes to tell Dr MacFarlane who is once again in the pub. By this point in the proceedings I don't think anyone can blame him. While they discuss Georgina's case a family in mourning enters. It transpires they have just returned from a funeral conducted at Glencorse churchyard, a lonely cemetery where few people ever venture. MacFarlane can't resist the lure of a new specimen he believes should be easy to obtain and sets off, with Fettes in tow. We get a fine dose of the gothic (and even the faintest suggestion, at least stylistically, of the Universal horror films whose cycle was just winding down at the time) as the two of them dig up the body of the recently deceased, wrap it in a sheet, and prop it behind them in MacFarlane's tiny carriage. As they head back to Edinburgh it begins to rain. The storm worsens, and MacFarlane believes he can hear Gray's voice, faint at first, calling his name, before the rhythm of the horses' hooves change the words to "Never be rid of me" repeated over and over, becoming so insistent that MacFarlane has to halt the carriage. As Fettes steps down MacFarlane insists the body has changed its appearance. He lifts the cover to reveal the corpse's face and in a flash of lightning both he and we see not the face of a recently deceased elderly woman, but the cadaverous face of Gray. The carriage sets off once more, the dead body of Gray buffeting the living one of MacFarlane as the lightning illuminates them both, the vehicle rattling uncontrollably over the uneven ground, until eventually it crashes. When Fettes gets to the wreckage all he sees are the dead bodies of MacFarlane and the elderly woman they dug up. Perhaps

in an attempt to restore some civility for the censor's sake after all the supremely unsettling mayhem that has just occurred, the film comes to an end on a quote from Hippocrates.

Gray plays a much more minor role in the original Robert Louis Stevenson short story. In that both Fettes and MacFarlane are the medical students charged with the job of receiving bodies from Burke and Hare, with MacFarlane doing some procuring of bodies himself, one of whom is Gray. The climax is similar, with the two of them digging up a fresh body in Glencorse churchyard and it taking on the appearance of Gray in the carriage on the way back to Edinburgh. In the story both men leap from the carriage and both of them survive, but they are haunted to the end of their days. The story proper is told in retrospect by Fettes, now an alcoholic, upon learning that MacFarlane has recently died.

the United Kingdom, where all references to Burke and Hare were ordered removed, as was some of the conversation between Fettes and Gray where Fettes accuses the man of murdering the street singer. The death of Joseph (and the subsequent reveal of his body) was also cut. Most significantly of all, edits were made to the climax so that only a brief shot of Gray's face is seen and the sequence where his body constantly bumps against MacFarlane's was removed entirely. For many British readers of this magazine, this will be the version they will have encountered on television screenings, including the Val Lewton season the BBC screened in the summer of 1981, as the film did not receive an uncensored release on video until the late 1990s. On its release in the United States the

In 1945 Boris Karloff was under contract to RKO and would eventually complete three pictures for Val Lewton—*The Body Snatcher* and *Isle of the Dead* (both 1945) with *Bedlam* following the year after. The screenplay for the Stevenson story was written with instructions to expand the character of Gray especially for the actor, and when it was suggested that Bela Lugosi would be good for marquee value, the character of Joseph was created and included as well. Filming took place over four weeks starting at the end of October 1944 at the RKO Pictures Encino Ranch in the San Fernando valley, using some of the sets from their highly successful adaptation of Victor Hugo's *The Hunchback of Notre Dame* (1939) starring Charles Laughton.

For such an effective film it's perhaps not surprising that *The Body Snatcher* ran into censorship problems, most notably in

film ran into trouble in Ohio, New York, Kansas, and Pennsylvania. US readers can now enjoy Shout Factory's 4K Blu-ray transfer which looks absolutely splendid.

The Body Snatcher was an early project for the then 31 year old Robert Wise, who got the film because he had helped Lewton out when the previous year's The *Curse of the Cat People* had run into trouble. His only full feature credit prior to the Stevenson adaptation was the Franco-Prussian war drama *Mademoiselle Fifi* (1944) which also featured the star of the two Cat People films, Simone Simon. Many years later, having accrued a filmography to be envied by many a successful director, Wise was asked to cite his favorites amongst the many films he had made. Unsurprisingly *The Body Snatcher* was on that short list. Widely recognized as one of the best horror films of the 1940s, and featuring one of the best performances of Boris Karloff's career, it's a film that endures. Made with the utmost skill and featuring the final scenes of Karloff and Lugosi together, it's a film that can comfortably sit alongside the story which spawned it as a true classic in its own right.

☠ ☠ ☠

ALLEN K. '08

THE BRIGHTEST HEAVEN

By John Llewellyn Probert

I FIRST MET RAYMOND TURNER AT A WEEK-END WRITING COURSE. You may wonder why I, a university lecturer who has had some success in both the mainstream and small presses, might have been attending such an event. A friend of mine had organized it and found himself a speaker short and thus it was that I found myself in a remote, fog-mantled, Victorian hotel in West Wales in the middle of January, preparing to fill, as a favor, the post-lunchtime graveyard slot. I was tempted to open with a joke along the lines of how the retitling of an August Derleth Arkham House anthology (for its UK Tandem paperback release) had nothing on the assembly before me, but then, as I surveyed the room of hopeful young writers of tomorrow I realized it likely no one present except myself had ever heard of *When Graveyards Yawn*, so I put up my first slide and got on with talking about The Construction of Dread in Horror Fiction.

After the hour was done and one lengthy and mostly irrelevant question from the audience had been answered, to my and everyone else's satisfaction if not the questioner, I left the floor to a colleague. Their opening salvo, a barrage of questions concerning gender roles in fiction, had me beating a hasty retreat to the bar to avoid being caught in the crossfire.

I knew Turner, of course—as someone who had enjoyed more success in this genre of ours than most British writers—but we had never spoken. We almost didn't this time. Later I was to wish we never had.

The main reason we nearly missed each other was his apparel. Writers, like any other artists, are a varied bunch with a corresponding panoply of dress tastes, ranging from three-piece designer suits to whatever greying potato sack happens to be closest to hand upon rising in the morning. Raymond Turner sported neither end of this range of apparel, and at that moment looked less like a writer and more like someone kitted out

to scale the north face of the Eiger. At least his garb provided me with an excuse to break the awkward silence.

"A visual aid for your talk?"

"I beg your pardon?"

I held out a hand and introduced myself. "You're Raymond Turner, aren't you? I think we were on successive panels at one of those conventions a couple of years ago but we never got the chance to meet."

"Oh. Yes. I see." He seemed terribly nervous. Perhaps his talk was next and the drink was fortification. Not all good writers are good public speakers and even those who excel at it can suffer from anxiety so crippling a last minute replacement is required. It was my reason for having been begged to attend in the first place, in fact.

He glanced down to the knapsack at his feet. A small pickaxe protruded from it. He tried to push it out of sight but only succeeded in creating a clanking sound that betrayed the presence of other tools within.

"Mountaineering horror?" I sipped my Penderyn and, seeing his glass was empty, offered to buy him another.

He refused. "I really should be getting along." He went to pick up the bag and then glanced over to the broad French windows to our right. We watched as the increasingly violent weather caused the rain to lash against the glass with such fury it was as if it was determined to get in.

Turner slumped back onto his stool. "Or maybe not. I'll never find it now, anyway."

I had no idea what that last remark was supposed to mean and so I ignored it. "It's what you get for holding something like this in the depths of Wales at this time of year." I took another sip and tried to make light of it. "Or any time of year, really."

"It has to be this time of year." Turner didn't seem to be talking to me as he tapped his index finger on the bar. "Has to be." His gaze returned to the awful weather outside. "Maybe tomorrow, but not much longer than that. Not much longer at all."

"Listen old fellow, are you all right?" Writers can go off the deep end. Manic episodes, spiraling depression and all kinds of other things. If that was what was happening here I felt duty bound to help out. "You're behaving a bit strangely, even for one of our sort." I laid a hand on his arm, tempering the action with what I hoped was a friendly grin. "Do you know where you are?"

"What? Of course I do!" Turner pulled his arm away and glared at me. My resulting expression must have been more shocked than I intended for he instantly begged forgiveness. It was the turning point in our relationship. He became friendlier, said that yes he would like another drink actually and yes I was quite right to be wondering what on earth a man like him was doing, looking as if he was about to go searching for the abominable snowman.

I laughed as I ordered fresh drinks for both of us, commenting that he was in the wrong country to be looking for the yeti anyway.

"That's true." He regarded his drink as if intending to down it, then thought better of the idea and instead nursed the glass with both hands. "But Wales is still a place of myth and legend. There are...things rumored to make their home here."

"Such as?"

A noise from the hotel foyer startled him. We turned to see the audience for Gender Roles in Horror Fiction being discharged early. Many of its attendees were making straight for the bar.

Now Turner did down his drink. "Later," he said, gathering up his clanking knapsack. "Perhaps after dinner?" He seemed to be contemplating something. "You might actually be able to help me." More contemplation. "We should probably wait until everyone's gone to bed to discuss it."

That wasn't a problem. "I'm supposed to be doing a midnight reading anyway," I replied, thankful that I had been reminded of that particular, likely to be poorly attended, slot I had agreed to when negotiating my free bed and board with the organizers. "Aren't you doing one?"

"I refused. Other things to do. But it doesn't look as if this weather's going to let up so you and I may as well chat instead. Shall we say after midnight in the lounge area, then?"

Two people turned up to my midnight reading.

For that dedicated couple, sitting nervously close to the exit, I made sure to keep it short. After twenty minutes they, too, were making their way out of the lounge area, stifling yawns as they did so.

Turner must have been waiting outside because he appeared as soon as they had gone, a large whiskey in either hand and two knapsacks slung over one shoulder. As he pulled up a table and took a seat it was the bags, rather than the drinks, that held my attention.

"Planning a late night expedition?"

Turner was quiet for a moment, allowing the sound of the persistent storm outside to penetrate through the thick curtains. "Not the right weather for it," he replied as he lifted the first bag onto his lap. It failed to clank, suggesting it was host to a different collection of items altogether.

The first was an iPod. I'm not familiar with how the things work myself but he had little trouble sliding it into the docking system on the table behind him.

"Just want to play you something." Turner set the device going. Immediately the sound of classical music filled the room. I motioned him to turn the volume down but he shook his head. "They're all asleep by now and besides this is far better than what they usually have on for late night parties."

I wasn't so sure, just as I wasn't sure what piece was playing, or why. He allowed it to continue for a minute or so before, to my relief, he turned the volume down to a level that allowed conversation.

"Are you familiar with Fingal's Cave?"

"The place or the piece of music?" I hoped my very complete answer would meet with his approval. It did.

"Both! Been there, have you?"

"Fingal's Cave? I'm afraid not."

"Pity. It's worth it. Makes you appreciate how Mendelssohn was moved to write this." He turned the volume back up for a split second.

So that's what it was. "Otherwise known as the Hebrides Overture?" I hoped this would make me look more learned in the face of having failed to recognize the music itself.

"Precisely! And do you know the background to its writing?"

I could guess. "I'm presuming he went there and that inspired him to compose it."

"It's said that he wrote down the main theme you've just heard as soon as he saw the place."

"It's wonderful when inspiration strikes like that." It had only happened to me once or twice in my entire career. "Most of us have to resort to the sweating blood technique to get our stuff on the page."

"Oh I know. But what if the event Mendelssohn experienced wasn't just a chance occurrence? His talent combined with being in the right place at just the right moment? What if it was something else, something greater than the sum of those elements?"

I was intrigued. "Like what?"

"Do you know what kind of geographical, and in fact I might even say geological, feature Fingal's Cave is?" I resisted the urge to say the obvious and thought it wiser to shake my head.

"It's a grotto. Are you familiar with the term?"

Only as a place where sticky-fingered children got to sit on Santa's knee in department stores and tell some poor underpaid employee what they felt they were entitled to get for Christmas. But that wasn't the answer he wanted and so I shook my head again, preferring to appear ignorant rather than obtuse.

"It's a type of cave. They can be man-made but the most interesting are the ones that were formed naturally, often by the movement of water eroding the rock. Of course I haven't asked you here at this benighted hour to discuss either geography or geology." Thank heaven for that, I thought. "If you've read your Greek and Roman history you'll know that some of them were rumored to be the homes of nymphs and oracles."

I was beginning to regret staying up for this. "That's all very interesting, Raymond, but couldn't we have discussed this at the bar earlier today?"

He shook his head violently but he didn't seem to be angry with me.

"Think about it," he said. "Oracles, nymphs, Mendelssohn being inspired to write the Hebrides overture."

"Oh, you mean they were home to muses?" It really was far too late for these sorts of games.

"Exactly! Now, wouldn't it be wonderful if you could discover a place like that, with a muse that might inspire you to create the greatest thing you would ever write, the work that would live on long after you had departed this earth, and cause you to be remembered long after your death?"

Needless to say, I had never given the matter any thought. The question of where the next sentence to go on the page was coming from was always foremost in my mind, followed closely by when certain literary bodies were finally going to pay me for work they had already published.

But none of that was important right now. As I regarded the gleam in his eye, as Mendlessohn played in the background, and as he began to empty the knapsack of its documents, newspaper clippings and one small and very old book, all the pieces fell worryingly into place. I chose my next words carefully.

"Raymond, are you proposing to go muse hunting?"

I expected a firm denial or at the least a derisive snort. What I did not predict was a cautious nod as he motioned me to look through the contents of his bag.

It was a curious collection of items. There were clippings and printouts of "one-hit wonders" in music, literature and other branches of the arts, as well as accounts of the fall from grace of the artists responsible. Drugs, alcohol, and in some cases suicide or death by "misadventure." Finally there was the book. It threatened to crumble between my fingers despite my holding it as gingerly as I could. Very old and filled with mystic symbols, much of the language uninterpretable to my uneducated eyes. But some of the pictures were not pretty. Not at all.

I laid the book down on the table in front of me, the juxtaposition of that old and rotting thing lying on the clean polished modern surface disturbed me, and I could not rid myself of the thought that if left there too long some malign influence would spread from it to infect the wood. I spoke my next words even more gently than I had treated the vile thing.

"Raymond, what does all this mean?"

"They found it." His voice was shaking now, whether from nerves or excitement it was difficult to tell. "All of them. But it was too much. They couldn't handle it. One great memorable work and they burned out, couldn't cope anymore, not with the work, nor the knowledge that they lacked the capability to achieve it more than once. Some of them."

I rubbed my temples. I was at a loss as to what to say and so I tried to reason with him.

"Are you suggesting that all these people," I pointed to the news stories scattered in front of me, "all went to the same place and encountered some kind of supernatural... force, for want of a better word? Something that made them come up with the work they're now remembered for?"

His fierce nodding did not reassure me.

"But not the same place." He picked the book up, handling it far less gently in his fervor than I had. Was it my imagination or did tiny particles of it fall to the table, stain his fingertips, discharge themselves into the air with the intention of making their way towards me? I moved my chair back just to be safe while at the same time chastising myself for being conducive to such madness.

"The muse—let us call it that—can manifest any time it wants, under any circumstances." He thrust the book at me. I could not help but recoil. He did not seem to notice. "They knew! They tried to document it, to find some pattern, some reason behind its movements."

"And what did 'they' conclude?" I was humoring him, and in doing so I hoped he wouldn't suggest I read that damnable thing for myself.

"The muse is mischievous. It is cruel. It 'strikes'—if we can use that word—at random because that causes it the greatest amusement. Or rather, the aftermath does." I urged him to explain. "It delights in the downfall of man. It feeds off misery and desperation, off the human need to reproduce that single golden moment of the purest creativity despite that moment now being an impossibility. It imbues man with the ability to create and then just as quickly takes it away."

"'Oh for a Muse of fire that would ascend the brightest heaven of invention'." My quote came out as a whisper but Raymond wrapped his arms around himself and began to rock back and forth at the words.

"Yes! Yes! Do you know the last time I produced a work of genuine quality?"

That was difficult to say. Despite my interest in the genre (and indeed, my own career) I tend not to keep up with recently published bestsellers.

"Never! I churn out rubbish under the guidance of my agent and my publishers but it's never what's truly inside me, the 'great work,' if you like, that I know is in there somewhere but which I am unable to access, like a deep seated abscess that needs lancing but which is so well hidden not even the most skillful surgeon can find it without terrible detriment to his patient."

"And you think that if you can find..." It

was all nonsense. "Even if it's true, surely, Raymond, the cost is too high."

"It is not too high!"

Thank goodness it was late and there was no one else in the hotel lounge or else we might have been thrown out for causing a disturbance.

"For that one moment, that single opportunity to create something approaching true quality, true greatness, after a lifetime of drudgery, of scrabbling for scraps of wit, striving to create an atmosphere of dread, or terror, just to be gifted the ability to write something of worth, just once. For that I would give anything."

"Even your life, or at the very least your sanity?" My efforts to calm him weren't working. I tried a different tack. "You claim these reports and this...book," I glanced at the horrible thing, still in his hands, still staining his skin, "they state that this muse can appear anytime and anywhere. How, then, do you hope to find it?"

He grinned in a disconcerting way as he tapped the book once more. "The people who wrote this may have been working with limited resources but they were clever, clever enough to detect patterns in the randomness, to determine where such an entity might make its home."

This was too much. "Oh come on! Are you seriously suggesting that the Muse of Creativity lives in Wales? Now I suppose you're going to tell me it lives in a cave close by and you're going to pay it a visit? Oh and let me guess, the entrance to the cave is buried, which is why you have the digging equipment. That and this little...guidebook of yours is going to help you find that cave, is that it?"

"It's a grotto." This time he sounded irritated at my misnomer. "And you haven't been listening. I told you the muse can appear at any time, can manifest in any place. The idea of there being some physical location where it resides is childish in the extreme."

Was that insult directed at me? If so it passed me by. "If this grotto is ethereal, then how do you propose to find it?"

"With this!" The book again. "It says you need to be near the sea." Admittedly the Welsh coast was just a mile or so away. "That the moon needs to be full." I had no

idea but I assumed it must be. "And that you must allow your desire to guide you."

That seemed rather non-specific. "And you think you're going to find it out there?" I gestured to the curtains.

"I don't know, but I have to try. It won't be the first time."

Oh dear. "How many times have you done this, Raymond?"

Now he looked embarrassed. "A few."

"Here?"

He shook his head. "Everywhere I've traveled. It's why I always accept invitations to speak. Over the last few years I've lost count of the number of conventions, panels and courses I've said yes to, both here and abroad."

"And at every one of these you've slipped out and..."

"...gone 'hunting' as you put it, yes."

I took a moment to ponder this. "Don't you ever get discouraged?"

He looked as if the thought had never entered his head. "Surely it's better to pursue greatness and fail than never go looking for it at all?"

I was about to reply that he might find more success directing his energies to the blank page than in this futile-sounding pursuit, but there isn't a writer alive who hasn't wished to find a source not just of inspiration but of, as he had said, greatness.

"I don't know what to say, Raymond."

"Say you'll come with me!" His grip on my arm was just firm enough for it to hurt. "Two of us together might stand a better chance!"

I was torn between feeling sorry for him and wanting to dismiss the whole thing as nonsense. But a part of me wanted it to be true, perhaps a larger part than I realized.

"But the rain," I spluttered.

"Has stopped."

We were silent for a moment. He was right. The storm had ceased. I went to the curtains. Outside, a full moon shone brightly through a dark hole in the cloud cover, lending a silver glow to the gently rolling hillsides and rendering them the landscape of fairytale.

Or myth.

It was nearly one o'clock in the morning,

we were two men approaching late middle age, and we were both supposed to be up early tomorrow for a discussion panel on "The Influence of Arthur Machen on Supernatural Fiction."

Turner picked up the second bag he had brought with him. This one did clank as he hefted it.

"You can't!"

He tore his arm from my grip. "It may be my only chance. I have to try."

I saw myself coming down to breakfast the next morning only to learn that his body had been found smashed on the rocks, and knew that if I couldn't stop him, I was going to have to go along.

IT TOOK ONLY FIFTEEN minutes for me to begin regretting my decision.

That was how long it took for water from the sodden soil to leak into my boots, for the chill air to worm its way through the numerous layers I had hastily pulled on before joining Turner outside our hotel, and for the pothole-riddled landscape across which we found ourselves trudging to trip me up for the umpteenth time.

We stopped for a breather in the middle of a field.

"Remind me again of how you know where to go," I panted.

I couldn't see Turner's face. The light from his torch rendered his entire form as mere shadow.

"I told you. Near the sea." I could just make out the susurration of waves in the distance. "A full moon." Despite both it and Turner's torch our journey so far had found us making our way through almost total blackness. "And to be led by my desire."

It was that last one I had misgivings about. "Was that all the book said?"

"And that it should be carried by the one seeking enlightenment." He held up a silhouetted hand gripping something recognizably tattered and blocky.

"Well I suggest we give it another quarter of an hour or so and if you don't feel anything we should make our way back."

I could see Turner's outline shiver as he agreed. He was obviously feeling the cold as much as I was.

We had reached a gap in a hedge beyond which lay the gentle incline of a hill when he stopped again.

"Are you all right?"

Silence.

"Turner, is anything wrong?"

His response this time was a muffled groan and he dropped the torch. I picked it up. The man looked doubled up in pain. After all that brisk walking in the cold I hoped he wasn't succumbing to a heart attack.

"Turner! Say something!"

He didn't speak, but he did gesture, holding out the hand that still gripped that ancient, rotting tome. I had visions of a myriad tiny book-eating parasites having scurried from its chill pages and buried themselves in the warmth of his skin.

The reality was somehow worse.

I shone the torch at his clenched fingers. The normal creatures of nature fluttered in its smoky beam, but what it illuminated on my colleague was not normal at all. I crouched to get a better look and my initial, fantastical suspicions were confirmed.

The book, that old, mouldering volume of what I now knew to be evil, had somehow fused itself to his hand. I tried to grab it, to pull it from him, but that led to a cry of agony. He begged me to stop. I explained I was trying to help.

"Leave it alone. It's supposed to happen," he said in between gasps of pain.

This was news to me. "Why didn't you tell me?"

"I never thought it would actually work. The book claims not just to be a guide but the key that will unlock the muse's grotto, and that must mean we are close."

Out of everything he had just told me I think those last words were the most chilling of all. We were on the trail of something mythical, something fabulous and yet utterly terrifying, and now we had a compass that had fused itself to flesh to make certain we got there.

"Can you stand?"

Turner nodded. I could see from his breath that he was still panting, but at least he was no longer crying out. When he next spoke his voice was thin and reedy but no less determined.

"It wants us to go this way."

He gestured to his right. The torchlight revealed an old wooden gate set into the hedge. He needed my support to reach it. Once we were there it swung open at his touch.

"Up the hill."

The incline was a lot steeper than it had looked from a distance. In fact I could almost swear the gradient was increasing beneath our feet as we climbed. But that was nowhere near as strange as what was about to happen.

Just as the hill was becoming so steep I feared we would have to proceed by crawling, the ground lurched and we fell to our knees. A second tremor had me wondering if Wales was being subjected to a mild earthquake which, in a way, it was.

"Look!"

I did not need Turner's urging to see what was happening. I was reminded of the old fairy story of the Pied Piper as I beheld, in the hillside just ahead of us, a shaft of swiftly widening white light appear in the soil, as if a door was being opened into the earth itself.

"Come on! Before it closes!"

It was the kind of thing writers like myself spend our days dreaming up, and here was just such a miraculous and fantastic thing happening right in front of me. How could I not follow my colleague into that blinding light? As we passed through, the book fell away from Turner's palm, becoming nothing more than ash before it reached the ground, its purpose fulfilled, its possession no longer necessary.

Thankfully it turned out that white glare merely signified the boundary between the world we know and one that usually remains hidden. Once we were past it our eyes quickly adjusted to our new surroundings. The cavern in which we found ourselves glowed with a cyanic hue. Stalactites the thickness of telegraph poles hung from the high ceiling but the narrow path on which we found ourselves standing was as polished green glass. I looked behind but could see no evidence of where we had entered. There was only one way to go and Turner had already set off.

Despite my best efforts to keep up, the distance between us quickly increased. It was difficult for my feet to gain purchase and it felt as if the ground was sliding in different directions all at once beneath me. What little progress I made was exhausting. I tried calling out, but instead of the echo effect one would usually expect from such surroundings it was as if my cries were absorbed by the blue-grey rocks that surrounded us. Soon Turner was little more than a matchstick figure in the distance, and while I could still see him and while the path he followed seemed straight, my own journey seemed beset by twists and turns.

The next thing I knew Turner was gone.

Then I heard the scream.

Suddenly I could walk. Suddenly I could run, the surface beneath my feet suddenly rough, the rock no longer trying to heed my progress. But, I asked myself as I hastened along the path, should I not proceed with more caution in view of what I had heard? On the other hand my colleague might be hurt, he could be dying. There was nothing else I could do but hurry to his aid.

As I ran, something began to happen, something even stranger than the previous conspiration of all that surrounded me to heed my progress. The environment itself began to alter. First it was the color, the rocks changing from cyan to a brilliant orange, as if caressed by sunlight from a source I could not identify. Their outlines, craggy and irregular before, were smoothing themselves, limestone becoming sandstone, or perhaps even soapstone, exhibiting such graceful curves that I found myself wishing I had the time to stop and touch their shining perfection. Beneath my feet the path changed from green to a brilliant blue so intense it hurt my eyes and gave me the delirious, glorious sensation that I was running across the sky. The temperature had increased as well, not to an uncomfortable level, but instead to a point where I felt great comfort.

But the greatest change was in my mind.

Amidst all the panic and confusion, all the concern for my still invisible colleague, the most beautiful images began to form in my imagination. Ideas I had never entertained now presented themselves, and I found myself yearning for the notebook I had left behind in the hotel, so I could write them down. This sudden cascade of sound and color, texture and ideas was almost too much for me, so much so that I had to shout aloud with delight just to release some of the creative pressure (I can think of no better term) that was building within my very soul.

The outburst served to clear my mind a little, and allowed the first feeling of concern to raise itself. Had Turner found the muse? Had it exerted its effect on him? And if so, was this why I was feeling this way? Had I, somehow, been "caught in the fallout" from what it had gifted to my colleague? If so I felt a little jealous but nowhere near as much as the worry I now felt for him. The sensations I was experiencing were like having been administered an overpowering drug whose effects it was almost impossible to resist. If I had only received a trace of it, what could it possibly be like to receive a full dose? To meet the muse face to face? Surely that could only lead to...

There was another scream from up ahead. I shook my head, slapped my face and did everything else I could to sober myself. I made my way through this beautiful, ethereal, comforting, stimulating environment, wishing I could pause but knowing I could not, until I found him.

He was lying near a pool of water so pure, so crystalline, I could have believed it was the first water gifted by the gods to the world, the mythic font from which all life began. I forced myself to stop dreaming and help Turner, who was almost unrousable. When he finally opened his eyes I knew he had seen that which I was glad I had not, and while part of me envied him his serene smile, his sense of near beatification, the part of me that remained firmly grounded in reality did not envy what I knew lay in store.

It was not long before he was able to stand, not long before I was able to help him to walk. Already the place was changing once more, its vibrancy and tactility diminishing rapidly now. As our surroundings grew colder and the light began to fade I worried for a moment that we would find ourselves prisoners in darkness. Instead the very solidity of the rock walls around us faded with the same speed as their less tangible effects, and soon we were back on that hillside, the curve of its slopes now returned to the gentle incline we had spied from a distance. Turner, now almost fully in control of his faculties, was able to walk back to our hotel unaided.

You can probably guess the rest. Raymond Turner, winner of numerous literary prizes for the one great work he produced after that experience, is no more. I do not intend to go into the circumstances of his death but I will tell you that I met him shortly before he passed on, and his was a mixture of emotions regarding what had happened. Elation at what he had been able to create, delight at the recognition he had achieved for it, and then a slow, insidious but perpetually increasing misery at being unable to repeat it, a state of mind he knew with crushing inevitability would eventually overwhelm him. And yet he wanted his public to know that he had no regrets, and that he always understood the inevitable price he would be paying for that one moment of stark, crystalline creativity.

As for me, caught in the blast of the muse's "blessing"? Well, as you have just read for yourself, once I had recovered from the initial experience, I felt only the tiniest of creative effects from it.

And yet...

With every story I write, every sentence I commit to paper, I feel a mounting sense of misery that despite my experience I will never be able to create something as memorable as Raymond Turner did, or so many others before me, and with every day that passes that feeling weighs heavier on my soul. At the moment, it is manageable. If it ever reaches the point where it is not, then I know what I have to do.

John Llewellyn Probert's latest books are the short story collection Chasing Spirits *(Black Shuck Books), the portmanteau novel* How Grim Was My Valley *(NewCon Press) and on the non-fiction front,* The Frightfest Guide to Mad Doctor Movies *(FAB Press). Coming up next will be a couple of novels, another short story collection and more film books, as well as articles for both US and UK film and literary magazines. He tries to fit in some sleep where he can.*

TRUTH LIES AT THE BOTTOM OF A WELL

BY STEVE DUFFY

A SMART, WASPISH WOMAN IN HER EIGHTIES, OLD MONEY FROM PORTLAND, TOLD ME SOMETHING ONCE: it was a passing remark, probably no more accurate than any other throwaway, but I'll leave it here for what it's worth. Gold rushes, she said, are all about excitement, flash and glamour; they make for overnight millionaires and generate gaudy, splashy tragedies that make all the front pages. Timber money, by contrast, is slower, dull and patient. Timber builds stodgy fortunes and staid dynasties, and if those dynasties go off the rails it happens gradually, over generations, in shadows and seclusion. But when they do go bad, declared my deep source with relish, they go big.

The Findlays were adduced as a case in point. A family who guarded their privacy with a doggedness that positively invited speculation, they'd left the highlands of Scotland in 1849, heading for America. There they made their fortune in timber, the mighty Douglas firs of the Pacific northwest. In the forests around the Findlay mansion the felled trunks tumbled in their tens of thousands down the skid roads cut into the hillside, heading for the mills on the shores of Puget Sound. But the trees that grew in the Findlay parkland were safe from the saw; they were there to shield the family, like the spike-topped stone wall surrounding the estate or the iron gate, the height of two tall men, at its entrance.

Within that wall, beneath the shadows of those trees, very few people outside the family gained admittance. Melanie Dressel managed it twice in the fall of 1966, thanks to the auspices of Time-Life Publishing. The corporation was at that time producing a popular series of illustrated large-format books on the theme "The Glory That Is...," each showcasing the architectural treasures of a given American city in vivid Kodachrome. Melanie's job was to provide the neat little blocks of text that went with those luscious color plates, and after Sacramento and San Francisco, Seattle was next up on Melanie's agenda. The Findlay mansion was an obvious candidate for inclusion, being one of the most photogenic, yet at the same time least photographed, of all the old family homes in the northwest. Admission to the estate was hardly ever granted, but word had it that a personal letter to the family from Mrs. Clare Boothe Luce herself had sealed the deal.

Melanie was cheerfully and openly dismissive of those who said, sometimes to her face, that what she did wasn't "proper writing." What did that even mean? If you were without glamor or expectations, the wrong side of thirty and reconciled to it, then a job was a job, and independence beat self-indulgence all ends up. Let the Bryn Mawr girls coddle their neuroses: that was a luxury outside her grasp. She was earning her way in the world, which to her understanding was a finer thing than relying on privilege.

Not that she didn't daydream (once in a while, and never on the company dollar) of a timeline in which she didn't have to cut her cloth according to her means. She was by no means bereft of an imagination, and given half a chance she'd have loved to monetize it in some way that was both artistically and financially rewarding. As it was, she had to be content to indulge it vicariously, through other people's experiences, other people's art. Loves books, loves to read, her mother had said of her, as if those weren't the same thing. "You and your books." *Yes*, she'd think, *me and my books. One day.*

Of course Melanie was smart enough to know that not everybody had, as the saying goes, a book in them, and that even those who did wouldn't necessarily have the wherewithal or even the plain good luck to make a proper fist of it. Rather than waste time chasing the ideal, she found a sort of freedom in making do with what she had, getting on with the business of living. She was perfectly happy and perfectly free, she told herself. Like Pinocchio in that song Barbra Streisand sang on her favorite record album, she had no strings to hold her down. She liked Barbra Streisand and Truman Capote, Atticus Finch and the songs of Bacharach & David, and she wasn't tied up to anyone.

And so, untethered, Melanie found herself at the gates of the Findlay estate, one bright morning in November '66. Her travels among the rich and reclusive had accustomed her to grandeur and magnitude, grace and splendor, otherwise she might have felt a little intimidated by the sight of the great house set among landscaped lawns and topiary hedges, the wooded hills rising behind it, a magical palace at the edge of a fairy-tale forest. The cameramen were delighted with the low sunlight skewing through the trees, busy testing lenses and filters, and she was in conversation with the family lawyer, a Mr. Crittenden, who'd driven up from the city to give her formal admittance. He'd already explained that the family were not in residence, and preferred all their dealings with outsiders to take place through his own intermediary services.

"Now, Miss Dressel, you understand that this is quite a privilege." He reminded her of an aunt she'd loathed in childhood, who would dispense charity to Melanie and her widowed mother at her place in New Hampshire. It had never seemed a particular privilege to Melanie to be sitting in a stuffy over-furnished drawing room when outside on Ashland Street there was the cemetery just begging to be explored, irresistibly seductive, filled with the memorious dead (a phrase she'd read in a Nashua city guidebook and instantly appropriated). Still, she'd eat any amount of crow for a free pass at the Findlay house, so she smiled cheerfully up at Mr. Crittenden and said "My gosh, yes."

"I've arranged for you to be shown around the house by Mrs. Seale, the housekeeper," Mr. Crittenden explained, "she's very knowledgeable, good on facts and dates. She won't expect a gratuity." Always as well to get the ground rules straight. "Obviously the family's private rooms will be off bounds, and we do ask that you not attempt to gain admittance to those, nor embarrass Mrs. Seale by asking her." *Well, heaven forbid I embarrass Mrs. Seale*, Melanie thought. Aloud, she said:

"That's marvelous, Mr. Crittenden. Shan't I have the pleasure of your company, though?" Fate had ordained it otherwise; politely yet decisively, the lawyer begged an urgent appointment in the city, and scuttled back to his chocolate-brown Mercedes as soon as Mrs. Seale appeared at the gates.

Melanie had been expecting Mrs. Danvers from *Rebecca*, and Mrs. Seale did not disappoint, at least so far as looks went. She was, however, less immediately terrifying in her manner than that fearsome old retainer, and she greeted Melanie civilly enough. She beckoned the Time-Life party through the gates, and asked how she could best be of service to them. Melanie explained that one of the photographers could be left to his own devices in and around the grounds, but that the other two would accompany her on a tour of the mansion. Mrs. Seale was agreeable to this, with one caveat: "The family would prefer it if there were no photographs taken of the private cemetery in the woods."

"Oh, of course," Melanie said, and to her crew, "You heard that, boys?"

"Yes, ma'am," agreed Waldo, the most loquacious of the three, and he set about his outdoors business. The others, Mike and Jeffrey, went with Melanie up the driveway in the company of Mrs. Seale. "Have you been here a very long time, Mrs. Seale?" Melanie asked, hoping it wouldn't be taken the wrong way.

"Since I was a girl," Mrs. Seale said proudly, and Melanie guessed that there was nothing in life she would have liked better. "How lovely for you," she said, not without sincerity. Mrs. Seale's exalted position, a little like her own, seemed to represent a victory of sorts, the triumph of practicality over monkeyshines. Seeing no wedding band on her finger, Melanie decided that the title of Mrs. was an honorific that went with the post; in fact it seemed entirely plausible that she'd exchanged vows of some sort with the estate, pledged honor and obedience before settling into a chastely unconsummated honeymoon of furniture polish and well-aired linen. With an effort, Melanie set aside this image, and tried to pay attention to Mrs. Seale's lecture on the history and composition of the celebrated Findlay flowerbeds.

Over the course of the next hour and a half, Mrs. Seale's commentary never once strayed from the authorized version. It was the guided tour of the house, no more and no less, which *objets* had been snaffled at what unimaginable expense, whose were the faces in all the old portraits, how long had they been dead, the minutely audited details of their contributions to the Findlay patrimony. Which was exactly what the customers would want, in all fairness—facts, just the right amount of them, a homeopathic dose of local color between wide margins on shiny coated stock. So Melanie followed the housekeeper dutifully, made notes in shorthand, asked all the right questions and only the right ones, while behind them trailed Mike, juggling lights and reflector, and Jeffrey, shooting and reloading, shooting and reloading his Pentax with aperture open wide.

If you can lay hands on a copy of *The Glory That Is Seattle*, you can see for yourself what that old place was like, pages 144 through 160. Had you not known that the Findlays made their fortune in timber, you could surely have guessed it from the decor. Oak and pine predominated, the rich deep tones of honey and amber and the sap at the heart of the tree. All the walls were paneled, and all the floors were parqueted; pillars of wood helped raise the ceilings high, and carved screens divided the rooms into secret nooks and corners. If from outside the house looked like a mighty cliff of stone, inside it seemed hollowed out of one enormous tree-trunk, with great craft and attention to detail. Fires burned in all the fireplaces, and autumn arrangements stood in vases on the mantels and the meticulously polished tables. But for whose benefit? Was it all meant to impress the readers who would spend an afternoon flipping through the pages of their coffee-table tomes in search of diversion? Melanie couldn't imagine a less *tenanted* house, somehow; couldn't picture people moving through these swept and dusted rooms, settling in an armchair with a good book from the library or watching the sun go down over the parkland. It all seemed such a waste.

It was while Mrs. Seale was shaking loose the dustsheets from a glass case of fine Meissen porcelain for the benefit of Jeffrey's lens that Melanie felt a tap at her shoulder. Behind her in the doorway, at an angle that rendered her invisible from inside the room, was an unremarkable woman of approximately her own age and height, with thick brows and a mop of thick black hair cut in no discernible style. A smile was tugging at one corner of her crooked mouth. She was beckoning Melanie out into the corridor. And after all, why not?

Melanie would have taken her for another of the staff, but her clothes seemed far too informal: a heavy shapeless sweater and slacks would certainly not pass muster with Mrs. Seale. Nor would the housekeeper have approved of her first words: "Has she bored the pants off you yet?" Her voice was low and confiding, and Melanie was warming to her already.

"Who are you?"

"I'm the daughter of the house," the woman said. "My name is Eilidh. E-I-L-I-D-H. That's Scottish, you know."

"I'm Melanie Dressel. It's lovely to meet you." She was ready to shake, but the woman made no move, just kept looking at her with a sort of detached amusement—not mocking, more conspiratorial, as if it was all just a perfect hoot. "I didn't mean to intrude on your private space, Miss Findlay, but I'm with the Time-Life party, we've been given permission to look around..." But wouldn't she be aware of that already? "It sure is a beautiful place," Melanie finished off. As a matter of fact, "beautiful" was not her abiding impression of the Findlay house, but it was impolite to say precisely what you thought to one's host, at least on first acquaintance.

"It's an old mausoleum," Eilidh said, still with that slight crooked smile. "But it's got some pretty things in it, I guess. Would you like to see them?"

"Mrs. Seale has been showing me around, Miss Findlay—"

"Mrs. Seale wouldn't know a pretty thing if it crept up behind her and whacked her on the head," Eilidh confided. "Look, can you come back tomorrow? I'll take you round myself. It's Mrs. Seale's afternoon off, so if you get here around two it'll be just us."

Melanie gulped. "There's more to see?" she said, stupidly.

"So much more. Old Sealey won't show you the best bits. It'll just be the two of us. Say you will. But you have to call me Eilidh."

She stifled a laugh, lest Old Sealey hear them. "Are you serious?"

"Terribly." Still with that twisted smile.

"I've been watching you. You deserve a break from Mrs. Seale and her inventories."

Melanie couldn't believe it. People would sell their own mothers for this sort of access. And here it was being offered to her on a plate, like the head of John the Baptist in that painting in the library (a Meissonier, picked up in fin-de-siècle Paris for a then-record price which Mrs. Seale had helpfully converted from 1890s francs to 1960s dollars). What sort of mutt would turn down an invitation like this? Not one who entertained hopes of one day seeing her photograph on the back flap of a dustjacket.

Inside the room, Mrs. Seale was chiding Jeffrey, "Hurry up, young man, we haven't got all day." That helped her decide, not that she really needed helping. However rule-abiding and practical you might pride yourself in being, sometimes you just have to snatch at an off-chance when it comes your way.

"Do you really mean it? Because I'd love that. Should I bring anything? A camera? Some Danish pastries? A party frock?" She hadn't been this hugger-mugger—this *flirty*—with anyone since grade school, let alone someone she'd only just met, and that under the most unlikely circumstances imaginable.

"Just bring yourself." Which of course is what all of us want to hear.

"This is like something out of a story," Melanie said, still a little dazed at the swiftness with which events were proceeding. "Nancy Drew Investigates."

Maybe Eilidh hadn't read any Carolyn Keene, because she didn't seem to pick up on the reference. Instead, she shrugged and said: "Oh, I've got stories that'll make your hair stand on end. And every one of them is true."

They giggled like schoolgirls playing truant. "Do you do this with all the guests?" Already Melanie felt perfectly safe in taking these modest liberties.

"Only the ones who'll appreciate it." We are all, of course, susceptible to flattery, and Melanie was no exception. "I'm perfectly happy with my own company most of the time, but you don't often come across a kindred spirit."

A kindred spirit.

She touched Melanie's forearm lightly. "I'd better go now—don't tell anyone about this. It'll be our secret. *Lunchtime tomorrow,*" a hiss, almost in her ear. And then she did a weird thing, but a thing that Melanie found thoroughly delightful: she reached up with the knuckles of two fingers and nipped her guest's snub nose, then showed her the tip of a thumb gripped between them, as if she'd nipped that nose clean off. It was a simple, almost childish prank; the sort of game that little children with friends probably played every day of their lives. Nobody had ever played it before with Melanie. Before she could even react Eilidh was gone, running noiselessly down the tasteful turkish carpet between the wood paneling and the frowsty portraits of Findlays past, eavesdropping in mute disapproval on their clandestine arrangement.

"And passing on from the main house," Mrs. Seale appeared just as Eilidh vanished around the corner, "we shall conclude our tour in the orangery, which is down the back stairs and along the north portico." She gathered Melanie back beneath her repressive wing, but the assignation had already been made, and there was nothing she could have done to stop it.

Were Melanie's motives entirely altruistic in all this? After all, she was, if not a journalist exactly, in the employ of a news-gathering organization, and it went without saying that an inside connection to possibly the most reclusive family in America might be leveraged to her considerable advantage. A fan of Truman Capote, Melanie asked herself: what would Truman do in a situation such as this? The answer, of course, was obvious. Follow the story. Be charming, keep his ears wide open, and follow the story wherever it led.

Then again, her curiosity was in part at least quite unselfish. She genuinely wanted to know what life was like for Eilidh Findlay; more than that, she genuinely liked her, even on this briefest of acquaintance. Eilidh's openness was both flattering and endearing, and it carried the thrill of acceptance as well as the lure of possibilities. It seemed to her entirely possible that Eilidh too had been told by her mother that she'd never find a man if she dressed that way; that she'd been unkindly compared to Nancy from the comic strips; that she'd been a wallflower at her own birthday parties; that she was always on the lookout for—what had she said?—for a *kindred spirit.* There were no rules when it came to friendship, no telling who a person might click with. And friendship, she told herself, wasn't the same as strings.

If Melanie had been another type of person, one without that wild hair of whimsy, then who knows? She would have finished up on the Findlay job and checked out of the Camlin Hotel that same night, probably, taken the overnight back to New York, gotten on with her life. But the ticket was open-ended, her copy was filed, she had no pressing work engagements, no friends were waiting on her return, and the thought of her empty apartment seemed more than usually unpromising, as she sat in her room on the ninth floor and looked out over Elliot Bay and the Olympic range. *Somewhere,* she thought, *in that blackness beyond the city lights, somewhere out there is the Findlay mansion, and a lonely girl a little bit like me.*

AND SO MELANIE FOUND herself back at the Findlay estate the next day, alone this time, having left no word of her destination. On finding no one at the gates to greet her, she positively refused to worry: Eilidh would appear soon enough, she was sure. Not even alone in her hotel room, far from the heavy enchantment of the Findlay place, had she doubted a single word her new friend had spoken. In the meantime, she tried to decide what she really thought of Eilidh's home, should the question arise later that afternoon. It seemed important that between them there should only be perfect faith and perfect trust.

Such an excessively gothic mass ought, it seemed to Melanie, have gathered enough strength to launch itself upwards into the treetops. It ought to have found expression in spires and turrets and pointed gables, like the mad castles of Bavaria. Yet the sheer bulk of the mansion seemed instead to have bound it to the earth, prevented it from rising more than three sullen storeys out of the damp and clinging clay. Out of nowhere, a remembrance from childhood and long-departed pets came to her: the way that a dead animal always seems to weigh heavier than a live one in your hands.

There was nothing airy about that place, nothing whimsical, just a great bluff of grey stone. In the grey light of an overcast midday, yesterday's sun lost in slow-moving slabs of thick cloud, everything about it appeared petrified with age. Even the tall tracery windows either side of the great front door seemed to have more of stone than glass about them, as if the old stained glass was only a special sort of rock worn thin and transparent with the passage of the years. *Stone outside and wood within*, thought Melanie, *like an altar tomb that holds a coffin*. Perhaps she wouldn't tell Eilidh everything she was thinking after all.

"There you are." A voice out of nowhere: it was Eilidh, of course, and the gates stood ajar, soundlessly opened for her alone.

Melanie had been out early that morning shopping for clothes at Frederick & Nelson, swapping her formal career-girl outfit of yesterday for blue jeans, flannel shirt in lumberjack check and a well-cut but practical fringed suede jacket, worn with sensible saddle Oxfords. She was glad to see that her instincts had been right, and that dressing down was still the order of the day. "Hello!" she said, slipping through the gate.

"You came, then." Eilidh sounded pleased. "I thought you might think I was the family lunatic."

"Oh, the family lunatic is always the most fun," she deadpanned. "Anyway, I had to come back for my nose."

"You understand, then." Gravely Eilidh returned the captured nose to her face and took her by the arm. "Come on, I want to show you something before it starts to rain."

They took one of the gravel paths that skirted the mansion and led into the silent pines, where the way underfoot turned to clean dry woodchip and pine-needles. "These woods go on for miles beyond the house," Eilidh said, "they're perfectly quiet on afternoons like this. Even the birds have stopped singing, listen."

"I sort of miss the birdsong," Melanie said.

"Oh, they'll start again once it's dark," Eilidh assured her. "Now I want you to tell me everything about yourself."

"How long is this path, anyway?" Melanie asked.

"It goes all the way to the cemetery," Eilidh said, which certainly seemed like a long way. Melanie did her best to entertain her host with a brisk and chatty run-through of her own story: "Mom drank," she explained, "and we didn't have a lot of money. I was told to forget about college, but then an uncle died and there was some money set aside in his will, which came as a surprise, and so I got to go to journalism college."

"Was your mother proud?" Eilidh asked.

"Mother…" Melanie let it hang, deciding how light she wanted to keep the conversation. *But why not*, she asked herself, and continued: "Mother always wanted a son, you see. There was a thing she used to say to me when she'd been drinking: 'you're certainly plain enough for a boy.'" She related it without embarrassment: things were as they were, after all.

"When I graduated—when I got the job at Time-Life, and wound up writing copy for the high-end publications—I think it bemused her as much as anything else. I think it almost made her angry, can you understand that? She'd never seen being a woman as anything other than…passive, you know? It's like, the only expectation she'd ever had of me was before I was born, that I'd be a boy, and not only wasn't I a boy, I wasn't even a pretty girl. Everything just wrong-footed her."

"So you kept on confounding her expectations."

"Every step of the way."

"Well, good for you," Eilidh said. "It's a little like that in my family: there isn't much to look forward to for the girls, only to do what's expected of them. But don't you just love doing the unexpected, sometimes?"

And with that they came out from beneath the cover of the trees into a clearing. Ahead of them lay the pleasantly unexpected, in the form of a small cemetery surrounded by wrought-iron railings. "Oh, how absolutely perfect," Melanie exclaimed. "I always used to try to slip into graveyards when I was a little girl."

"You left that out of your résumé," Eilidh said, unlatching the gate. "But I might have guessed it, really."

The graves were laid out in a series of semicircles, facing inwards. Around them the grass was mown closely and neatly in roundels, to match the curve of the rows. At the center, where you might have expected to see a massive memorial stone or perhaps a piece of religious statuary, there was of all things a humble brick well, complete with winch and rope beneath a conical shingled witch's hat of a roof. "Well," Eilidh said, and for a moment Melanie misunderstood her, "here we all are. Meet the Findlays."

"But not all of you." Melanie was stooping to read the inscriptions on the slabs.

"No, not quite," Eilidh agreed. "I mean, you won't find me here."

"But here you are."

"It's a pretty place to wander," Eilidh said dreamily. "See, the graves are arranged by generations. This outer row is being filled in one by one with the current family, their parents are back here, and so on all the way back to the center, where it all began. Those half-dozen graves around the well are the patriarch and his clan: the original Findlays who came over from Scotland and settled right here on this spot. It's like the Inferno," she added, almost as an afterthought, "the closer you get to the center, the worse it gets."

"What's with the well?" Melanie wanted to know.

"Oh, the well," Eilidh said. "The well's at the center of everything, so far as the Findlays are concerned."

"Is it the family crest or something?"

"I'll tell you the whole story," Eilidh said, "if you'll be good and wait."

At that moment the heavens opened. Melanie, kneeling by the slab of the patriarch, Alistair Findlay ("also Jessie, wife of the above"), saw the first few raindrops fall like shiny pennies on the rough dove-grey granite. "There it is," she said, getting to her feet. "I just hate to get wet, don't you?" But Eilidh was already running, yelling over her shoulder "Come on," and Melanie hurried after her down the resin-scented path beneath the trees. Remembering something

her aunt had once told her, she stopped for a moment to close the gate of the graveyard behind her.

They collided with the door of the orangery, forcing it open between them and tumbling through to the quiet inside. Absent Mrs. Seale's juiceless commentary, Melanie was better able to appreciate its dry earthy smell, the patterned Victorian tiles underfoot, the way the light filtered through the stained-glass skylight down the rows of late blooming exotics. "That's a cobra lily," Eilidh told her, "and that's gloriosa. The orchids are over there."

"They really do look like some kind of reptile," Melanie marveled. "Is that a pitcher plant there, with the fat little forked tongue?"

"I'd really like to grow toadstools," Eilidh said, leading the way through the glassed portico, its windows running with the heavy slanting rain. "They're practically the state flower." Melanie followed her host along a succession of corridors to the great hallway where the silence lay, packed tight like wadding, muffling the world in thick grey lint.

"Come and see the special room," Eilidh told her. At some point she must have kicked off her shoes; her footsteps made no sound on the polished oak floor as she ran across the hallway to a high wooden door twice her height. It opened to her touch, and for a moment Melanie felt a little throb of unease— this wasn't one of the rooms she'd seen on her guided tour. Nevertheless, she followed her host inside.

"This is old Alistair's study," Eilidh said. "Practically nobody was allowed in here when he was alive, and nobody comes here now, even when the family spend their summers out west. Except Mrs. Seale with a duster, of course," she added cheerfully. Her amusement sounded all wrong in that room.

The patriarch's personal space, his holy of holies, was not a place for laughter. The wood in here—and there was a lot of it, it was all wood—was dark with coat after coat of thick stain, varnished almost to black, threatening to swallow up the afternoon light that seemed suddenly to have dwindled, as if an eclipse was underway and the sun might forever after hide behind the moon. Outside, through mullioned windows with drapes half-drawn, the tops of the trees swayed fitfully in the wind that had blown the rain in from the bay.

The study was on two levels: its rear half was raised five feet or so above the rest, with eight wooden steps on either side leading up to the great desk. From that eminence, Alistair Findlay must have sat like a king on his dais or a priest at the high altar, light streaming in from the tall windows at his back on to the supplicants that came before him. Melanie wondered how anybody could live like that, what sort of a mind would take pleasure in such absurd shows of dominance.

Eilidh, quite at home amongst the grandeur, flopped into a two-seater chesterfield of rubbed red leather at one side of the room. She motioned Melanie into its twin, and they sat facing each other either side of a gently crackling fireplace. Standing in the hearth was an old-fashioned oil lamp with glass chimney.

There were no books in the room, which came as a surprise to Melanie; but there were pictures on the walls, lots of them, covering almost every panel. Grim compositions in oils, their varnish crackling with age, forests and rivers and stags at bay on hilltops, ruins of castles and broken battlements; black-and-white photograph studies of loggers at work, women in bustles with parasols, whiskered old men in high-crown hats and waistcoats bursting with prosperity. The lives and times of Alistair Findlay and his generations, Melanie thought, captured on the old man's wall like so many butterflies under glass.

The walls curved back towards the desk, for the room was the shape of a semicircle, and Melanie mentally fitted it into place on the ground plan of the mansion. Seen from above, the Findlay place took the form of a long rectangle with a circle at its middle. The great hallway at the entrance to the house took up half that circle, more or less, and its back half was the patriarch's study.

Aloud, she said: "When I was a little girl, I always wanted to live in a tower. I was just fascinated with the idea of a round room, round walls surrounding me. I guess this is halfway there."

"Little Melanie in her tower," Eilidh said. "Just like Rapunzel."

"I didn't have the hair for Rapunzel," Melanie confessed, tousling her pixie cut.

"And Rapunzel wanted to escape, didn't she?"

"Well, the witch was coming to get her," Melanie said, "that would have been at the front of her mind, I guess."

"Aren't you afraid of the witch, Melanie?"

She scoffed. "If I can face my editor at Time-Life, I can face anything."

"The version I read," Eilidh said, "ended up with the old witch trapped in the tower instead. I was the sort of girl who thought that was unfair."

"I guess you're the opposite of Rapunzel," Melanie said. Conversations with Eilidh were, she thought, a little like a maze; you got to where you were headed in the end, but by fun and unexpected ways.

"The Findlays don't run to towers," Eilidh said. "All we've got is a well—that's like the opposite, right?"

"Aren't we just the perfect contrarians?" Melanie laughed. "What an extraordinary room, though." She leaned back on the couch, looked at the pictures above the fireplace. "Oh, the well! There it is again! That is the one, right?"

Faded sepia on a cream card mount, blown up big. A gathering in the nineteenth century, old light caught in silver and iodine and mercury. A grassed slope, tall trees in the background, and a babe in arms, and at the center of the composition a family: father, mother, youngsters grouped around a well resembling in every respect the one she'd seen in the Findlay's graveyard.

Eilidh studied it as if someone had hung it while her back was turned. "Yes," she said after a little while, "that's the well—but it's not the one you saw out there among the graves. That's the *real* one."

"How many wells do you have?" Melanie asked in amusement, and Eilidh only smiled. "The one in the graveyard is for show," she said. "It's just bricks and tiles; there's no real shaft going down into the earth. It's quite a story."

"You're just cram packed with stories," Melanie said approvingly.

"This room is full of them," Eilidh said, gesturing at the pictures on the walls. "You're looking at the entire history of the family, from before we left Scotland, even. Down through the generations, all the way back to the stories told by grandmothers about the days before the family Bible or the parish register. Forget about what you saw on your tour, all that bric-a-brac, the heirlooms and mementos, room after room full of old junk. This is the real inheritance. It's all here in this room. The stuff that nobody knows."

The frustrated New Yorker correspondent inside Melanie emitted a long low moan, and she honestly wondered whether it might not be audible from across the hearth. Visions of Capote danced across her brain, of herself in mod monochrome and mask at the Black & White Ball, a last-minute addition to the guest list, a fellow nonfiction novelist and new journalist. Practical Melanie, Miss Make Do and Don't Complain, was far away at that moment, and her saddle Oxfords were kicking in thin air, a long way off the ground.

"One of the nineteenth-century Findlays thought to compile a family history," Eilidh told her. "He used to work on it right here in this room, it became quite an obsession with him. He never did finish it, but I suppose history never is finished, is it? Who's to say when the tale is at an end?"

"I guess," said Melanie, wondering when Eilidh's tale was going to begin.

"So we really ought to start back in Scotland, back in the days when the Findlays were working the forest of Glen Affric, in the highlands. The waters in the forest streams run down to Loch Ness, where there are kelpies and monsters, and a lot of the stories about those streams have to do with their inhabitants.

"The kelpies will lead you to your death, they say; they'll take on a pleasant form to fool you and lure you down to the water where you drown. Near by Loch Ness is Loch Morar: it's dark and deep, and Morag lives in the deepest part. She's very sneaky, and hardly anybody sees her, but when they do, it means a death in the family. Nobody really knows what she looks like, because nobody dares to tell."

"All these stories," Melanie said. "A kid would be afraid to get in the bath after hearing that stuff. It's enough to put you off water for the rest of your life."

"But you can't do without it," Eilidh said. "Old Alistair found that out—the Findlay who went west, who uprooted the family and sailed for the New World.

"You have to understand, Alistair had never amounted to much back in Scotland. He had just enough cash to pay his passage, and a pittance left over for the journey overland in a covered wagon. One in ten died on that Oregon trail. Every time those pioneers crossed a river, they took their lives in their hands; out along the Platte in Nebraska the water was bad, and cholera was running riot in the camp, people falling sick and dying all along the way.

"Alistair Findlay thought he'd sell his soul for a mug of good clean water from the ice-cold streams of Affric. The thought of it maddened him, night after night, and the family would wake to find him muttering over a dying campfire, his eyes like black holes with a spark of fire at the bottom, and it might have been the firelight, or it might have been his soul. Nobody liked the look of him; nobody wanted to be alone with him, and it was just as well that he was so wrapped up in himself. They all thought they were pretty much doomed, but they kept on out of sheer Scottish cussedness.

"They didn't die, somehow, and they made it over the mountains, down into the damp green Oregon territory. Alistair wasn't for stopping at the first good place they came to, though: he kept on rolling until he found himself in amongst the big timber, here on the shores of the Salish Sea. Only the Denny party were here before him, out on Alki Point. Where are we going, the Findlays would ask old Alistair whenever they got up the nerve, and he'd tell them he'd seen the place in a dream, that he'd know it when he saw it.

"This was the place, of course." Eilidh pointed to the photo on the wall. "Right here. There he is, Alistair and his wife, standing where he planned to build a mansion, on land to which he'd signed his name forever and ever.

"That well was the dot at the end of his name. Do you know, before he chopped down a single tree out here he dug that well, lined it with stone, threw in a silver penny for luck? People thought it was something that he'd been dreaming of, out along the trail; part of his vision of the more abundant life here in America. His wife Jessie knew better: she knew what it really meant. You see, there'd been a well very much like it in the glen back home, and she knew the story the village children used to tell, a tale they'd all heard before their noses reached the table.

"Long ago, before Alistair's time or even his grandparents', the Glen Affric folk used to graze their sheep on the common land around the well, and the story went that each crofter that used this common had to offer up a sacrifice to the spirit of the well. That sacrifice was the first ewe-lamb of his flock, the first one that was dropped each year. If he didn't make the sacrifice, then his sheep would sicken and die, half of the flock gone by the end of the grazing season with the braxy or the daising, lying by the well in the morning with their eyes pecked out by the corbies."

"So they'd actually sacrifice a lamb? My God!" Eilidh certainly knew how to tell a story, Melanie thought.

"The first-born ewe-lamb," she confirmed. "It was always the first-born, in the old stories. They're alike in so many ways, those old wives' tales: there's always a sacrifice, there's always a death. Do you know the rhyme about the rivers of Scotland? My mother used to tell it. 'Bloodthirsty Dee, each year needs three, but bonny Don, she needs none.'" Eilidh sounded very Scottish as she recited the rhyme, as if it had been the language of her youth and it didn't need much prompting for her mouth to shape the words the way it used to, the old way, as was only right and proper for the old tales.

"Each year needs three—three what?"

"Three deaths, what else? The river demands it. They used to say it about the Spey as well, that it had to claim a victim each year or it wouldn't be satisfied. 'Bloodthirsty Spey, from the loch to the bay.' So whether in the well or in the river, even out to sea where there was, oh, just unimaginable danger, the spirits that lived in the water were always cruel, and they always needed buying off, and the only thing that satisfied them was blood. You must give of your best to the well, that's what they used to say in the glen; you must give it your most treasured possession. Your most treasured possession," she said, and her voice became faraway.

"Why, it's enough to send a person clean around the bend," Melanie said, her eyes wide and round.

"Absolutely," Eilidh said, as if rousing herself from contemplation. "That's the thing you have to understand about old Alistair, you see: he was quite mad, however much he tried to hide it—and he did manage to hide it from everyone except his own family. To the world at large he was a driven man, a go-getter, a pioneer who'd gone west and built an empire with his bare hands, but his family knew him for who he really was, and they feared him, I tell you; they feared him.

"I really think he was crazy even before he left his home and almost died out in the wilderness: I think it was always in his blood. There was a weird streak about the Findlays, that's what they said in the glen. Respect them, do business with them, but never marry into them. Alistair had that against him from the start, the Findlay inheritance, such as it was, but he was all the way crazy by the time he reached his destination, what with one thing and another." She was staring at the old photograph. "And it all centered on that well."

"Which is not the well we just saw," Melanie was trying to follow the thread, "but some other well."

"The real well," Eilidh confirmed. "The true well, the one Alistair sank here among the trees, as part of his offering to the old gods. Would you like to see it?"

Melanie nodded eagerly.

"Are you sure?" Eilidh was smiling. "You haven't heard the whole of the story yet."

"But you're going to tell me, right?"

"I wouldn't leave you dangling." She thought for a moment, then began again. "Remember that old wives' saying, 'You must give of your best to the well'? Now what do you suppose was Alistair's best? What do you suppose he gave to his well?"

Melanie was shaking her head. "I really don't know."

"Look at the photograph." All of a sudden she scrambled up on to the high fender rail around the fireplace. She reached up on tiptoes and lifted the photo from its hook, hopping back down to lay it in Melanie's lap. "That's Alistair, of course, and that's his wife Jessie." An unsmiling woman, lath-thin and narrow-eyed, grimacing at the camera. "You saw their grave just now. The children—" she pointed to each in turn—"that's Struan, that's Gordon the eldest, little Dugald, and Cameron, just a baby then."

"All boys," Melanie said. She hadn't noticed that out among the graves. "No girls."

"All the boys bar Cameron were born in Scotland," Eilidh said. She hunkered down beside the chesterfield with the fire at her back, head pillowed on the padded leather arm. "They made the crossing with their parents, and amazingly none of them died along the way. But there was another child, one who's missing from that photo, conceived on the trail, born a few months after they reached their destination, just five short years before that photograph was taken. Eilidh—it runs in the family alongside madness and secrecy, it's the customary name for the first daughter—Eilidh's missing. Little Eilidh, the first Findlay born in the New World."

"The first-born of the flock. The little ewe-lamb," Melanie said. Connections were flashing like dry lightning on the horizon. "Oh no. No, he didn't."

"It was his understanding of what was necessary," Eilidh said. Her hand sought Melanie's own, tightened around it. "Those first few years were so hard, barely existing, scraping a living on alien soil, trying to build a new life out of nothing much, and always, always the fear of failure.

"You see, Alistair knew he couldn't ever return, there could be no journey back from here. He'd thrown the dice for the last time, and wherever it landed, that was where he had to stick, and make the best of it. There could be no second chance for them: if not here, then nowhere, if not then, never. Do

or die. And along with all that fear, the madness. Ever present, surging in his brain, bubbling like black water from a bad spring, like the stagnant waters of the Platte that made men sick and crazy when they sipped it, but Alistair? He was drinking deep; he was swimming in it. It was his element. Do you see?"

"He was totally crazy," Melanie was struggling to take it in, "and nobody stopped him?"

"Nobody stopped him," Eilidh confirmed. "He took little Eilidh to the well one afternoon in the springtime, and he came back alone. The birds had stopped singing, or so the story goes; everybody noticed it and wondered what was wrong. And in that silence Jessie asked him where their daughter was, and he told her.

"Imagine that tableau, Melanie. Imagine Jessie, knowing what Alistair had done, knowing too that no punishment would ever fall upon him in this life, that he would kill her too, kill all of them, before he let any outsider interfere with his little kingdom among the trees. She had four more children to think of, four more little hostages to fate. And so Eilidh was never spoken of again, and her death became the great and shameful secret of the Findlay family.

"And the family prospered from that point onwards. Lumber revenues doubled and doubled again and went through the roof, a tiny settlement on the bay became a city, and inside ten years Alistair Findlay's name was a byword in that city for industry and wealth. Within twenty years he was the richest man in the Seattle region bar old Henry Yesler. He and Yesler brought the railroad to Seattle, the Great Northern, and the railroad brought the people. Ten more years and the ground was broken for the building of this mansion right here, and Alistair lived on for another decade under its roof before he was gathered unto God, as it says on his gravestone. Long enough to found a dynasty; long enough to set down rules for his sons and his grandsons, to share the secret of his success with them and them alone.

"He made his sons promise to do just exactly as he had done, and at least one of them hated him for it, left the family home and never came back till he was in his coffin. In life poor Dugald might have loathed his father, but in death there was a space reserved for him at his side, and the family saw to it that it was filled, irrespective of Dugald's wishes. Gordon, though: he was his father's son, so totally under his influence that even as a child he'd accepted the necessity of Alistair's sacrifice. There was something about Gordon, his pale blue eyes, you didn't like to look at him for too long, or to have those eyes rest on you. Anyway, Gordon grew up and married, brought a wife back to the Findlay mansion, and once she fell pregnant, he spent a long time shut away with his father, talking late into the night.

"Gordon's first child was a girl, and he named her Eilidh, after his dear departed sister. Poor little Eilidh! She died, they said, of the Russian flu, but you won't find a grave out there in the cemetery. She's an afterthought on Gordon's stone, that's all, 'Eilidh, an infant'. That summer, the great fire of Seattle burned down every single wharf and mill from Union Street to Jackson, killed a million rats, or so they say. All that destruction, and not a stick of Findlay property was harmed, not one single shed. Coincidence? You be the judge.

"Gordon's second child, young Alistair Junior, fathered only boys, but there was another brother, James, who lived in Paris, where he married a dancer in the Folies Bergère. The society pages have her pregnant on departing France to meet the family in Seattle; after their return, the pregnancy is never mentioned again, but soon after the wife is placed under psychiatric care in a sanatorium on the Lac d'Annecy. Was it a girl? and if so, what became of her? Did they name her Eilidh as well? The great war and the depression leave the Findlay fortunes untouched, of course. The luck of the Findlays.

"The next generation perfected the art of concealment, and very little is known outside formal announcements in the births, deaths, and marriages sections of the papers. But I have my suspicions." Eilidh smiled, but there was no mirth in it. "So there you have it. Now you know our greatest secret. What do you think of us now, Melanie?"

Melanie didn't know what to say. She could barely sit still with excitement. This kind of story was career-changing, a blockbuster in the making: it would land like *In Cold Blood* or *The Death of a President*, it would put her on front pages and TV shows. Most importantly, it would make her a writer, for real this time, not a company hack, not a copy-poppy, but an author— a bestseller. It would complete her.

There was only one thing, and it wasn't a small thing, it was critical. Would Eilidh play ball? Melanie was acutely aware that everything she'd heard had been spoken in confidence between friends—not friends of long standing, either, the newest of acquaintances. At no time had Melanie asked her if she was speaking on the record; at no time had there been any suggestion that their tête-à-tête was for public consumption. All that Eilidh had told her had been meant to establish trust, she thought; and now the first thing she was thinking of was how to break that trust.

The only way she could see around it was to go in deeper: to keep Eilidh talking, to strengthen the bond between them to the point where she was no longer thinking like the daughter of the house, but as an independent woman, a free spirit like Melanie herself. To really become that friend to whom she could tell everything. Didn't she want it to come out, after all? Why else would she have confided in her?

"And all of this happened without any trace?" she wondered aloud. "There was never any evidence, nobody suspected?"

"We're a very private family," Eilidh said. "We're good at keeping secrets."

"It seems, I don't know, sort of impossible that nobody ever guessed."

"Guessed what?" Eilidh scoffed. "That the biggest fortune in Seattle was built on insanity and blood sacrifice?"

Despite herself, Melanie shuddered. "They can't have covered up every single clue."

"Maybe they didn't. Who knows what Dugald might have let slip, drinking himself to death in a New Orleans whorehouse?

Who knows what James's wife the dancer told the doctors at the sanatorium? But you'd need to know what you were looking for, even to begin to search, and you'd have to know where to look." Eilidh thought for a moment. "Take another look at the picture." She took Melanie's hand and traced with her finger the details in the failing afternoon light.

"That photograph doesn't tell the whole truth. Look close. Can you see where Dugald has his hand a little way out from his body? See how he looks kind of uncomfortable, not a natural sort of pose? Look here, alongside him, how there's a sort of blurriness to the background. As if they had it retouched, maybe; or maybe they didn't need to. Maybe it just faded away of its own accord."

"Was there someone there?" Melanie strained to see the detail. "Did they airbrush it out? Was someone holding his hand, someone who went missing from the photo?"

"Well, I can show you the answer to that as easy as tell you," Eilidh said. She took a spill from the fireside and lit the oil lamp in the hearth. "Would that suit?"

"Yes, of course," Melanie said eagerly.

"Come on, then." She was halfway up the steps to the raised dais, and Melanie had to hurry after her.

"Look," she said, pointing to the desk, holding the lamp so Melanie could see in the gloom. It was not a cluttered desk: there was a pewter penholder—in the shape of a well, Melanie saw with revulsion—a blotter bound in leather, and a framed photograph. At least, she assumed it was a photograph: it was hidden behind little folding wooden doors, facing the old man's high-backed leather chair.

"This is the original," Eilidh said, opening the wooden flaps. "They blew the other one up from this." There was the family grouping from the enlargement that hung above the fireplace, except that here Dugald's hand was not suspended in thin air. Here, it was holding the hand of a pale little girl, her face a blur beneath a wide summer bonnet. "There she is," Eilidh said. "The daughter of the house, the first-born."

"Oh, my, God..." Melanie stared at the photo open-mouthed. Before the truth of it had really sunk in, Eilidh had picked up the lamp and skipped down from the dais by the other set of steps. "Come along," she called, and Melanie followed after.

Eilidh was fiddling at the wooden paneling beneath the low railing that ran the length of the dais. Her free hand was searching up and down; there was a click, a creak, some movement of which Melanie caught only a glimpse before the panel swung back, revealing a door some four feet high and a dark space within, a hollow underneath the dais.

"Oh for Pete's sake," Melanie said, "not a secret chamber." It seemed just too perfect, too gloriously, gothically inevitable. She wondered whether someday her readers might assume she'd made it up for effect.

"*The* secret chamber," Eilidh corrected her. "The secret of the Findlays."

Melanie was choking with curiosity. "Well?" Eilidh prompted. "Aren't you going in?"

"You've got the light," Melanie objected.

"More of a surprise if you go first," Eilidh said, and giggled. It hadn't struck Melanie before, but she really was quite childish in some ways. And another thing: Eilidh wasn't nearly as tall as her, either. Shouldn't she have noticed that already? Her impression, her fancy, had been that they might have been sisters, non-identical twins. But maybe it was that high-ceilinged mausoleum of a room that made everybody look smaller; such high ceilings, and such a tiny door.

"Go on," Eilidh was saying. "You're not scared, are you?"

Uncertainly, Melanie moved past her into the doorway, the light of the oil lamp behind her. Stone steps, going down into darkness.

She had to duck a little as she descended: even for her, the way was low, and above her head was rough unfinished stone. Stone to right and to left, as well, so close that her outspread hands could touch it on either side, until it suddenly wasn't there anymore and the floor came up to meet her in that disconcerting trick of the very last step, making her gasp for breath and grope for support that wasn't there.

"Go *on*," the girlish voice behind her said. "Slowly does it. There aren't any more steps or anything." But there was a damp, mouldy smell, as if they'd lifted up a rock with some awful sort of rottenness underneath. Cold, too: a dismal cold, crawling and unhealthy, and a wetness that actually seemed to reach out and envelop her.

Melanie advanced one step, two steps, three steps. Just as she became totally unmoored from her surroundings, she stubbed her toe against a solid object and almost lost her balance. She grabbed at it with her outstretched hands, felt more rough stone, found what seemed to be the top of it, so it was maybe waist high at most. The smell was stronger now, much stronger. "Eilidh!" she shouted, and her voice echoed in the dark. "I need a light in here!"

And light came from behind her, from the top of the steps. The darkness resolved itself into deep shadows and half-glimpsed shapes: she was standing in a circular chamber maybe twelve feet across, its ceiling higher than the passageway but not much higher.

Now she could make out the thing she'd come hard up against. It was a well, a real honest-to-goodness well just like the one outside in the graveyard, just like the one in the photo.

"Here we are," Eilidh said, and somehow, instead of being behind Melanie, she was in front of her, the cold black maw of the well between them. Her voice sounded very thin and childlike; it carried a strange sort of resonance, as if it came from some reverberant depth. "Now you've seen nearly all our secrets." There was a musical inflection in her speech—was it a Scottish lilt? She rather thought it was.

"Is this—" Melanie's own voice came out high and cracked, and she had to try again— "is this the real well?"

"Of course," said girlish Eilidh. "This is the well that Daddy Findlay dug, to drown his little daughter in. The well of sacrifices. This is the source of all his wealth and power, and he built his house around it, he couldn't bear not to be near it. He loved his well, much more than he loved his daughter —I think he might have been a little afraid of her, in the end. What she'd become.

"Every day he used to come down here; he'd get up off his throne and come down the steps into the well-chamber and stand right where you are now, looking down into the dark water, where he'd cast his little Eilidh. I can see him now, leaning over the edge, dropping pennies just to hear them plop. It can't have been for luck, can it, because he already had all the luck in the world, the luck of the devil. I think perhaps it was an offering to the spirits of the well, a guarantee that Eilidh would stay put, that she wouldn't come out. He wanted her in there forever.

"And guess what? Poor little Eilidh had got so lonely down there that she became glad to see him, almost. The sight of his face was better than nothing, better than the darkness and the cold and the wet. Even when they brought her company, her little niece, her great-niece, it was still such a lonely place to be."

"But she was dead," Melanie protested.

"She was that," the little-girl voice agreed.

Though Melanie's own shadow obscured her view, it was plain to see that this wasn't the grown woman who'd met her at the gates, who'd been talking to her just minutes before in the study. The figure on the far side of the well was no taller than a child, and it spoke with the voice, not of a woman, but a girl, a little Scottish girl.

"And when Daddy Findlay finally died, nobody came to visit the well, and nobody was there to stand watch in his study, and so Eilidh—the other girls too, not just poor Eilidh by this time, all the little Findlay lambs—they found that if they were quiet, and picked their times, they could sneak out of hiding, just for a little while. They couldn't go far from the house, and they could never go beyond the gates, but by then they didn't really want to. The well was their only home. It still is. They've become accustomed to it, bless their souls," the little figure said in an eerie singsong, leaning over the edge of the well. Her tiny voice set an echo ringing in the depths. Or was it an echo?

Out of nowhere it occurred to Melanie: *where's the light coming from?* She swung around, expecting to see modern-day Eilidh, her Eilidh, standing at the top of the passage, holding up the lamp, showing a way back to sanity.

But instead there was Mrs. Seale, firm and implacable, the lamp outstretched in her hand, and the way was everlastingly blocked.

"Shut the door, Sealey," the voice from the well commanded. "Quickly, lock her in." And giggled, and all the voices in the well giggled too as the paneling slammed back into place and everything was swallowed up in dark.

Steve Duffy lives and works in North Wales. His most recent collection of weird stories, The Faces At Your Shoulder, *was published by Sarob Press in 2023; he's already in the process of putting together his next. Steve was the winner of the International Horror Guild's award for Best Short Story 2000, and in 2015 he received the Shirley Jackson Award for Best Novelette.*

Get Away

All arrangements made by your local travel agent **RAY CLULEY**

Calvin tried to enjoy the morning breeze coming in from the Indian **Ocean.** He tried to enjoy the view: the unblemished sky; the water that went from brochure-blue to turquoise to entirely clear as it neared the pier. It lapped at the stilts beneath and passed under his feet to move slowly through the shallows and up the white sands of the shore, where palm trees waved him to their shade.

The Maldives. Every bit as beautiful as it had looked online.

Their overwater bungalow was one of only a dozen at this particular resort, each of them thatched and connected by a single long pier curving out from the island to give an uninterrupted view of the ocean. The beautifully clear, beautifully gentle, ocean. It reflected the morning sun in spectacular dazzles and flashes as slow waves rose and then fell, but Calvin's attention was suddenly caught by a more specific blink of light.

There it was again.

He moved down their private deck, looking for what it might be. From his new position he could see across to one of the other bungalows where a woman rested against the railings of her own deck. She appeared to be scanning the water for something, too. She moved up and down the walkway, sometimes leaning over to look down at where the sea passed under her feet. Perhaps she'd seen some interesting fish. Or perhaps she'd seen something else, flashing in the light, as Calvin had.

As if she'd sensed being watched, the woman looked up and saw Calvin.

She was an attractive woman, about his age but looking better with it. She wore a kimono over a colorful one-piece swimsuit. Calvin waved and she waved back. It was friendly, but not the hello that his had been: she went back inside.

Calvin turned his attention back to the sea, unbuttoning his linen shirt to catch some of the cool air before the day warmed up. Later he'd need to slather himself with lotion, but he'd wait until Nina mentioned it. He disliked the oiliness on his skin, and how it made his bald head shine.

There. That winking flash again. Something bobbing in the water, catching the light.

A bottle.

He was surprised to see it. A lot of the world's oceans were polluted, of course, but the resort had been remarkably clean. Pristine, even, as you'd expect of paradise.

And yet there was another one.

And there.

Bottles.

Dozens of bottles.

They were lifting with each wave, then bobbing back down again as the wave dipped, held in tidal limbo. It looked like there was a curl of paper inside each one.

With little more thought, Calvin went to the steps leading into the sea and descended. It was cold at first, shaded by the pier, and he sucked in a sharp breath as the chill clutched at his thighs and higher until, in a moment of sudden bravery, he dunked under completely, washing away the remaining fug of sleep and a hangover. Then, wading further out, his wet shirt billowing around him like the bell of a jellyfish, he made towards one of the bottles.

It was clear glass, with no sign of ever having had a label. The rolled note inside was protected from the sea by a screw-top lid that had never been cracked open. Calvin twisted the lid where he stood and tipped the paper to his palm. He dropped the bottle

and with wet hands unfurled the note.

I hope you're okay with me contacting you like this. We should meet up for a drink or something and talk about what happened. I understand it might feel awkward, but I think it could be good for us, for everyone, *if we talk about it...*

"What?"

He looked around for someone, saw no one, and read it again.

I hope you're okay with me contacting you like this...

"What the *hell*?"

He recovered the bottle bobbing beside him and emptied it of seawater as he searched for another. The water was so clear that he could see the flitting shapes of fish and his feet in the sand, but he could not see any other bottles. Not a single one.

There had been so many of them a moment ago.

He tucked the note back inside its bottle and made his way back to the bungalow to look again from a higher position.

He found the woman from the neighboring bungalow waiting for him.

"What did you see?"

She was British, her accent one Calvin associated with money. Closer now, she looked exhausted, like she hadn't slept much lately, either. She was holding her kimono closed with crossed arms.

"I saw you looking," she told him.

Calvin apologized. "I didn't mean—"

"You were looking at the water. What did you see?"

Calvin wondered what was wrong, why she was asking. He wondered what she might have seen herself.

"Bottles," he said. "With notes inside."

He expected some understanding in her expression, perhaps some relief at having seen the same thing, but instead she frowned.

"You didn't see the jellyfish?"

"Jellyfish?"

"Yes," she said. "The ocean's ghosts."

Calvin shook his head. "No. No, I just saw bottles." He remembered he was holding one and showed it to her, tipping the note out to show her that as well, though he didn't unroll it for her to read.

"Sandra!" a French man called from the woman's bungalow. "I have made breakfast!"

But the woman, Sandra, was already retreating from Calvin.

"They have my mother's face," she said.

She wiped a tear from her eye and forced a smile before heading back.

The French man waved at Calvin, and Calvin raised his hand to wave back. It still held the note he'd found.

I hope you're okay with me contacting you like this...

He was about to take another walk around the bungalow to see if there were more when the glass doors behind him slid open—

"There you are."

—and Nina emerged with two glasses of strikingly bright orange juice, a large slice of fruit clinging to the rim of the glass. She handed one to Calvin as he pocketed the note.

"Our own little sunrise," she said.

"As in, tequila?"

She laughed. "Sorry. Just juice." She noticed he was wet. "Morning swim?"

He nodded. "Trying to wake up."

She clinked her drink to his and stood beside him at the railing. She was wearing one of his shirts, unbuttoned to show off her bikini beneath. It was as strikingly bright as their drinks.

"Do you like it?" she asked him.

Calvin looked away and attempted a sip of his drink. He flinched from the protruding garnish, plucked the orange slice away, and took a long, deep mouthful. "Yes," he said. "Very nice."

"I meant the bikini."

Nina stepped away and spread the shirt open to give him a slow turn, lifting the shirt at the back.

"Very nice," he said again.

It was enough.

Nina nudged in close. "It's so beautiful here, don't you think?" She gave a hesitant smile, looked as if she might say something else, then gave up on both and linked her arm with his. She rested her head against his shoulder and looked with him out to sea. "I love you," she said.

Calvin squeezed her arm then kissed the top of her head, but that was all.

"The Maldives is made up of more than one thousand, two hundred islands," Nina read from her phone. "It's an...archy-pelar-go? Arki-pella-go?"

"Ark-a-pell-a-go," Calvin said. "It's a group of islands."

"An archipelago of some twenty-six atolls..." She glanced at him.

"Ring-shaped reefs or islands."

"Thank you. Twenty-six atolls with a tropical monsoon climate and—"

"Neen?"

"And I should put my phone down and just enjoy it." She smiled at him and put the phone on the table between them before lying back into her lounger. She no longer wore Calvin's shirt, just her bikini. She'd unfastened the straps to tan her shoulders.

"The bikini was named after an atoll," Calvin said.

"Yeah?"

"Bikini Atoll. It's where they tested atomic bombs. Whoever invented it—the bikini—thought it would have the same kind of impact. Metaphorically speaking."

She squinted at him, shielding her eyes with one hand when her sunglasses were right there in her hair. "Do you want me to put some more lotion on?"

"Well, I did enjoy watching the last time."

It was a joke that surprised them both, but whereas Nina responded with a grateful smile, Calvin chose to add, "I think everyone enjoyed it," and Nina's smile faded.

They'd given up the privacy of their deck for the patio and beach of the small island's bar because Nina liked the infinity pool and Calvin liked the cocktails. It wasn't a coping mechanism if you were on holiday. Besides, there were quite a few other couples enjoying the cocktails, too. Most of them were Calvin's age or even a little older, but a few were in Nina's range. The women were as preened and perfect as magazine advertisements, while the men looked like they'd stepped straight out of a gym or an action movie. Calvin had watched them watch Nina as she applied lotion to her body.

"I meant do you want me to put some

more lotion on *you*." She shook the bottle at him, then flipped the lid open. "Come on," she said, beckoning, "bow to your queen."

Calvin tipped his head and Nina rubbed lotion into his scalp. It was cool on his skin. "You've caught a little sun," she said.

"Yeah."

"How's the view?"

Bowing towards her, his view was entirely cleavage, but all he said was, "You've caught a bit, too."

She leaned away from him and adjusted the cups of her bikini to see. "Bit pink," she agreed, and rubbed in the leftover lotion from her hands.

Calvin looked for who else might be watching.

"You know, we could always go back to bed for a bit," Nina suggested.

But Calvin settled into the comfort of his lounger. He closed his eyes. The leaves of the palm trees leaning over them whispered in the breeze while barely-there waves washed up the nearby shore with a soft, lullaby hush.

"Cal?"

"Mm?"

"We don't have to sleep."

It was almost too late for Calvin. The bar's quiet music, and the palm leaves, the sea, were combining with the heat of the sun to ease him into drowsy peace.

It was a man's voice that startled him awake.

"Nina! Hello!"

Calvin was suddenly alert—he knew exactly who this would be—but the bronzed man in the bulging Speedos wasn't anyone Calvin knew, just as the French accent should have told him, but he was still standing so close to Nina's lounger that it was practically foreplay.

"Cal," she said, leaning around the man. "This is…"

"Jacques," the man said, and stepped aside to face Calvin with an apology. He sat on the edge of a vacant lounger beside them and offered his hand to shake. His grip was too firm.

"We just met," Nina said.

Calvin had sort of met him, too. He'd called over to Sandra about—

jellyfish

—breakfast.

"He kayaked past our bungalow when you were in the shower," Nina explained.

Jacques pointed at the bungalows. "I am over there. One, two, three from you."

"Yes," Calvin said, though he didn't look.

"Did you enjoy the kayaking?" Nina asked.

"Yes, very much! There are so many beautiful fish."

"Sounds nice."

"What kind of fish?" Calvin asked.

Jacques shrugged.

"Groupers? Fusiliers? Batfish?"

"You are a fish expert!" Jacques declared. "They were blue and yellow, like this." He mimed with his hands, one color above the other.

"Fusiliers," Calvin said.

"You like fish? Do you dive?"

"We do," Nina answered.

"Ah. You will love it here, there are so many fish, and there are sea turtles, and rays. Manta rays?" He made floaty waving motions with both hands. "And there are sharks." He made a fin of his hands over his head.

Nina was appropriately shocked— "Sharks?"—and Jacques laughed.

"Most of the time, they are not dangerous."

"Most of the time," Nina repeated, and Jacques laughed again. He was a happy man, this Jacques. He made another hand-fin, adding the theme from *Jaws*. This time Nina laughed with him.

"Are you going kayaking again now?" Calvin asked.

Jacques turned his smile on Calvin and said, "No, not today." Then he saw someone over Calvin's shoulder and stood, calling, *"Viens ici mon amour!* We are here!" before beckoning to someone who had just arrived at the bar.

It was the woman Calvin had seen that morning. Sandra. She was wearing the same one-piece swimsuit but with a flowery sarong wrapped around her waist now instead of the kimono and a large sunhat keeping her face shaded.

She waved as she approached.

"This is Sandra," Jacques said, and greeted her with a kiss before completing the introductions, adding, "Calvin likes fish."

"Have you been to the shipwreck?" Sandra asked him.

"No shipwrecks," Calvin said.

"We just arrived," Nina explained.

"Oh, you *must* see it. There's all this beautiful, colorful coral, and so many stunning fish. Butterfly fish and damsels and—"

"Sharks," Jacques said again, hands in a fin once more to menace Nina.

"What about eels?" Calvin asked. "They can be territorial. They bite."

Jacques snaked his arms together and turned the shark fin of his hands into a snapping mouth that he clapped at Calvin. Calvin flinched.

"Okay!" Jacques said. "Drinks!"

"They seemed nice," Nina said.

The sky had deepened to indigo for their slow walk back to the bungalow, the surf an ongoing sigh beside them. They were carrying their sandals, the evening sand cool beneath their feet, and occasionally Nina pulled them to the water's edge to enjoy how the wet sand squeezed between their toes. Calvin watched the footprints they left behind fill with water and disappear in the emerging moonlight. The moon was bright and low and full, and it prompted Nina to sing a quiet line about pizza pie from *That's Amore*. She was clinging to Calvin's arm with both of hers, leaning against him.

"Do you really want to go diving with them tomorrow?" she asked. "Or were you just being polite?"

"Why? Don't you want to?"

"No, it's fine, it'll be fun. It's just..."

"Just what?"

Nina waited a moment. Calvin thought he knew what she was going to talk about, and he dreaded it, but she proved him wrong when she asked, "Did Sandra tell you her mother died?"

Ghosts of the ocean, he thought.

"That's sad," he said. "Recently?"

"I don't know. But time goes a bit funny when someone dies, doesn't it? It probably feels recent."

Calvin agreed.

"She said Jacques works a lot, like you do, but they came out here so she could get away from everything for a bit. I just don't want to get in the way of their holiday. Like, maybe they should spend this time together."

"They invited us," Calvin reminded her, trying not to bristle at her comment about work.

They were approaching the pier. The lights beneath the railings were on, casting a glow across the boards, and lanterns at the walkways to each bungalow cast their light onto the sea in beautiful halos, gentle wavetop nimbuses reflected and diffused by the motion of the ocean.

"So beautiful," said Nina, and tried, "So romantic."

She pulled Calvin to a stop and kissed him. Calvin felt her tongue briefly just before he pulled away.

"Let's get inside," he said.

Nina nodded, her eyes as bright as the lantern light. "Yes."

She took his hand, pulling Calvin from their stroll into something more urgent.

"What's the rush?"

"Come *on*."

Buoyed by the alcohol and the atmosphere, and for a moment remembering only how they used to be, Calvin let her lead him. They were almost running. It felt good to be running *towards* something.

At the walkway to their bungalow, though, a dazzle of light on the water caught Calvin's eye. He stopped abruptly and Nina's hand was surprised out of his by the sudden halt.

"What is it?" she asked.

Calvin leaned to look but saw only the dark, vague shapes of fish zigzagging beneath their feet.

"Cal?"

"Just a moment."

There.

No.

There.

Nina was at his side again, taking his hand.

"There's a bottle," Calvin said, pointing. Could it be the same one as before?

"Where?"

"There. See it? I think there's a note inside."

Nina laughed—"A note?"—but she at least pretended to look with him.

"It's right there," said Calvin, pointing. "Look."

But it wasn't. It was gone.

"Stop teasing," Nina said, and again she led him back towards the bungalow. She paused at the door. "Wait here. I have something special to show you." She kissed him again, a quick one, and went inside, saying, "I'll call you in when I'm ready."

Calvin went to the deck's railing and scoured the water for the bottle he'd seen, wondering at the message it might hold. He checked the whole perimeter but all he saw in the water was the silvery light of the moon.

He checked again.

He checked a third time.

A light came on at one of the other bungalows. Sandra's, he realized, because there she was outside, looking at the water from her decking just like him. He waved but this time she didn't see him. Jacques came out to her and the two of them exchanged a few words before Jacques went back inside with a dramatically dismissive gesture. Sandra waited a moment, then followed.

Trouble in paradise, Calvin thought.

He returned his attention to the sea, but despite another thorough search, followed by another, he found nothing.

By the time he went back inside, Nina was asleep on the bed, curled on her side. She was wearing something diaphanous over lingerie he'd never seen before, and he could tell from what remained of her makeup that she'd been crying.

CALVIN WOKE in one of the hammocks on the deck. The sun was shining directly into his eyes. Blinking away the glare, it took him a moment to see Nina standing in the light.

"What time is it?" he asked her.

"Still early. You slept here all night?"

He sat up and put his feet on the deck before the hammock could toss him out. "Must've done. Sorry."

She said nothing.

"You look nice," Calvin said.

She was wearing a halter twist bikini top and short shorts that sat low on her hips to show the ties of her bikini briefs. A flowy black cover up completed the ensemble. It was a seemingly modest outfit, especially compared to what she'd worn yesterday, but the sheer black of the loose cover up actually seemed to draw *more* attention to what she didn't wear beneath. Much like the lacey thing she'd worn over lingerie last night.

"There's some orange juice there for you," Nina said, pointing to the table. No slice of sunrise this time, but he was grateful.

"Thanks. My mouth is all sand."

"It's the last of it, but I'm off to pick up a few things so I'll get some more."

"I'll come with you."

"No. You stay and wake up properly. I won't be long." She hesitated, then added, "I've left my phone."

Calvin slapped at her behind as she turned to go. It was meant to be a playful apology for abandoning her last night, but he accidentally struck a little too hard, which surprised them both. He was even more surprised by the noise she made, and the excited way she looked at him.

"When I get back," she said, and smiled a bright smile, and he knew he was forgiven. There was hope in that smile.

She took it with her, leaving Calvin to hydrate and take in the view.

He rubbed sleep and sunlight from his eyes, blinking into the morning. He examined the criss-cross marks in his skin from the hammock netting, the rope lines and knot marks, and he thought about the way Nina had just sort of squealed, just sort of sighed, when spanked. What else did she like? Either she was still something of a stranger to him, or she had become one.

He guzzled half of the orange juice and carried the rest with him as he walked the perimeter of the bungalow, trying to clear his mind. Wisps of cloud striped the sky at the horizon, but the sun was shining, and the water twinkled little signals that flashed like Morse code and—

Yes.

There.

And there.

More of them, each with a message demanding his attention.

He tried to ignore them but knew he wouldn't manage for long.

WHEN NINA RETURNED, she was with another man. Calvin was waiting on the deck, watching for her, and at the sight of them both he thought: it's him.

It wasn't.

The man was helping Nina carry her loaded beach-bag between them. He was middle-aged, younger than Calvin and a little heavier. His chest and arms were silver-haired and tattooed. He saw Calvin looking and gestured Nina's attention towards him. Nina waved with her free hand.

"Here he is," she said, as they neared the walkway, "my sleepyhead husband."

Calvin gave a curt nod.

The other man handed Nina her bag as she said to Calvin, "Honey, didn't you say this resort was adults only?"

"No kids allowed," Calvin confirmed.

The man with Nina sighed. "I'm going to have to put in a complaint, then."

"David's in the one just over," Nina told Calvin, pointing to the next bungalow. "There were kids running up and down the pier all night, yelling and screaming."

"And we came here to get away from all that," David said.

"Of course," said Calvin.

"You got kids?"

Calvin shook his head. Nina said, "Not yet."

"Don't. That's my advice. I love mine, I do, but just...don't."

Calvin wondered if the man regretted his chest tattoo as well; two baby faces smiling over where his heart beat. Darren and Skye, according to the scrollwork.

"Did you hear them, honey?" Nina asked. To David she explained, "He slept on the deck last night, under the stars."

"Slept right through," Calvin said.

"Yeah, my wife too, both nights. She thinks I dreamt it."

"You got the orange juice there, Neen?"

"Yeah." She hefted the bag, and took the prompt, telling David, "It was nice meeting you. I hope you get a better sleep tonight."

"Yeah, me too." He saluted them. "Enjoy your dive."

Calvin stood aside for Nina to pass and considered slapping her behind again to hear the noise she'd make. He wondered what other noises she made he hadn't heard yet and when she might have made them last.

"You excited about it?" she asked.

"Excited?"

Nina slid the door open and said, "Diving." She headed towards the fridge with the provisions she'd picked up. "With Jacques and Sandra."

When she turned to look at him, Calvin was standing in the lounge area. It was a large space with comfortable white cushions on wicker sofas and an open section in the floor offering direct access to the water below. There was a glass table next to this, and Calvin gestured to it with both hands. He'd lined up all the bottles he'd retrieved from the sea, a note rolled inside each one.

"Look what I found."

Nina frowned.

"What do you mean, found?"

She went to the table and picked up her phone.

"I told you I'd left it," she said, unlocking the screen. "Did you check it?"

"What? No."

"Because you can keep checking if that's what it takes." She offered the phone to him.

"I don't need to."

"Good," she said, "because there's nothing to check." But still she offered the phone, and so he took it.

"I don't need to check because it's all in the notes."

"What notes?"

"The notes," he said, "the Goddamn notes, in the Goddamn bottles!"

Nina didn't look at the notes or the bottles. She only looked at Calvin.

"Stop shouting at me."

Calvin growled in frustration and threw Nina's phone to the table. He missed, though, and it flew straight through the floor and into the sea.

"Thank you," Nina said. "That's great." She went back to the fridge, thrusting items away. "I guess you won't be checking anything now."

She was close to tears.

"I hope you're okay with me contacting you like this," Calvin recited.

Her tears came then.

"Don't," she said.

"We should meet up for a drink or something and talk about what happened."

"Please don't."

"I understand it might feel awkward, but I think it could be good for us, for *everyone* —that bit was underlined, I suppose he meant me—good for *everyone* if we talk about it. So, let's talk about it, shall we?"

Nina stood with her head bowed, hand still on the open door of the fridge. "Again?" she said, quietly. "Shall we talk about it again?"

"Humor me."

She closed the fridge to face him. "I'm sorry, Cal, I'm really sorry, and I've said I'm sorry *so* many times. Please believe me. It was one time, and—"

"No, it wasn't."

"Yes. It was."

"He was very explicit about how many times, if I remember the rest of the message correctly."

For a moment, he was thrilled to see that hurt her.

"One night, then," she said, crying. "But it was a stupid mistake, a *huge* mistake, and I told him that, and then I told you, and I never spoke to him again, or messaged, or anything. Please, Cal. We've talked about this. We're here to get away from it all, aren't we?"

He let her cry and watched for a while, hoping her tears would stir something in him beyond…whatever it was he was feeling. Or not feeling. He didn't know anymore. Everything he used to feel had been blasted away. Nina's tears were just a familiar part of the fallout.

She was crying so hard now that she hitched for breath and snipped her words.

"You keep…keep saying…we're going to…going to be…okay."

He did keep saying that. He was trying to persuade himself it was true.

Looking at her sobbing, all the anger suddenly drained away, and Calvin only felt hollow again.

"It *is* okay," he decided. It was the only lie he kept telling her.

"We'll be okay," he said. He wasn't sure about that one, but he said it anyway because he hated to see her cry—most of the time, he hated to see her cry—and he didn't know how else to comfort her.

"We better get ready," he said.

Nina nodded, but otherwise didn't move except to wipe her tears.

When Calvin came out from the shower, buttoning a fresh shirt, Nina's phone was sitting on the table in a bowl of couscous that had plumped up around it. A substitute for rice, he supposed, though the phone was likely beyond saving. Some broken things could never be fixed.

Nina was outside on the deck. She'd stripped down to her bikini to retrieve the phone and was drying herself under the sun.

Calvin looked back from Nina to the table and her phone in the swollen couscous and realized all of the bottles were gone. If she had thrown them back into the water, they were nowhere he could see, and maybe that was for the best.

THEY MET WITH Sandra and Jacques and rather than pay for a guided dive they rented a boat and diving gear between them. "We've already done it," Sandra said. "We can show you."

"For only a fraction of the price," Jacques joked, reaching as if to take money. He was attempting to break some of the obvious tension, Calvin realized. Not just between him and Nina: there was something brittle between Jacques and Sandra, as well. It wasn't long, though, before the four of them were bumping over waves that turned into spray as they sped towards the hidden wreck, the boat's engine too loud for any conversation, and by the time Jacques slowed them to a stop, much of the tension had been swept away by the exhilaration of the boat trip.

"From here we will swim," Jacques said, and they focused on the process of gearing up and checking each other's equipment. When they were ready for the water, each was abuzz with excitement.

"*Suis-moi!*" Jacques cried, then jumped. He hit the water feet first, body ramrod straight, hands at his mask.

Calvin and Nina took a less dramatic

approach and rolled backwards together, tanks leading them into the sea.

It was a different world below the boat, a full rainbow of colors teeming with life—"Like swimming in an aquarium," Nina would say later—and they took turns pointing out one fish after another: beautifully chevroned triggerfish; striped sweetlips; clownfish. There were so many, it was breathtaking. They saw giant clams, too, more iridescent in color than either of them had imagined, gathered like a flowerbed in the ocean. A majestic manta ray sifted the seabed for food. They even glimpsed an octopus, but it swept up a sandy cloud to hide itself, blending its colors into camouflage. There was an anxious moment when Nina swam too close to the fan-like fins of a lionfish, but Calvin guided her away. He would explain later about the venomous spines hidden within its flowing mane.

Yet as varied and vibrant as it all was initially, as they neared the hulk of the wreck the environment began to change. The previously colorful coral paled, colors fading so that before long they were swimming amongst a landscape that was only ghostly white. It was a strange development and unexpected. Even Sandra and Jacques seemed surprised, judging by their body language. Sandra looked back at Calvin and Nina as if to gauge their reaction. Jacques swept his arms wide, all encompassing, as if to say check this out, before giving an elaborate shrug.

Rising out of the white like it was mired in hoary frost was the dark bulk of the wrecked vessel. It was as if the ship had been caught by the coral, trapped in a vast, spindly spider's web that clutched it to the ocean floor. Large sections of the ship were missing. Rust-crusted beams leaned and curved in skeletal shapes. Spaces gaped, vacant. Nothing moved. It was a metal net that trapped only shadows. Calvin had expected to see fish flitting in and out of the ruin, but the bright assortment of life they had passed through earlier was entirely absent.

A sudden flurry of movement beside him startled Calvin.

Sandra was thrashing.

She kicked her legs and swept at the water with both arms, trying to propel herself backwards, and Calvin's first thought was: shark!

He scanned the area on full alert, searching for the silver-grey streak of a sleek body threading through the darkness of the wreck. Openings in the vessel that should have been enticing now filled him with dread. He saw no danger, though. Only Jacques, oblivious, passing over the bleached field of coral, and Nina, wide-eyed in her face mask, hand at her mouth as if to hold the respirator in place.

Calvin pulled at the water and kicked to where Sandra was swatting at nothing, slap-boxing in a panic that would have her hyperventilating if she wasn't already. He checked around them again for danger, checked for sharks, for moray eels, for the translucent tendrils of—

the ocean's ghosts

—a jellyfish, but there was nothing that he could see. He thought, narcosis. But they weren't deep enough for that. Something wrong with her oxygen? He put himself in front of her to show there was no danger. He held his hands up to calm her.

But then Jacques was suddenly there as well. He shoved Calvin and made to do so again, thinking him the source of Sandra's fear, but she grabbed his arm and shook her head, ending the ridiculous underwater tussle before it could begin, and calming herself in the process. Calvin made an okay at her and she nodded, eventually giving the okay back and nodding some more. She gave the same to Jacques, but then pointed up and back the way they'd come. She turned on the spot and finned for the boat.

Jacques followed, patting Calvin's shoulder as he passed.

Nina was sweeping her arms wide and slow-kicking to keep herself in place. She, too, made the okay but Calvin couldn't return it.

Behind Nina, coral sprouted from the wreck's remains like white mould from something rotten.

BACK IN THE BOAT, Sandra tried to dismiss the entire incident. "I thought I saw something," was all she said as they stripped of diving gear. "I feel silly now."

Calvin and Nina let it go at that, comforting her when necessary, but Jacques persisted with his questions, even speaking to her hurriedly in French at one point, which she ignored entirely. Some of the earlier tension of the morning crept back.

"What was with the coral?" Nina asked, trying to steer the subject away.

"Coral bleaching," Calvin said.

"Like, pollution?"

"It happens when the ocean gets too warm."

"El Niño," Jacques said, the Spanish sounding strange with a French accent. "Only it was not this color a few days ago."

"It was all alive," Sandra said.

Jacques nodded. "I do not think El Niño happens so quickly."

Calvin remembered reading that the Maldives had suffered a bad El Niño a few years ago that destroyed something like ninety percent of its coral, and it took a long time to recover. If it hadn't been for the wreck, he would have simply assumed Sandra and Jacques had taken them to the wrong location.

Suddenly Jacques said, "Nina! There is La Niña, too!"

"Yay me!"

"But it is when the sea is cold."

"That's all right," said Calvin, "because then El Niño comes, and she is warm again."

He was trying to maintain the levity Jacques was using to lighten the mood but something about what he'd said or the way he'd said it seemed to sour the attempt, at least judging by Nina's reaction.

"Warm?" said Jacques. "She is hot!"

Nina laughed. She struck an exaggerated modeling pose.

"Yes, she is too hot to be La Niña," Jacques decided, and gave Calvin a thumbs up as if he had achieved something.

"Can we go back now, please?" Sandra said. "I need a drink."

"But of course!"

To Calvin and Nina, Sandra said, "Please say you'll join us?"

Nina, eager to keep the mood light, said, "But of course!" with the same accent and enthusiasm as Jacques, who laughed.

Sandra only smiled and looked overboard as Jacques started the boat engine.

She watched the water the whole way back to the island.

BACK AT THE BAR, after a drink, Sandra confided to Calvin that she had seen another jellyfish.

Nina and Jacques were in the pool. Nina had disrobed to her bikini immediately, wading in, and Jacques had called to the others in the water, "Watch out! La Niña is coming!" She'd splashed him. He'd splashed her back.

As they frolicked, Sandra said, "Thank you for trying to help me back there."

Calvin toasted her with his drink. He didn't want to say anything else about the incident in case it embarrassed or upset her, but she said, "I thought I saw a jellyfish."

"Well, that would panic me a bit, too."

She gave him a tight smile, and he thought that might be all, but after a long moment of silence between them, disturbed only by the banter in the pool, Sandra spoke again.

"We went out to that wreck three days ago. On one of those guided dives. I think we told you?"

Calvin nodded.

"The guide told us about all the things we might see, and afterwards all the things we *had* seen, and it was him who called jellyfish the ocean's ghosts. He only meant because they're see-through, I think, and because of how they move, but it sounded quite poetic, and it stuck with me. Then I started seeing them everywhere."

Calvin thought of bottles, winking at him from the sun-dazzled sea.

"Not just jellyfish. Ghosts. Because all of them, every jellyfish..."

They have my mother's face, Calvin remembered.

"Ah, shit," Sandra said, and wiped at new tears.

Into the awkward silence, Calvin said, "I'm sorry about your mother."

Sandra said, "Thank you. Me too. But it doesn't help much, does it?"

No, Calvin thought, looking to where Nina and Jacques played in the pool. Because sorry never changes anything.

"I thought going there today with you two, things would be different. I thought it might stop me seeing…anything strange. And it worked, at first. Now I can't even bring myself to look at the pool in case it's full of jellyfish. In case my mother's face is there, floating in the water."

What Calvin saw was a pool full of bottles. Nina was waist-deep in them, glistening wet at the far end of the pool, staring from its infinity to a horizon Calvin couldn't see.

THE WIND PICKED UP in the afternoon until it was no longer a gentle breeze that stirred the palm leaves and by early evening they were thrashing against each other violently. Lines of sand began snaking up the beach, striking the low wall of the patio to be cast up like spindrifts that had everybody poolside blinking or putting their sunglasses back on despite the fading light.

Jacques suggested to Sandra that they go back to the bungalow, but she argued it was too early and accused him of using the weather as an excuse to get some work done, so they stayed and tried to put up with it, repositioning their loungers out of the wind. It wasn't long, though, before they admitted defeat.

"It's not supposed to be like this," Nina said.

"No," said Calvin, meaning more than the weather.

"Are you staying?" Sandra asked.

"We'll try a bit longer," Calvin said, but soon the wind was strong enough to scatter furniture and he and Nina left as well, retreating while staff hurried to retrieve parasols and joked, "Monsoon!" It wasn't yet the season but remembering the coral that had bleached itself dead in a matter of days, Calvin thought: time goes a bit funny when something dies.

At the pier, with less need to shield themselves from the sand, the change in the weather was more tolerable, and the wind, blocked by some of the bungalows, less ferocious. There was more chop in the water beneath their feet, though. Calvin could hear all the bottles in it, clinking together.

"It'll be good to get inside," Nina said, and Calvin agreed, but at the walkway to their bungalow, he stopped.

"You go," he said. "I'll be back in a few minutes."

Nina said, "No," as if she didn't believe him. "No, Calvin." Then, "Calvin, please."

"It's okay," he said, the lie he kept trying to make true. "I'm only going to the end of the pier."

"I'll come with you."

"No, you go in. Put that new lingerie on again."

Nina hesitated.

"I promise I won't sleep in the hammock."

She still didn't move, but she let her hand slip limp from his. "Please stay," she said, quietly, but Calvin pretended not to hear and walked away.

He pretended not to hear the bottles, either, bumping against each other under the pier. Instead, he felt for the one in his pocket. It was a tonic bottle he'd pocketed from the bar, and inside was a rolled napkin he'd written on.

"Jesus *Christ*," someone called, "just go to *bed!*"

The shout came from one of the other bungalows.

"Darren! Skye! *Shut* the *hell up!*"

Calvin looked around as if there may have been a couple of children he hadn't noticed running up and down the pier and he saw Sandra, standing in the glow of her bungalow's welcome lantern. She was leaning on the railing, facing the wind with a drink in hand. "Long time no see," she joked.

"You okay?"

She gave him a sad smile. "Just chatting with my mum." She nodded at the water, but Calvin didn't look to see what she might mean.

From behind him came another cry for Darren and Skye to be quiet.

"No one else can hear them," Sandra said. "They're like the jellyfish, I expect. Or your bottles." She raised her glass and drank.

"Where's Jacques?"

"On the phone to work, apparently."

She gestured behind and Calvin saw Jacques in the bungalow, pacing. He was talking with some urgency, phone pressed to his ear. When he noticed Calvin he raised a hand in hello, then switched ears with the phone.

Except it wasn't a phone.

"On the way back, he saw a message in the wet sand," Sandra explained, "asking him to call."

Jacques was holding a large shell to his ear, talking into a conch and listening to whatever came back.

Calvin looked behind at his own bungalow and saw Nina in silhouette, standing at the glass.

"She'll start to think we're having an affair or something," Sandra said, and smiled to show she was joking, that she couldn't ever compare to someone like Nina, but why not? Maybe he should kiss her right now. Maybe he should take her right there against the railings. Jacques probably wouldn't even notice; he was so caught up in…whatever he was doing.

"You okay, Calvin?"

He mumbled something that was both an embarrassed apology and a hasty goodbye and resumed his walk to the end of the pier, looking to the horizon.

A line of cloud was rolling in, a hurrying dark upon the dark. There was so much of it, tumbling over itself in its hurry to reach the island, that it looked like a special effect from a film, and as he watched, the clouds lit up with a pulse of lightning so bright it seemed to flicker through everything, through the whole world, before it was gone.

Calvin wished the past could be gone so quickly, but the past lingered. It didn't disappear like footprints in wet sand. It was more like a shipwreck, hidden beneath the surface, rotting on the ocean floor and casting ruined pieces of itself back upon the shore. It was the tide itself, the to-and-fro of eroding waves, wearing Calvin down to his bleached bone core.

Another bright flash scattered beneath the clouds, and this time, as the lightning chased itself away, thunder rumbled.

Calvin leant against the railings at the end of the pier and watched the coming storm. Every bright strike of lighting reflected back at him from a sea choked full of bottles. They rolled in with the tide and thunder and, coming with them, in the next flash of lightning, Calvin saw a man on a jet-ski. He was steering with one hand while the other tousled at the long hair which the speed of his travel threw out behind him. A mane of hair, tossed around in the wind and rain like the spines of a lionfish.

From behind Calvin came a cry, sharp and desperate, but he kept his eyes on the jet-ski tsunami bumping over the bottle-strewn waves. An eel was emerging from the man's shorts now, hanging huge and glistening.

A moray, Calvin thought. There's always a bigger fish.

When the world seems to shine, like you've had too much wine, that's…

"Calvin!"

But he kept his eye on the man, this storm-brought El Niño, who, when he came, brought the sopping wet thrashing of a monsoon with him, and though he was too far away to see clearly, Calvin knew who it would be. He'd brought the man with them, after all.

"Cal!"

At last, Calvin turned to face what was behind him and saw Nina. She was running, a nightdress clinging to her skin in the rain, and though she held an arm across her body for modesty she was clearly naked beneath. Her other arm reached for him, but under her feet the boards of the pier stretched on and on and she ran without making any progress. Another special effect, like she was trapped in a dolly zoom.

Calvin still held the tonic bottle with the message he'd written. One word split in two, scrawled on a napkin. A holiday word turned instruction.

Get away.

He didn't know who it was for.

Calvin held the bottled message in one hand. The other he raised, either to reach for Nina or to keep her distant.

"I can't get back to you!" she cried.

"No," Calvin said, and wondered how long she'd try. 💀 💀 💀

Ray Cluley's work has appeared in various magazines and anthologies. It's been reprinted several times, including in Ellen Datlow's Best Horror of the Year, Steve Berman's Wilde Stories 2013, and in Benoît Domis's Ténèbres series. He has been translated into French, Polish, Hungarian, and Chinese. He won the British Fantasy Award for Best Short Story ("Shark! Shark!") and has since been nominated for Best Novella (Water For Drowning) and Best Collection (Probably Monsters). His second collection, All That's Lost, is available now from Black Shuck Books.

JOHN M. NAVROTH'S FEAR IN FOUR COLORS

THE HIDEOUS HISTORY OF AMERICAN HORROR COMICS

#1- PREMONITIONS AND PRECURSORS

LIKE CREATURES EMERGING FROM A SHADOWY MIST, HORROR COMICS CREPT SLOWLY OUT OF THE DARKNESS, and would only appear, fully-formed years later. Their obscure beginnings were difficult to detect, but they finally clawed their way through the gauntlet of detectives and superheroes until finally, they were revealed in all their grisly glory.

Comic books are direct descendants of newspaper strips, followed closely by the pulps, those lurid and delectable tomes that were available in titles and subjects to satisfy anybody that could read and had ruled corner drug stores for almost two decades. Then someone got the idea to package a bunch of newspaper comic strips together and sell them as a book. The idea caught on and the rest is history.

Comic book publishers were (and still are) a fickle lot, and they'll stick with a subject until sales tell them otherwise. As a result, horror was first thought of as a risk, if it was considered at all. But the detectives and superheroes had their day, and after World War II they began to lose their popularity. That's when horror came shambling in.

At first ranging in content from anemic to tepid, they eventually became a force to be reckoned with. Suddenly, stories were brimming with panels of blood, gore, and dismemberment, which entertained the hell out of readers but shocked the conservative strata of respectable American society—so much that the entire industry was eventually forced to turn on its decapitated head. But before all that, horror comics enjoyed a few halcyon years with some of the most remarkable and unique tales written for the four-color page by talented writers and artists who are still being discussed with reverence today.

So how did horror comics come to be both loved and maligned? Let's crack open the musty tomb of time and find out...

A LEADING CANDIDATE for the earliest introduction of horror into the world of comics was in the final issue of *New Fun Comics* (#6, October 1935). The tabloid size (10" x 15") *New Fun* has the distinction of being the first comic to contain all original stories rather than reprints from newspaper strips.

Influenced by "occult investigators" in the pulps, "Dr. Occult, Ghost Detective" was "sworn to combat supernatural evil in this world." The first episode has all the teeth-marks of a classic vampire story, with dialogue right out of a Hollywood horror film (MGM's *Mark of the Vampire*, starring Bela Lugosi, had been released only a few months earlier).

Dr. Occult returned in the pages of Centaur's *The Comics Magazine* #1 with the name, "Dr. Mystic," then travelled through the ether where he appeared once again as Dr. Occult in *More Fun Comics* #14 (October 1936) through #17 (January 1937), published by National Allied Publications, a forerunner to National Periodicals (aka DC Comics). In this series, he journeyed to another world with his friend, Zator, where he donned a cloth around his neck and wore an inverted triangle emblazoned on his chest. This uniform (as it was called in the strip) certifies him as the first-ever comic book superhero to wear a cape.

The Dr. Occult series was written and drawn by "Leger and Reuths," not readily recognizable names even at that time. However, if a reader cared to notice the bylines of the Dr. Mystic story in Centaur's comic, they would have seen that the writer and artist were credited for the story with their real names, Jerome Siegel and Joe Schuster. Leger and Reuths were the pseudonyms

used by the soon-to-be-famous pair who would create one of the most recognizable comic book super-heroes on the planet, Superman! Siegel and Schuster had been developing the character since the early thirties and a comparison between the likeness of Dr. Occult and Superman reveals a remarkable similarity.

Another early glimpse of horror appearing in the comics was from a company called Fiction House. Founded in 1921 by John B. Kelly and John W. Glenister, Fiction House published pulp magazines exclusively until later in the 1930s when they tried out their first comic book, *Jumbo Comics* (September 1938) under the imprint Real Adventures Publishing Company. So called for its 10.5" x 14.5" page size through the first eight issues, its content was supplied by Will Eisner and Jerry Iger's Syndicated Features Corporation, then well-known as the go-to studio for providing "packages" of complete comics to publishers who wanted to enter the developing market but didn't have the funds or the staff to create their own. Eisner, best remembered for creating *The Spirit* full-page Sunday newspaper strips and his later graphic novels, became highly influential in the comics industry. While he was part-nered with Iger, the page rates and the sheer volume of work they produced made them wealthy men who were at that time barely in their 20s.

Left: Eisner at work. Top: Dr. Occult and (inset) Superman (both by DC Comics). Previous page: EC Comics' The Vault of Horror #30.

Jack Kirby

The stories in the early issues of *Jumbo* were not original; they had been collected and published from Sunday comic strip supplements for *Wags*, a U.S.-produced tabloid for distribution in the U.K. and other foreign markets, hence the title heading was shown on each page of the story in the comic book.

The first issue of *Jumbo* contained work by Eisner and Iger, as well as a humor page by Bob Kane, who would only months later create the legendary Batman with writer Bill Finger in *Detective Comics* #27 (May 1939), and a young Jack Kirby (as Jack Curtiss). Although usually considered science-fiction, one of Kirby's stories, "The Diary of Dr. Hayward" (as Curt Davis) was a continuing series that featured a mad doctor conducting ghastly experiments, one of the sinister trademarks of the "weird menace" pulp magazines that became popular after *Dime Mystery Magazine* replaced its mystery stories for horror in October 1933.

Another horror crossover in this issue was a loose adaptation of Victor Hugo's 1831 novel, *The Hunchback of Notre Dame*. Possibly inspired by the upcoming, second film version by RKO Pictures in 1939, the five-page story was illustrated by Dick Briefer, who we will learn more about shortly. Not knowing how the future film Quasimodo (Charles Laughton) would look, Briefer patterned his after Lon Chaney from the first film version in 1923. With a total of twenty-six pages, *Hunchback* ran from #1 through #8 and returned for the last installment in #10.

When *Jumbo* reduced its page size closer to the standard Golden Age comic book format with #9, "Weird Tales of the Supernatural," a new, quasi-horror series was introduced. Scripted by an unknown writer and drawn by Lou Fine, it was reprinted from an Australian edition of *Wags*. Fine's straight-forward, no-frills style was admired by many, and even Eisner commented, "I had respect for his towering kind of draftsmanship. He was the epitome of the honest draftsman. No fakery, no razzle-dazzle—very direct, very honest in his approach." The title was changed to "Stuart Taylor in Weird Stories of the Supernatural" in #10 and, interestingly, Curt Davis was credited on the heading. Since the name was a pseudonym used by Jack Kirby, one could speculate that it might have been Kirby who was the scriptwriter, or that Kirby drew the breakdowns with Fine completing the work. The series continued until #14 (April 1940). The art for the last of the stories was completed by Charles "Chuck" J. Mazoujian, who was also working on *The Spirit* Sunday strip at the time. Mazoujian filled in the rest after

Fine's first five pages. Fine might have left to join Fox Comics.

Jumbo ran for 167 issues, from 1938–1953, and Fiction House would keep one small foot in horror comics later with their titles, *Ghost Comics* (ten issues, 1951–1954) and *Monster* (January 1953), retitled *The Monster* in the second and last issue (June 1953).

DRAWN BY THE prolific George Tuska, the cover of *Weird Comics* #1 (Fox, April 1940) pictures a deranged scientist preparing a syringe from a potion he has concocted. Flanked by a chained girl and a gorilla, the scene implies he is about to engage in some sort of interspecies experiment. An image clearly inspired by the weird menace pulps and their signature cover art, the title suggests horror is ahead. Unfortunately, it does not entirely deliver.

The story is from a continuing series, "Dr. Mortal," a "Creator of Human Monstrosities." Crudely drawn by newspaper cartoonist Bert Whitman, each episode has the Mad Doctor trying his best to create man-beast hybrids and other monsters that would put Dr. Moreau to shame. For instance, after having escaped a fire that would have otherwise ended the evil doctor's career, in #2 he finds another laboratory "off in the hills." With the help of his trusty assistant who exhumes two bodies from a nearby graveyard, he combines them with a batch of lion entrails in a steam cabinet (!). What emerges after the requisite "treatment" is a hybrid lion-man that goes on a murderous rampage around the surrounding countryside. Seeing that his experiment is a success, he quickly whips up a batch of a few more, at which point the reader should be left wondering, "Where did he get all those lion entrails?" Luckily, Dr. Mortal and grisly beasts such as these are foiled at every turn in each issue. The episodes are truly weird, but not quite horrifying.

Another series begins in this issue that qualifies to a degree for a horror theme is

The Voodoo Man. Artlessly illustrated by an unknown person named as "Allen Spectre", the portentous beginning leads with the text panel, "To Haiti, island of mystic Voodooism, where black magic reigns and dead men walk as zombies, sails Bob Warren, young doctor." The title character, however, is not Warren, but an indigenous "witch doctor" who practices said black magic on any number of victims in order to bend them to

his evil will. *Voodoo Man* was likely inspired by William Seabrook's, *The Magic Island*, a sensational 1929 first-person account of voodoo and zombiism written while he was traveling in Haiti. Another possible source is *White Zombie*, the 1932 Halperin Brothers production starring Bela Lugosi based on Seabrook's book. Contrary to Seabrook's sensitivity described in a number of his passages, *The Magic Island* has not stood up well under scrutiny for its suspected inaccuracies regarding the Haitian religion or characterizations of its oppressed people of the time. Purposefully or not, the stories in *Voodoo Man* follow the same contemporaneous tendencies, and would make any latter-day revisionist reach for a pair of scissors.

Dr. Mortal ran for sixteen of *Weird's* twenty issues, through January 1942, and *The Voodoo Man* managed to last through eight, when it was replaced by an even less horrific, jungle series, Marga the Panther Woman.

Matt Baker

Not noted for overwhelming newsstands with horror comics in their twenty years of business, Fox Comics (aka Fox Feature Syndicate) instead became better recognized for their abundant use of what later became known to comic book collectors as "good girl" art. Typically drawn by Jack Kamen and Matt Baker (an early African-American comic artist) for titles such as, *Blue Beetle*, *Rulah*, *Phantom Lady*, and *Dagar, Desert Hawk*, good girl art comics now command high prices as a result of their provocative imagery. Condescendingly characterized as "headlight comics" for their brazen habit of emphasizing women's breasts, these titles would end up facing the white heat of being

singled out along with horror comics and others being declared as unfit for a young comic book reader's consumption during the infamous Senate hearings of 1954. (Don't worry, this debacle will be covered to a greater extent in a later installment).

It's hard to imagine that the monster from Mary Shelley's immortal story of *Frankenstein* would end up in a comic book sandwiched between superhero stories with names like Dr. Frost and the Green Llama, but it did. "New Adventures of Frankenstein" rose up from the slab in *Prize Comics* #7 (December 1940), an imprint of Crestwood Publishing Co. Signed with the humorous pseudonym, "Frank N. Stein," the creator was Dick Briefer.

Briefer was born and raised in New York City. His original career path was to become a doctor, but when he was a pre-med student at NYU, he suddenly took an unusual turn (his parents probably thought it

was more of a nosedive) and went to work at the Eisner/Iger Studios drawing comics for five dollars a page! One wonders if he thought he could be more creative with a pencil than a surgeon's knife.

Briefer churned out science-fiction, superhero, and crime stories, all produced solely by him. "I never assisted anyone, nor did I have any assistants," he later wrote in a letter to comics historian, Jerry de Fuccio. "I wrote, penciled, inked, lettered, erased [sic] all my stuff."

Briefer's Frankenstein was a gruesome sight to behold, and far afield from the familiar image seen in Boris Karloff's popular film versions designed by monster makeup master, Jack Pierce. However, Briefer did, in a later version of the series, tip his hat to his Universal counterpart by adding a character to one of his stories named Boris Karload.

experiments to his girlfriend, Betty (later changed to Elizabeth in #9), the monster crashes through the window and, again as in the novel, instead of killing his creator, he threatens to make him suffer along with him, promising more misery to come.

Frankenstein appeared in several different titles and guises throughout his comic career. With the exception of #10 and #55, he appeared in *Prize Comics* from #7 to #68 (February-March 1948). In #33 (August 1942), Briefer re-invented his character with a new storyline and persona and dropped the horror theme for lighter fare. With an emphasis on the cartoon style most fans today are familiar with, Frankenstein returned in 1945, starring in his own title that ran through #33 (October-November 1954). Briefer said that he liked this version the best and the test of time has proved him out. The monster was resurrected once more, again as a horror character, in *Frankenstein* #18 (March 1952) through #33 (November 1954). With its cast of various monsters, ghoulish plots, and grisly deaths, the first *Frankenstein* series is rightly credited as the first all-horror, continuing series in a comic book.

Although set in the 1930s, the first episode bears a resemblance to Shelley's novel with the monster's creation scene, his escape from the lab and his subsequent terrorizing of the countryside. He comes across a blind man and it's hard not to overlook the obvious similarity to a scene in Universal's *Bride of Frankenstein* (1935), including when a man enters the cabin in hunting garb and shoots the monster with his rifle. The Monster's next stop is the zoo, where he encounters a pair of young boys at the lion cage. Overhearing them wonder what it would be like if they were in with the lion, Frankenstein innocently obliges and pulls apart the bars. The lion spares the kids and attacks Frankenstein instead. He manages to escape... riding an elephant! In a sequence emulating RKO's *King Kong* (1933), he scales the Statue of Liberty and makes it up to the observation tower, where he shockingly tosses out a couple to their death. In a convenient coincidence, Dr. Frankenstein happens to be on hand and spots his creation. That night, while the doctor is coming clean about his

Dick Briefer

A casualty of the great comics purge of the 1950s, Dick Briefer's *Frankenstein* was finished until it received another jolt of life when it became a popular title with collectors just over a decade later. Briefer had also experienced another setback when it was discovered he was drawing a comic strip for the communist newspaper, the *Daily Worker*, under the pseudonym, Dick Floyd. The storyline was about communists and their battle against the Nazis during World War II. While he got a pass during the time the strip was published, it is generally considered that it was this association with the Communist Party that led to him being blacklisted during the McCarthy era. Discouraged, Briefer left comics and went into commercial advertising to finish off his career. In an instance of unintended irony, the future of the entire comics industry was foreshadowed on the cover of the last issue of *Frankenstein*, where we see the monster on a tower with his back against a clock face threatened by a man wielding one of the clock arms as a spear. The title reads: "Death O'clock."

In 1942, Fiction House decided to try out their version of a continuing horror strip. The publisher had enjoyed great success with anthologies such as *Planet Stories*, *Wings* and *Jungle*. Another title, *Rangers*, was re-tooled for #8 (Dec. 1942) with some series dropped and new ones added. One of these was "Werewolf Hunter," arguably the first continuing horror series featuring lycanthropes. Written by an unknown writer with the quaint name of Arman Weygand, it is presumed illustrated by the Austro-Hungarian artist, Gus Schrotter. Although none of the stories could honestly be called horrifying by today's standards, they did often meet the criteria of horror by using familiar plots found in genre movies of the era. Set in the steamy bayous of Louisiana, they contain the familiar fare of a wizened professor with the arcane knowledge to track down and destroy the werewolf in each episode. While the rest of the strip is drawn fairly well, the werewolf is almost laughable. There was little improvement with the art of George Tuska, Saul Rosen

and (possibly) Jim Mooney over the next few issues.

"Werewolf Hunter" was likely inspired at least in part by Universal's release of *The Wolf Man*, released just the previous year. Screenwriter Curt Siodmak single-handedly set the template for the modern werewolf legend by establishing certain conventions (full-moon transformation, death by silver bullet, etc.) that are still used today.

The Fiction House series steered clear of these (possibly concerned with copyright infringement) and created its own rules about werewolves. As an example, the werewolf in the first episode could only transform under the full moon if it had rained earlier!

In *Rangers* #14 (Dec. 1943), a new artist took over, one of the most intriguing to come out of the Golden Age of comics. Answering an ad from Fiction House, art student Lily Renée was hired and assigned the job of illustrating "Werewolf Hunter," not because she wanted to, but because nobody else wanted it! There was one problem: Renée didn't like to draw wolves. She somehow convinced the writer to use other supernatural creatures instead.

Lily Renée

Transformed by the beautiful and talented Viennese artist, the series became one of the most underrated strips that Fiction House ever produced. Her decorative use of panel design and fluid ink lines made a lot of other artists look like hacks. One could almost describe her as the female Will Eisner. Criminally overlooked, Lily Renée deserves wider recognition.

"Werewolf Hunter" ran until #41 (January 1948). The series never got the cover spot since *Rangers* had always been primarily a military-themed comic. The fact that it even found itself in this title is a mystery unto itself.

Gilberton Corporation's *Classic Comics* had the market cornered on adapting popular young reader's novels and story collections to the comic book page. In #12 (June 1943), they published two stories by Washington Irving. The second is an adaption for *The Legend of Sleepy Hollow*, written by Dan Levin and illustrated by Rolland H. Livingstone. The next issue (#13, August 1943) is considered the first all-horror comic with the adaptation of Robert Louis Stevenson's *Dr. Jekyll and Mr. Hyde*, written by Evelyn Goodman and drawn by Arnold L. Hicks, who also illustrated the frightening cover. Several editions were printed, including one with a painted cover and new page art by Lou Cameron.

One of the trio of stories appearing in *3 Famous Mysteries* (*Classic Comics* #21, July 1944) was an adaptation of Edgar Allan Poe's, "The Murders in the Rue Morgue," scripted by Dan Levin and drawn by Arnold L. Hicks. Gilberton would follow up in December 1945 with an adaptation of Shelly's *Frankenstein*. The covers and interiors were penciled by Robert Webb and inked by Ann Brewster with the story faithfully written by Ruth A. Roche. *Frankenstein* would stay in print

FAMOUS TALES of TERROR

IN THESE PAGES OF YELLOWJACKET COMICS, WE PRESENT WITH PRIDE AN OLD MASTERPIECE ADAPTED TO COMIC CONTINUITY... THE FIRST IN THE SERIES OF FAMOUS SHORT MYSTERY STORIES IS EDGAR ALLEN POE'S, THE BLACK CAT!

THE STORY I MUST TELL YOU, IS ONE WHICH I CAN HARDLY HOPE YOU WILL BELIEVE. BUT, AS YOU CAN SEE, I AM GOING TO DIE-- TOMORROW, AND TODAY I WOULD UNBURDEN MY SOUL!

for the next twenty-six years in nineteen editions. Translated into twenty-two languages and sold in thirty countries, it is likely the most widely-distributed horror comic in history.

The Frank Comunale Publishing Company also used horror story adaptations in their superhero title, *Yellowjacket Comics*. Under the heading, "Famous Tales of Terror," the first appeared in #1 (September 1944), with Poe's "The Black Cat," illustrated by Bill Allison, who worked out of the Iger Shop (all the Poe adaptations were scripted by unknown writers). The next installment was in #3 (November 1944) and featured Poe's "The Pit and the Pendulum," with art by Gus Schrotter. Poe's "The Fall of the House of Usher" was adapted in #4 (Dec. 1944), again with art by Schrotter. Due to the war shortage of paper, *Yellowjacket* took a publishing hiatus for most of the following year, and the next "Tales of Terror" resumed in #6 (Dec. 1945) with "The Tell Tale Heart," illustrated by Rudy Palais and Arnold Hicks.

Subsequent edition of *Classic Comics* #26, under its later and more familiar name.

Then, something interesting happened in #7 (January 1946) when the Poe stories were replaced with a new and original horror story, "The Avenging Hand." Written and drawn by Alan Mandell, it's a simple story of a gangster with a guilty conscience. What makes it unique, however, as well as significant in the history of horror comics, is that it is book-ended by a host—and not just any host—it's a character called the Ancient Witch, who was referred to in later stories as the Old Witch. This exact set-up would be adopted and made famous by EC Comics in their legendary trilogy of horror titles… only it wouldn't be until six years later! Indeed, if it had been drawn with a little more sophistication, with the style of dialogue and the surprise ending, it could easily be taken as a story by EC's Old Witch. It is interesting to note that Bill Gaines, the publisher of EC Comics claimed the horror hosts were his idea and it's hard to believe he wasn't aware of these stories. Three more "Famous Tales of Terror" (written by George Mandel and drawn by Alan Mandel) introduced by the Old Witch would appear in *Yellowjacket* until the title folded with #10 (June 1946). In another twist, both concepts were precluded by a radio show that began in 1931 called *The Witch's Tale*. Produced and written by Alonzo

Dean Cole, each episode was hosted by Old Nancy, the Witch of Salem. Two issues of a pulp magazine, *The Witch's Tales*, published by Carwood Publishing Co. in November/December 1936, were based on the show. On a side note, the colophon publisher, The Frank Comunale Publishing Co., was renamed Charlton Comics, Inc. in this issue.

A few other comics titles worth mentioning that showed signs of horror themes in one form or another were: *Suspense Comics* (first issue December 1943, Continental/Et-Es-Go Magazines, Inc.), had a penchant for lurid bondage covers, including the infamous Nazi/KKK ritual sacrifice cover of #3; *Spook Comics* #1 (1945, Baily Publishing Company), with a zombie story; and *Spooky Mysteries* #1 (1946,

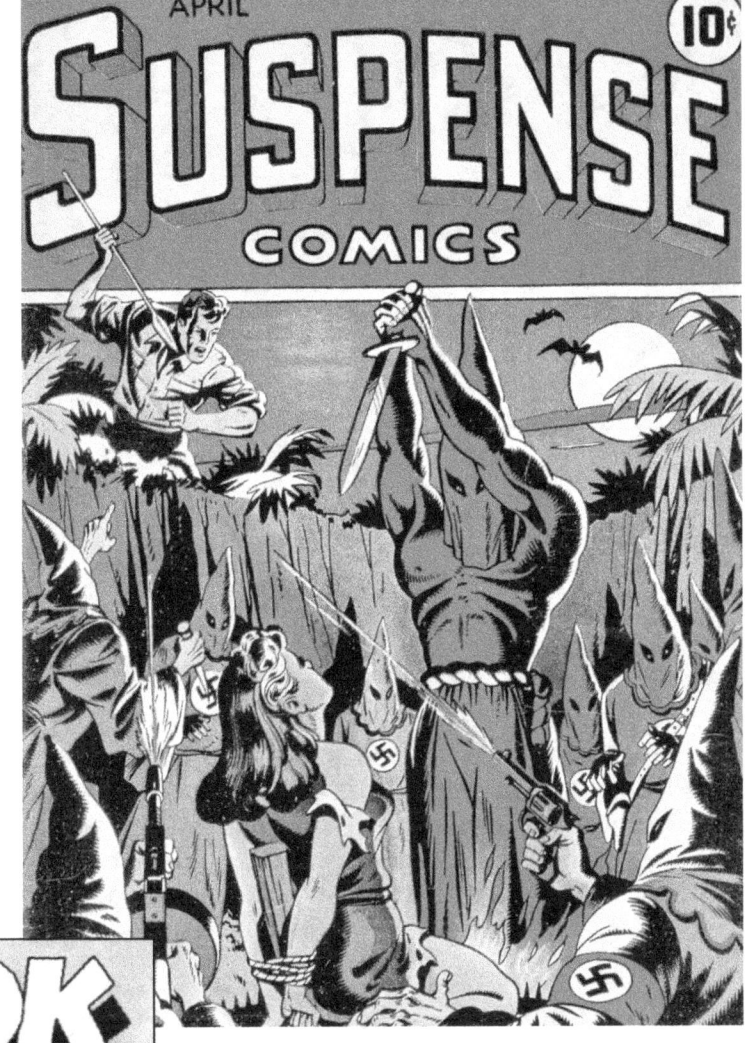

Your Guide Publications, Inc./Lev Gleason), a humor comic that is "spooky" in name only.

☠ ☠ ☠

Next: "THE PRE-CODE PLAGUE"

John Navroth has been a fan of comic books since he was a young lad during the Silver Age. When word got out that the same 12-cent books were becoming far more valuable than their cover price, he immediately stopped folding them over while reading them and saved up enough for a stock of plastic bags and backer boards. For readers who are interested more about vintage horror comics visit John's blog at: monstermagazineworld.blogspot.com

And don't miss John's history of *Famous Monsters of Filmland* in *Black Infinity: Creature Features*.

SUNDOWN IN DUFFIELD

By Steve Rasnic Tem

JOHN CONVINCED HIS GRANDSON TO TAKE HIM ON THIS TRIP EVEN THOUGH FRANKLIN HAD HIS DOUBTS. John felt apologetic. He knew he was asking a lot. Franklin was a fine young man, and had always been a loyal and dutiful grandson, but clearly John's progressive disease frightened him. John persuaded him this was his final opportunity to see the house where he'd lived as a child—"before my mind goes"—and so reluctantly Franklin agreed. It was a shameful manipulation. John felt embarrassed for the man he once was.

The old homeplace was near Duffield, Virginia off Pattonsville Road. Scott County, deep into the southwest corner of the state. The population had always been small, and now was down to a tiny community of seventy-three, according to Franklin. He'd looked it up on wiki-something. John had lost the ability to use the computer. He didn't miss it.

John couldn't remember how old he was when his family left the house, fleeing in the middle of the night with time only to throw a few things into the car. But it had been at least sixty years. He'd been nine or ten. Maybe eleven. He'd never gone back, not until today.

His sister died a few months ago, and much to his surprise he discovered she still owned the place, and now it was his. How did that happen? He couldn't follow the legalities involved. He hadn't seen his sister in years.

Were they estranged? Certainly, they'd been strangers. Was he being unkind? In any case the state was about to take the property for unpaid taxes. Let them have it—he certainly had no use for it. John just wanted one final look.

THEY HAD A MAP from his sister's lawyer. They couldn't have found the house otherwise. The road was gravel, dirt, and weeds. Franklin kept saying, "it's a jungle in here," and each time he said it John felt guiltier. Franklin's vehicle had a high ground clearance, but it wasn't designed for off-road travel. John lost his license some time ago and couldn't share the driving. Although it was for the best, he supposed, he still resented it.

John was about to suggest they give up when Frankin cried, "There it is!" and stopped. "It's only a few yards. We can walk the rest of the way. You can hold onto me just in case."

Despite his misgivings, John could tell his grandson was enjoying himself. He was still at an age when inconvenience felt like an adventure. Franklin unloaded a backpack, snacks, and a powerful battery-operated lantern he bought especially for this expedition. He reserved a yurt for the night at the Natural Tunnel Park a few miles away. John was confused at first—he thought the word referred to a kind of drink. Then Franklin explained it was like a tent. He seemed quite excited about it. John didn't want to sleep in a tent. Camping had never appealed to him, not even when he was a boy.

No doubt Franklin would want to see the Natural Tunnel itself, which William Jennings Bryan once called the eighth wonder of the world. Of course, Bryan had been a bit of a blowhard. Hundreds of thousands of years of a stream running through the limestone carved it out, and like every other natural tourist attraction in the U.S. it had its own Lover's Leap, and a tragic story of star-crossed Indian lovers to go with it. Or he'd want to hike up to the Devil's Bathtub, a natural depression in the bedrock full of water. Nature took multiple millennia creating these wonders and human beings spent fifteen minutes manufacturing semi-appropriate metaphors. John would remain back in the yurt during any such sightseeing if Franklin let him.

The land here was rampant with porous limestone, sinkholes, and caves, many of them hidden or undiscovered. You never knew when you might step off the trail and into a hole. John had no intention of risking any broken bones, certainly not at his age.

"Damn! No reception." Franklin kept pushing buttons on his cell phone.

"Do we really need that thing?" Franklin gave John a cell phone for Christmas. It was still in its box in a drawer somewhere.

"If there's an emergency, yes."

"I guess we'll have to avoid emergencies."

John couldn't see the house, but he couldn't see a lot of things if there were trees or other distractions around whatever he was looking for. He counted on his grandson to lead the way. Instead, Franklin had John grab his left arm and they walked together. John wanted to say he wasn't blind, at least not yet, but it seemed silly to fuss.

They kept away from the road's deep ruts and pushed through thick growths of chickweed and bull thistle, button weed and spotted spurge. How come he could remember the names of all these weeds and yet so little of anything important?

A patch of gray ahead of them evolved into the side of a house with all the paint worn away, the structure difficult to distinguish at first from the overgrowth and the shadows among the trees. John couldn't remember the original color, white or a light blue, but even back then the paint hadn't been kept up.

So many places to hide, whether you were a victim or someone intent on doing harm. The leafy trees smothered the light. He imagined it always felt after sunset here. He didn't know if his grandson kept a gun in his car—most of the locals did. John should have asked.

Like many older homes in the area the house dated from the Civil War. The house still wore the remains of the fancy gingerbread fretwork and medallions and eave brackets of that era, split and half-rotted. The brick and stone foundation was losing its integrity, splitting into its component blocks in parts. The ancient shutters were shredded or missing. The windows were all broken, reduced to black rectangles of rotted screen. The porch roof sagged several feet on one end and the porch floor itself had fallen onto the ground. Pieces of a shattered swing hung from rusty chains. The fence in front of the house was missing its rails, leaving a few posts covered in thick layers of vine.

John knew time had been the chief perpetrator here, but his eyes kept searching the greenery for evidence of others.

"Was that your family's car?" Franklin pointed to the corroded skeleton of an automobile beneath a collapsed shed.

"No. Daddy drove us away in his Bel Air. That was grandaddy's. Daddy always said he'd get it running someday."

The warped metal roof of the house was rusted brown and there were large holes where sections had fallen in. The old cook stove sat in the side yard. John supposed someone had tried to steal it for scrap but given up because of its weight. Nearby, the balcony which once hung from the second story lay spilled through the weeds.

"We only have a few hours before losing light. You're not sundowning are you Grandad?"

John knew the term well but refused to acknowledge it in relation to himself. "I'm just fine."

"Okay, I'm going to check inside and see if it's stable enough to be in there. If we go in we should be quick about it, though. Think about what you want to see, if there's anything you want to get, whatever you want to accomplish here. That'll make things go faster. But don't go wandering around."

"Whatever you say." John tried to keep the irritation out of his voice but didn't think he succeeded, given the way his grandson was looking at him. He could feel his annoyance rising like a fever he could not control. Along with it was a rise in paranoia. He didn't want to be left out here alone.

"I'll be quick." Franklin tested the boards of the porch before putting his full weight on them, then stepped side to side as if looking for soft spots. The front door stuck for a moment, but then he put his shoulder into it and disappeared inside.

John meant to ask his grandson if it was spring or summer. For the life of him he couldn't remember. But asking such a question would have been a big mistake.

He was of two minds. His grandmother used to say that. But in his case one mind was sharp and clear and the other overflowing with bewilderment. John never knew at any given moment which one was going to show up.

With Franklin gone John could listen to his surroundings. The wind through the trees. The songs of small birds. He used to know his birdsongs. Not anymore. If there were larger animals around they were holding their peace.

Then the distinctive trickles and burbles of running water became evident. Of course. A branch of the Clinch River ran behind the house. He and his dad used to go fishing there. He was suddenly thrilled, and took a few steps in that direction before stopping himself. If he weren't here when his grandson came out of the house the child would have a fit.

The river flooded a few times while they lived here, bringing water, and whatever was in the water, almost to the edge of the house. John remembered he and his sister being so excited to see fish splashing in their backyard, but Mother wouldn't let them go near the flooded stream. He wondered if there had been worse flooding since then.

But they didn't leave because of the flooding. They fled the house in the middle of the night because of something far, far worse. If John could only remember what it was.

"Okay, I think it's safe enough," Franklin said. "It's more stable inside than it looks. We can't take the staircase to the second floor—we'd fall right through—but the main floor should be okay."

The interior looked nothing like the pictures in John's memory. Stain patterns on the walls and ceiling resembled badly healed wounds. The checkered kitchen linoleum floor appeared vaguely familiar, like a kitchen he'd once encountered, but not lived with. The kitchen chair seats were caked in layers of fallen plaster. Vines grew down the kitchen walls from a rent in the ceiling.

For a moment he thought he saw his mother standing there, staring at a pot on the stove with a blank look on her face. It happened more than a few times. She'd forgotten what she was doing. After a while Daddy took over the cooking. Both would be dead less than ten years later.

The walls were much closer than he remembered, and there was a bush growing in one corner of the living room. Spicebush, he thought. They used to grow outside the house, and the berries tasted peppery.

A collapsed couch near the flaking brick fireplace appeared too filthy to touch. If it once belonged to his family John didn't recognize it. Some sort of abandoned animal den was evident inside the fireplace, scattered small bones left behind. Either the animal itself or what it ate.

They shouldn't be here. John was suddenly convinced.

Franklin was in another room, poking at things, looking for heirlooms John might want to retrieve. He was going to tell Franklin this might not be the right house, even though he was sure it was, when he saw the mirror standing in one corner of a shallow alcove off the living room.

His mother's old dressing mirror leaned against a background of split and moldy wallpaper. He recognized the scrollwork around the bottom edge. When he was small he'd held onto that edge while his mother modeled some new dress she'd made. This might have been her sewing space, although his fragile memory told him the sewing room had been upstairs. Moisture had gotten into the silver backing creating mirror rot. He could see parts of himself, but the rest was shadow and distortion. From certain angles the mirror cast bad reflections across the room. Out of the corner of one eye he glimpsed things creeping from the walls.

He caught a peek of his head in an unspoiled spot in the glass. His hair looked crazy, and he hadn't buttoned his sweater right. Usually, Franklin fixed those things for him. He hastily moved his palm across his hair and fumbled with the top of his sweater. Another hand came up behind him and brushed the hair off his right ear. He twisted around. There was no one there.

"So, did your family grab the important stuff when they left?" Franklin stood a few feet away.

"Pictures mostly, some jewelry and a few changes of clothes, whatever money was in my dad's wallet. My sister and I each grabbed a favorite toy. I can't remember what I took. By the time we reached my uncle's house upstate I know I didn't have it whatever it was."

"Why did you guys leave exactly?"

How many times was his grandson going to ask him this question? "I don't remember. But I know my folks had their reasons."

There was soiled and sour-smelling clothing scattered throughout the downstairs. John didn't think they belonged to his family. They looked a little too new. Some had gray and fading reddish-brown stains on them. There were numerous signs of squatters: candy wrappers and food packages, indications of a fire along one wall, women's undergarments, pornographic magazines. There were long rips in the walls where scavengers had removed copper wiring or pipe. John started to pick up a plastic bag off the floor when his grandson told him to stop. "It might have had drugs in it, Oxycontin, or something worse." John couldn't remember what Oxycontin was but heeded the warning nevertheless. All this evidence looked several years old. The squatters were long gone.

"Just let me know when you're ready to leave."

John knew that meant his grandson was eager to abandon this pile of wreckage. "I won't be long. I promise."

Despite his grandson's warning he wanted to go upstairs where his and his sister's rooms had been. A taste of his childhood. A reminder of the rare things which brought him joy. But he didn't dare try the mossy stairs.

In a back corner of the first floor, he discovered a sagging armchair in the middle of a vacant room, a place to sit and watch the house disintegrate at one's leisure. A rotting pile of lovely old books made a smelly mound by the chair. He remembered his father had a small study where he liked to hide. Was this it? He would have liked to sort through these books to see what his father liked to read, but he was afraid to touch them.

John knew his father had stopped reading sometime before the family ran away from here. The reason he remembered was because it was such a dramatic change. Used to, John's mother had to drag Daddy out of that chair for dinner or for most family activities. But after he stopped Daddy looked so sad. John overheard Daddy telling Mother he still liked looking at these old books and turning the pages, but he could no longer follow the sentences.

The bedroom by the kitchen had been his parents'. He was eager to see it. After the family left this house things were never the same. They'd moved around the South, losing much of what they owned along the way. He didn't even have photographs of them.

The air in the room was dusty, the room dark, and it was difficult to tell which details were actual objects, and which the random effect of overlapping shadow. Jagged timbers poked down from the broken ceiling.

A portrait hung on the wall by the door. A woman's body, but she had lost her face. Something had scrubbed at the paint until all her features were erased. He thought she might have been his mother, or his grandmother, but thanks to his failing memory she'd been demoted to the anonymous dead.

He often had trouble determining distances in the dark, but today seemed worse than usual. Was that a wall or a shadow? As he stepped further into the room he was assaulted by an awful stench. The drapes sagged with mold. Corrupted bedding hung off the side of the blackened mattress like ruined folds of skin.

John took another step, and the floor sank an inch or so. He was suddenly having balance issues. This sometimes occurred, but usually in a safer setting. Everything felt soft underfoot. He looked down and was alarmed by the amount of seepage from the cellar underneath. The floor swayed as if floating. Things began to fall off the walls and slide toward him. He didn't dare move because of the mess and the peril. He wanted to call for his grandson but at that moment he could not remember his grandson's name.

Layers of wall began to fall, revealing the naked lathing beneath. The shadows painting the walls began to drip.

"Grandad, I don't think it's safe for you to be in here." Franklin, of course. His name was Franklin. His grandson grabbed his hand and pulled him from the room. Glancing back, John saw the room was a terrible mess, but nothing extraordinary. Light was bleeding through tears in the window shades.

"Is it morning yet?"

"No, Grandad. It's late afternoon. Sometimes the late afternoon light and the morning light look the same. I know that must confuse you, but it's okay, really."

They were about to pass the cellar door when Franklin grabbed the knob and tried to pull it open. John barely suppressed a warning scream. But the door was either locked or swollen shut. *Good*, he thought. *Let it be.*

He watched a memory leak out of the cellar door: his father shouting at him to run away, something tall coming up the cellar stairs behind his dad. But his dad kept blocking whatever it was so John couldn't see. Then his dad shook his head back and forth until his dad's face went away.

But Franklin wouldn't give up. He kept twisting and yanking on the knob. John, anxious the door not be breached, though he couldn't have explained to his grandson why, grabbed that sweet child's arm and began to screech "no no no!" until his voice went thin.

"Please step back, Grandad."

"Don't tell me what to do boy!" John could feel the anger rising from his chest into his head. He wanted to stop it but could not. Franklin squirmed out of his grip and John almost fell. He stared at this young man. "Is it morning yet?"

"No, Grandad. It's almost sundown. I think we should get you to the campsite."

"What's wrong?"

"Nothing's wrong, but you're getting tired. We'll check into our yurt, get something to eat, and then a good night's sleep. We can still come back here tomorrow if you feel you need to."

"I sleep too much during the day. That's why I get confused. That's the problem."

"Maybe. Maybe it is. We should go now."

Franklin hurried John along the dirt road and into the car, but he couldn't get the engine to turn over. He tried and tried, but all he got out of the vehicle was a rapid clicking sound. John sat quietly, afraid he might say the wrong thing.

"I always keep blankets in the car. You taught me that, remember?"

John did not. "I did? I'm glad I at least taught you something."

"You taught me lots of things, Grandad. You've always been…so wise. I've also got two air mattresses. We'll camp out in the house where there's more room. Maybe the car will start in the morning. If not, we'll figure something else out. Everything will be okay."

John smiled and nodded but knew better. In his experience, when someone says "everything will be okay" it usually won't be.

Franklin found a broom in a debris-filled closet and used it to sweep out the living room. John kept getting up and pawing through the more interesting bits discovered by the broom until his grandson persuaded him to sit in the kitchen. It was embarrassing, but John had just enough sense of himself to know it was necessary. His brain was filling up with wreckage, and sometimes he couldn't find the right memories, or the thoughts he needed, because all that wreckage was in the way.

Every few minutes John stared at the cellar door. He kept seeing his father running up those steps, something tall and borderless following him from below. Unfortunately, it was the clearest picture he had of his father. It was a memory which threatened to erase everything else the man ever did.

Both his parents died when John and his sister were teenagers—first his mother and then his father. The disappearance of his mother's mind had already begun in this house. In retrospect the evidence was clear. The same was true of his father, although his father was at least able to hang on until he got them out of the house.

They died hooked up to machines, having forgotten how to swallow or breathe. John didn't really know how his sister died. He should have stayed in touch, but that was as much her fault as his.

They made their beds on the floor with the lantern between them. The dark came quickly, rushing up to the very edges of the lantern light. In recent years it had become increasingly difficult for John to perceive objects in the dark. In his eyes, things were either visible in his world or they were lost to the shadows. But he understood the shadows were still there, waiting.

Either because he was nervous himself or because he wanted to distract John from the demons which came to him most afternoons as the sun went down, Franklin began a seemingly endless monologue about his work at the bank, the young woman he was dating, possible plans and their alternatives, what he remembered about his grandmother (John's wife, who had been fading so quickly from his own memories he barely remembered being married), and much more.

John interrupted. "It's okay, Franklin. I'm feeling relatively calm."

"Are you? I'm glad. We're both okay then, aren't we?"

"Yes we are," John said, although he'd suddenly forgotten why they were here. His grandson had obviously wanted to go camping, but why? John was always losing the thread of things. It was becoming tiresome.

"Was it always this damp?" his grandson asked.

"Damp? What do you mean? Is it raining? I don't hear any rain."

"This house. It smells of damp. I know there's a river nearby. But this floor? Doesn't it feel—I don't know—wet?"

John felt cold and tried to shake it off. "I remember the cellar always flooded. There were cracks at one end, and a cavity that went, well, who knows where it went? Did I tell you there were caves all around here?"

"You did. Water carves its way through limestone. Hundreds of thousands of years."

"That's right! They call that kind of landscape *karst*. That's a new word for you, child! Sinkholes, caves, all kinds of cavities in the rock, and under your feet. Daddy said we got water in the cellar because of that, and rats too, all sorts of creatures living inside those caves.

"I used to *hate* that damp smell! It got into your head, and it made it hard to think straight. You had to make an effort to push your thoughts through. I'd walk around the house numb and not feeling much of anything. I felt rubbed out."

Franklin stopped responding, and soon John could hear the boy snoring. But John kept talking. It comforted him to hear a voice, even if it was just his own.

John opened his eyes in the middle of the night and thought himself outside the house. The roof over his head was full of holes, and full of stars. Everything was creeping toward him. Everything his grandson had swept to the side was now sliding in John's direction.

He twisted around and found Franklin sitting up on his air mattress, staring at the cellar door. "Franklin, are you okay?"

"Grandad, is that you?"

"Of course it is, son. What's wrong? What's bothering you?"

"Where are we? I have no idea where we are."

"We're. We're." But John could not speak because of the cellar door. Which was open. He hadn't noticed it at first, but the door was now wide open, showing them the way into the emptiness beyond.

💀 💀 💀

Steve Rasnic Tem is a past winner of the Bram Stoker, World Fantasy, and British Fantasy Awards. His novel Ubo (Solaris Books), a finalist for the Bram Stoker Award, is a dark science fictional tale about violence and its origins, featuring such historical viewpoint characters as Jack the Ripper, Stalin, and Heinrich Himmler. He has published over 500 short stories in his 45+ year career. Some of his best are collected in Thanatrauma and Figures Unseen from Valancourt Books, and in The Night Doctor & Other Tales from Macabre Ink. You can visit his home on the web at www.stevetem.com